TALL DARK AND WICKED

The Wickeds Book 5

KATHLEEN AYERS

❧ I ❧

*L*ondon

Lady Petra Grantly observed the room of people gathered for the marriage of her brother, Rowan, to Lady Arabella Tremaine. The gathering was small and intimate, with only family and close friends in attendance. Her parents, Lord and Lady Marsh, had been pressuring Rowan to marry for years. Today should have been a happy one.

Alas, it was not. At least not for Lady Marsh.

Mother wept and clung to Father's hand as if the greatest of tragedies had befallen the Earl of Marsh and his countess. Petra supposed in Mother's eyes, it had. Last night, Mother's sobs had echoed down the hallway like the wailing of an Irish banshee. She'd declined breakfast this morning, declaring herself too distraught to eat. As the vicar began the ceremony uniting Rowan and Arabella, Father had to hush her by pressing a handkerchief to her lips.

Arabella was not her mother's choice of wife for Rowan.

The Duke of Dunbar, brother of the bride, and also related to Lord and Lady Marsh by marriage to Petra's cousin, watched Rowan take hold of Arabella's hand, shock clearly stamped on his rough-hewn features. His mismatched eyes, one azure blue and the other brown, stared in rapt attention at the bride and groom, clearly fascinated by the proceedings. Perhaps the duke thought he was dreaming for he certainly hadn't thought someone as sour as Arabella to ever wed.

He wasn't alone in his assessment.

No one in London had believed any man would ever marry the Duke of Dunbar's sister, especially not a gentleman of Rowan's charm, intelligence and good looks. How the pair ended up at an inn together with Arabella in a state best described as *disheveled*, had London guessing. The duke had made up a clever story to entertain the *ton*.

Petra believed none of it.

The *ton* hardly seemed to believe the story either; wonder over *how* exactly the Duke of Dunbar coerced Rowan, for certainly Rowan wasn't marrying Arabella of his own accord, was thick in the gossip circles. According to the betting books at White's, of which Petra was supposed to know nothing, odds were Rowan would flee to the Continent before reciting his vows. She expected several gentlemen would lose their wagers today when the news reached their ears that Rowan and Arabella had indeed wed.

The duke's wife, Petra's cousin, Jemma, still and brittle, watched the proceedings with pained resignation. It was common knowledge the duchess had no love for her sister-in-law. Petra thought the duke's home to be fraught with tension due to the animosity between the two women. She imagined the hurling of insults and biscuits as the two women fought for control, the stoic duke caught in the middle. She did not envy His Grace.

Petra's own feelings about her new sister-in-law vacillated between fear and dislike. Arabella had never been nice to Petra, though to be fair, Arabella was rarely nice to anyone.

Petra kept her distance, avoiding Arabella as much as she could. Of course, now it would be impossible to steer clear of the woman. Holidays were bound to be awkward.

Her brother stood tall and handsome, his voice resonating with some undefined emotion as he spoke his vows without a hint of hesitation. Regardless of what her parents or anyone in London thought, Rowan *wanted* to marry Arabella. The desire for his new wife was evident in the warmth of his eyes and the longing for Arabella etched across his face.

Well, there's no accounting for taste, Petra mused. Her brother did like a challenge. But Petra sensed there was more to Rowan's feelings for Arabella. He'd hovered protectively over her as the guests had filled her parents' home to witness the wedding, his fingers curling around her elbow as family and friends were greeted. Arabella, for her part, watched Rowan with a possessive glow in her dark eyes until he looked in her direction. Even Petra, as innocent as she was, saw the simmering hunger the pair seemed to have for each other.

She found all of it very interesting.

The vows finished, her mother's wailing finally subsided into pained sniffles. Petra sat back in her chair, carefully folding her hands into her lap as she'd been taught to do since the age of six. Her expression was perfectly smooth, her back straight as a pike, awaiting the vicar to end the ceremony.

A prickling sensation ran up the base of her neck.

Pretending to smooth the pale green of her gown, Petra lowered her eyes and discreetly snuck a glance at the right side of the room. She was not unaccustomed to appreciation from gentlemen, but she'd not thought to garner *his* interest.

Eyes the color of sapphires were focused rather intently on her bosom. An interesting development to be sure, since Petra's bosom was not large and her neckline incredibly modest. She straightened again, resisting the urge to fan herself. The room had grown warm and a window needed to be opened. She could barely hear the vicar over the loud thumping of her heart.

The Earl of Morwick uttered a soft, barely discernable chuckle, not in the least put off at being caught ogling her bosom. Though she could not see his face, she imagined he smiled at her discomfort; it was hardly a surprise, for he had struck her upon their initial meeting as a bit forward. Upon being introduced, his eyes, the most startling shade of indigo ringed by lighter blue and shot through with gold flecks, had run down her form without regard for politeness. He'd held her fingers a trifle longer than necessary. Even now she could still feel the press of his lips against her knuckles.

Incredibly forward.

His manner was to be expected; Lord Morwick *was* cousin to Arabella.

Petra pushed aside thoughts of Lord Morwick and forced her attention to the vicar as he recited some platitude about the institution of marriage.

How horrified Mother would be at Lord Morwick's impolite interest in her daughter. Petra knew little about him, only what her brother had told her. He was the youngest son of the thrice-widowed Lady Cupps-Foster, Arabella's aunt. He rarely ventured to London, preferring to stay a recluse in the wilds of the Peak District in Derbyshire. He had studied at Oxford or Cambridge, she wasn't sure which, and was thrown out due to his propensity for brawling. Some of the *ton* gossiped he was actually the product of Lady Cupps-Foster and a gypsy lover, but Petra didn't believe a word of it.

Petra dared another look at him. Morwick was also *dreadfully* handsome. If one preferred tall, dark men with broad shoulders and piercing blue eyes.

Despite her initial dislike, Petra found him fascinating. He reminded her of an exotic animal forced into the confines of her parents' town house, only waiting for the proper moment to burst free and attack. Morwick appeared ill at ease in his expensively tailored clothes. He tugged absently at the neck of his shirt and rolled his broad shoulders, stretching the dark blue superfine of his coat until the seams looked as if they would pop. The chair on which he sat was dwarfed by his large form, creaking with protest at the slightest move. His ebony hair was an unruly mass of curls, far too long and in desperate need of a cut. The dark hair paired with his deeply tanned skin *did* give Morwick the look of a gypsy. Or maybe a pirate.

Petra was so immersed in her thoughts of the Earl of Morwick, she didn't notice most of the guests had risen and were making their way to the dining room where a wedding feast, carefully prepared by Cook, awaited them. She was startled to find Morwick had been placed next to her at the table.

Petra waved over a footman and requested a window be opened. The dining room was nearly as warm as the main drawing room had been.

Morwick ignored her, settling himself and immediately signaling for wine. Perhaps he was a sot. That would be disappointing, but not unexpected given his penchant for fistfights in taverns. Heat emanated from his large body, searing Petra's arms as if she stood close to a fire.

As a well-bred young lady, manners dictated she engage him in conversation.

"Are you enjoying your stay in London, Lord Morwick?" Petra ventured, spearing a sliver of thinly sliced potatoes in cream sauce.

"Not in the least." The flecks of gold in his sapphire eyes flared and sparkled at her before he turned away.

Well, that was uncommonly rude. "How unfortunate," she said.

"I don't find it so." He drained his glass and waved for another.

Good Lord, he is a sot. "If I may make a suggestion, Lord Morwick, the brunch may last several hours." She pointedly looked at his empty wine glass. Mother would positively have fits if this large, rough man became drunk and disrupted the entire room.

A mocking smile crossed his lips. "What would you know of such things? I doubt you've ever had anything stronger than tea. May we end this painfully awkward attempt at conversation?"

Petra opened her mouth to speak and found she couldn't think of anything remotely polite to say. She'd never had a gentleman address her in such a way.

"Good." He nodded at her stricken look. "We are in agreement." Morwick then turned his attention back to his plate of food. Lord Kilmaire, to his left, said something and the two began speaking in earnest.

Mortified at having been cut down during her own brother's wedding brunch, Petra turned back to her plate.

What an absolutely horrible man.

After finishing brunch, the ladies all gathered in the large drawing room. The air filled with the laughter of Lady Kilmaire as she teased Arabella. Petra knew the two had been close since they were children. Lady Cupps-Foster, Arabella's aunt and Lord Morwick's mother, regaled the room with details of the Duchess of Canfeld's ball the previous week with the other women all chiming in to comment.

By the time Arabella took her arm and brought Petra to the Dowager Marchioness of Cambourne, Petra had nearly put Morwick and his discourteous behavior out of her mind. She congratulated herself on having maintained a polite demeanor throughout the exchange with the impolite Earl of Morwick, thankful her exposure to him was brief.

After nearly a half hour of being peppered with questions by the Dowager Marchioness of Cambourne, who considered herself to be something of a matchmaker, the elderly woman finally sat back and regarded Petra with amusement. "Forgive me for speaking my mind, Petra, but such a thing is the advantage of old age; that, and the benefit of a cane to wield." She lifted up the head of the cane leaning against her skirts. "You've spoken highly of many of your suitors, yet I do not sense an excess of regard for any particular gentleman. I understand your mother favors Lord Dunning."

"Lord Dunning has asked to call on me," Petra said carefully, not certain where Lady Cambourne's line of questioning would take her. Her mother favored Dunning, but Petra did not.

"Humph." The older woman's fingers flitted against the top of her cane. "I do not think Dunning to be your choice of husband. He's closer to me in age." She chuckled.

"Mother finds him to be suitable." Petra had already decided to encourage several other gentlemen she'd met in hope of distracting Mother from Lord Dunning.

"A practiced answer." The older woman leaned forward. "Your life is very well-ordered, isn't it?" She glanced toward Petra's mother as disapproval colored her words. "With military precision."

"I suppose so, my lady." Petra demurred. She'd been cautioned by her mother repeatedly to *never* offend the Dowager Marchioness of Cambourne.

"Would you like to know what I think?" The Dowager's gloved hand tightened on her cane. "That is a rhetorical question, my girl. For I shall tell you what I think whether you wish it or not. You, Petra," Lady Cambourne leaned so close Petra could smell the lavender in her hair, "fairly *simmer* with rebellion."

Petra jerked back in surprise. "I don't know what you mean, my lady."

"Pish. I am well-versed in playing demure and obedient as I did so myself for many years. Do not be so quick to allow your mother to make all your decisions. It is *your* life, after all, not hers." Lady Cambourne gave her a kindly smile. "Follow where your heart leads, as your brother has."

Petra nodded slowly, confused by the comment. "Forgive me, but—"

"I realize my advice is contrary to what society dictates. I assure you," she said with a laugh. "And I am considered a bastion of propriety. But I like you, Petra Grantly, and would see you happy as your brother is. You remind me a bit of myself, when I was busy being perfect."

"I—" Petra closed her mouth, uncertain as to what she could say to such a statement. Her entire life had been dictated by her mother. But that was no different from any other young lady of her acquaintance. True, Mother's rules had begun to chafe at Petra, and there *were* times when Petra could feel her ladylike decorum begin to slip before she steadfastly pushed it back into place.

Thankfully, Mother had been too busy agonizing over Rowan's choice of wife to pay too much attention to Petra as of late. Petra had stretched her wings, so to speak, and taken note that all marriages need not be passionless. Incredibly, an image of Morwick flitted through her mind. Her nose wrinkled as she pushed such a thought aside. *Surely not.*

"So there is someone." Lady Cambourne murmured.

Petra composed herself. "No, there's—"

"My lady," Mother said from behind Petra, "might I borrow my daughter for a moment?"

Lady Cambourne glanced up at her mother. "Of course, Lady Marsh. Petra and I have had a wonderful chat. I commend you on raising such a lovely young woman. She is a true credit to you and Lord Marsh."

"Thank you." Mother gushed at Lady Cambourne's praise.

Petra stood and dipped politely to the Dowager. As she lifted her head, the older woman winked at her and Petra smiled back.

"Whatever were you discussing with Lady Cambourne?" Mother sniffed at Petra suspiciously as the feather in her headdress quivered in accusation.

"Nothing at all. She wished to know about my Season and the various gentlemen I'd met," Petra said smoothly. "I believe she has a match in mind for me." The last bit was a lie, but one Mother would immediately latch onto.

"Very good, Petra. It doesn't hurt to have her ear. She's known to be an excellent matchmaker. I mentioned Lord Dunning to her, but she seems unimpressed by him. Perhaps he will not be as good for you as I first thought." Mother's brow wrinkled as she led Petra toward the door. "Dearest, Lady Cupps-Foster has gone missing. The gentlemen will be joining us soon to bid goodbye to Rowan and," Mother swallowed, obviously finding it difficult to say the words, "his wife. I would go myself, but I need to shepherd everyone out. I believe she wished to refresh herself but has perhaps become lost."

"Of course, Mother." Petra clasped her hands, obedient as always, telling herself to ignore the flash of irritation at the request. Mother *could* have sent one of the servants.

Heels clicking smartly on the freshly polished tiles of the hall, Petra headed in the direction of one of the smaller parlors which had been set aside for the ladies' use.

Passing the library, Petra slowed at the sound of Lady Cupps-Foster speaking to someone. She started to announce herself but then heard the dark rasp of Lord Morwick's voice.

Petra stopped, surprised at the sudden flapping of butterflies in her stomach. Mother's voice echoed in her mind, instructing Petra to turn around, as ladies did not eavesdrop on private conversations.

Petra, careful to step lightly, ignored her mother's imagined voice and moved closer to the door, which had been left ajar.

"Can you not behave for the length of time it takes for your cousin to be married?" Lady Cupps-Foster reprimanded.

"Is that why you've pulled me aside like an errant youngster?" A masculine snort.

"You drank far too much wine at brunch."

"The only way to tolerate my dinner companion."

"Petra is a lovely young woman, and much sought after. I marked your interest in her. You could stay a week or so more, Brendan. Perhaps call on her."

"Are you joking, Mother? Perfect Petra? She's yet another empty-headed pea-wit whose only purpose is to land a titled husband. A porcelain doll, lovely but lacking a brain. My boredom in conversing with her was only made palatable by the wine."

Lady Cupps-Foster made a dismissive sound and marched out of the library as Petra sank into one of the alcoves.

Of all the unmitigated gall. First ogling her during the ceremony then dismissing her out of hand during the brunch when she tried to be polite. She was still fuming when Morwick walked out of the library. He paused, clearly sensing her presence, and turned in her direction.

Her hands crawled from her sides in an attempt to clasp themselves demurely, as she'd been instructed, and failed.

"I thought properly bred ladies didn't eavesdrop." Morwick moved closer, leaning against the wall, clearly amused by the mounting rage that must have been visible on her face. He loomed over her, large and intimidating, like an angry bear or some other beast. "What are you going to do? Call me a dreadful cad?"

Red flashed before Petra's eyes, and she had to restrain herself from stamping her foot. Later, she would count the moment as one of the few times she'd ever lost her temper.

"I am not a bloody pea-wit, you *monster*." Petra had the momentary satisfaction of watching his eyes widen at the anger she threw back at him. "Possibly *you* are accustomed to dim-witted women as I cannot imagine any young lady with a modicum of intelligence expressing the slightest interest in you. A *gentleman* would not comport himself in such a way. I only wish I could have availed myself of the wine to blot out *your* presence. Perhaps become—"

The remainder of her diatribe was cut short as Morwick's mouth fell on hers. He placed his hands, palms flat, on the wall behind her, neatly trapping Petra between his arms. His lips were relentless and hungry, demanding her surrender, ravaging Petra until she felt light-headed. Her hands flew out to grasp the lapel of his coat, holding on for dear life. The kiss deepened, becoming gentle and coaxing until Petra tentatively kissed him back, mimicking the movement of his lips on hers.

A growl of satisfaction sounded from the large male holding her captive.

"Lady Cupps-Foster." Mother's voice sounded from further down the hall. "Goodness, have you seen Petra? I sent her after you. Where has she gotten off to?"

Morwick broke the kiss, eyes burning with blue flame, and took a step back, regarding her with an odd intensity.

Petra swallowed, her fingertips flying to touch her swollen lower lip. She moved down the wall until she had put enough distance between herself and Morwick, hurrying toward the sound of her mother's voice. She'd never been kissed in such a way nor felt such...a *stirring* within herself. It was as if she'd been out in the snow for hours and was suddenly in front of a hot searing fire. It was unsettling and uncomfortable.

And wonderful.

Shaken, Petra went to her mother's side. She dared not look back or lift her eyes as the guests shouted congratulations to the bride and groom, too afraid she'd catch his eyes.

Petra never wished to see the Earl of Morwick again.

ix months later.

"When Lord Pendleton extended an invitation to visit his estate, I'd no idea we'd be traveling into the wilds of England. I hadn't realized his estate was quite so far away. Goodness, I feel as if we are in a different country," Mother said, smoothing down an errant fold in her skirt.

Petra grasped the window ledge as the coach listed dangerously to one side. The roads were excessively rough and full of nothing but ruts and potholes. She was certain the springs of her father's coach were on the verge of being ruined forever. He'd have fits when they finally returned home and he saw the damage. "Derbyshire is still in England, Mother. It is not so very far."

"We should already be planning your wedding from the comfort of London." Mother's lips formed a tiny hill of disapproval. "Traveling all this way when the end result will be the same."

Petra absolutely hated that particular expression of her mother's. The pursing of Mother's lips all but decreed Petra was about to be chastised in some way.

"My request is not an unusual one." Petra murmured and pressed her forehead into the glass window. "I only wished to meet Simon's family and spend some time with him to make sure we suit."

"Lord Pendleton has made his intentions toward you clear. There was no need for us to come all this way." Mother sniffed. "Apparently he feels you *do* suit."

"I wish to be certain. It is my life, after all, Mother." Marriage was a daunting proposition even though she'd been preparing for such a thing her entire life.

"Petra," Mother admonished her, "I'm not sure what is the cause of your foul mood; perhaps your distress is caused by nerves."

"I was fine until dinner last night. I believe the stew didn't agree with me."

"Nerves, Petra. I ate exactly the same stew as you and have suffered no ill effects. You are only anxious at meeting Lord Pendleton's family. I don't blame you, of course. I was nervous the first time I met your grandparents, knowing your father would propose we marry." Mother nodded her head. "We are all in agreement Lord Pendleton will make you a most adequate husband."

Petra frowned at the word. She didn't wish to marry *adequate*.

"I feel as if you and Father are rushing me into marriage because Simon has offered for me," Petra answered. "Surely—"

Her mother puffed in frustration. "You *like* Lord Pendleton. He's been courting you for weeks. Good Lord, he was the very best of the crop of bachelors this Season and is quite taken with you. Don't you want to marry him?"

"Of course I do." A least she thought she did. When he'd first made his intentions clear, Petra had been certain, swept away in the excitement of having the attractive viscount court her. "But I've known him such a short time."

"You're concerned, I can see it. You worry if Simon's family and you don't get on, he will rescind his offer of marriage. Do not worry, dearest. Our visit is only a formality, I promise."

Petra's stomach ached. That was Petra's concern. Her parents had been *thrilled* when Simon asked permission to court her. Viscount Pendleton was a prominent member of Parliament, highly respected and quite dashing. He had also chased off Lord Dunning, the man her mother had originally wished Petra to marry. Petra had been incredibly grateful. Dunning was twice her age and prone to gout. Simon's attention had seemed a godsend at the time.

"I like Simon very much but —" But what? How could she explain to her mother what was wrong when Petra didn't know herself? She'd pled her case to Father, telling him she only wished more time. Simon's courtship of her had happened so fast. Father had acquiesced. The betrothal papers had been drawn up and reviewed by the Marsh solicitors, but nothing would be signed until she returned to London and Petra gave her agreement to the marriage. *Father had promised*. She shot her mother a mutinous glance. "Surely, a bit more time, or even another Season, would have made little difference if Simon and I suit."

"Petra, you are one and twenty. Nearly *ancient*. Waiting would have served no purpose other than potentially losing Pendleton's interest and possibly labeling you a spinster or worse. You might never have another suitor of such standing. The match is incredibly advantageous for all concerned."

"I have not accepted Simon's proposal." Advantageous. More so for her parents than for her. "Father has promised I am allowed the final decision."

Her mother looked away. "You and Simon are perfection together."

"As I recall, Mother, you felt much the same about Lady Gwendolyn as a wife for Rowan."

Her mother pursed her lips and sat back against the squabs. The return of the tiny hill above Mother's lip told Petra she didn't care to be reminded of such an utter failure in matchmaking. Her mother detested having her wishes disregarded. "Your brother's marriage to Arabella was not exactly what Lord Marsh and I envisioned. That much is true."

My God, that was the understatement of the century. Her mother's dislike of Rowan's wife was so well-known it had sparked rumors in the *ton* that her brother was contemplating an annulment, or even more scandalous, a divorce by order of Parliament so that Rowan could marry Lord White's daughter, Gwendolyn.

"Arabella is no longer so unpleasant." Mother's eye twitched a bit as she spoke. "I believe marriage to your brother will soften her further with time."

Petra pressed a hand to her lips to keep from snorting in disbelief. Arabella was many things—controlling, devious and possessive of Petra's brother—but certainly *no one* would describe Arabella as *soft*. Petra had not always liked Arabella, but the last few months had given her a grudging respect for her new sister-in-law. Arabella possessed a ruthless nature and was brilliant in business, much like Petra's brother. Rowan, for his part, eyed his wife as if she were a giant tea cake he wished to devour.

A love match. I am surrounded by them, though Mother doesn't consider such a thing of import.

Perhaps that is what had given her pause in agreeing to Viscount Pendleton's suit. She liked Simon very much, but she wasn't in love with him. And he didn't look at her like a tea cake either.

"Dearest." Lady Marsh took Petra's hand, stretching her plump figure across the coach. "You and Pendleton make a *very* attractive couple, and he's completely besotted by you."

"Yes, so you keep telling me." Besotted was a rather strong word. Mother acted as if Simon had been composing love sonnets and plying Petra with trinkets and flowers. He had done no such thing. He'd told her once that he believed an excess of emotion would be frowned upon by his peers. Simon was incredibly conscious of anything smacking of impropriety. The most Petra had ever received from him was a brotherly peck on the cheek.

"I find him delightful and well-mannered," Mother continued. "Mature beyond his years. Pendleton will make you a fine husband."

"Then perhaps you should marry him, Mother." Petra's obedient manner finally slipped. She was exhausted with Mother's litany regarding the wonderfulness of Simon. Everyone, especially Mother, expected Petra to be so bloody *grateful* Simon wanted her. The entire *ton* had congratulated Petra on her good fortune.

Mother gave her a hard stare. "I'll tolerate none of your missish behavior, Petra. I see a streak of rebellion in you of late I do not care for."

Fuming at her mother's chastisement, Petra took a deep breath, her gloved hands automatically crawling into her lap. Clasping her fingers had been ingrained in Petra for so long, the action was nearly second nature: a sign of a well-mannered young lady, one who is seen and not heard.

"I feel I don't know Simon as I should. If I'm going to agree to be his wife, I would like to know better the man whose children I must bear. If the Pendletons are to become my family, should I not come to know them better?"

"Bearing Simon's children is the privilege of his wife." A humph of frustration. "And that is *why* we are traveling to his estate, Petra. So that you may come to know each other better. At your insistence." Mother shook her head and went back to her book. "This change in your usually obedient nature has been most noticeable since your brother's marriage. I blame outside influences."

Mother was referring to Arabella.

Petra turned her attention back to the window. Marriage to Simon *would* be incredibly advantageous. He was wealthy, intelligent, and highly respected, even if some in the *ton* considered Simon a bit tightly laced. He was charming. Unfailingly polite. Handsome. But she hadn't any great passion for him. There was no glancing at him with longing from across a crowded ballroom. Nor the racing of her pulse when he drew near.

Perhaps only time was needed. Away from London, in the country, Petra was hopeful passion would bloom between them, or at the very least, something more than friendship. Perhaps she was being unrealistic, for most marriages began with little affection.

I want what Rowan has with Arabella. A spark.

That's why she'd insisted on this tedious journey to Simon's home. Petra was determined to be hopeful.

I felt such mad desire once and it only took a moment.

The wild scenery of the Peak District flew past the window and transformed into an image of a large, broad-shouldered man with eyes the color of sapphires. Rude and ill-mannered Morwick may have been, but Petra had relived the kiss he'd given her thousands of times. She'd called him a monster and instead of being offended or apologizing, as any true gentleman would have, Morwick had *kissed* her. And worse, she'd enjoyed the press of his lips against hers, the way his larger form had trapped her against the wall, as if he were claiming her. Morwick hadn't even touched her, except for his mouth, but her skin heated and pulsed as if he had.

Petra pressed a hand to her stomach as her insides took an unwanted turn. She forced herself to focus on the beauty outside the coach window.

Her knowledge of the area was woefully lacking. This part of England was divided into the Dark Peak and the White Peak. The Dark Peak consisted of cliffs and hills of gritstone which rose above the moors to overshadow portions of the White Peak, littered with fields of limestone. What little she knew of the area was the result of information Simon had imparted over dinner with her parents several weeks ago. The area east of Castleton, where Simon's estate lay, was home to the only known deposits of Blue John. The mineral was known for the distinctive purple, yellow and blue banding and was incredibly rare. Many years ago, Simon's father had found a vein of Blue John on the land surrounding Brushbriar, and the Pendletons had become quite wealthy as a result.

The Marsh home possessed two vases made of Blue John, which Mother had proudly shown to Simon after dinner.

"I doubt I could be happy here," Petra said, mainly to irritate her mother. "It's quite dreary." Perhaps Mother would take the hint and order the coach be turned around. She and Simon could continue to court when he returned to London and Petra could make her decision in familiar surroundings.

"I quite agree. I've never cared for the moors. Thankfully, Lord Pendleton spends most of his time in London. He's become *very* important in Parliament," her mother reminded her for the hundredth time, not looking up from her book. "He has a lovely house in Mayfair across from a park. A wonderful address to be sure. Think of the dinners you'll preside over."

Petra tried to imagine herself as a politician's wife, hosting dinner parties for London's elite, but didn't find the role as appealing as her mother did. Politics bored her, although Petra was involved in several charities and concerned especially with reforms affecting children. That was what had first attracted her to Simon; she'd heard him speak at a ladies' luncheon on the subject. He'd been so *passionate* about the subject matter. Petra had found him incredibly appealing.

As the coach came over a rise in the road, an immense lake came into view, the water studded with large boulders, sparkling in the meager sunlight. Birds swooped down across the expanse, calling to each other. It was a serene, peaceful scene and Petra's mood calmed. She had a sudden longing to kick off her shoes and race through the tall grass as she had before Mother had begun to groom her into the young lady she now was. It was tedious being demure all the time.

"I do hope Agnes and Tessie arrived at Lord Pendleton's with no incident and have not shirked their duties. I shall want a lie-down when we arrive, and our clothing aired. I was unsure about sending them ahead of us, but possibly it was for the best. I'm not sure what else we could have done with you feeling ill and lingering in bed." Mother's brow wrinkled. "I do hope Lady Pendleton doesn't find the appearance of our servants without us to be ill-mannered."

"I am sure Simon's mother is most understanding." Mother was obsessed with appearances and the merest hint of impropriety horrified her. "You wrote her a note, after all." It was apparent Mother's biggest concern was Lady Pendleton and *not* Petra's physical state, for she hadn't asked Petra how she was feeling since the coach had left the inn some hours ago. "Since you asked," Petra jabbed at her mother, "I'm feeling marginally better."

Mother leaned over her. "Nerves, Petra, nothing more. Why don't you shut your eyes and try to take a nap? I'd hate—"

Mother's words were cut off as the coach lurched violently

to the left, then to the right, knocking Petra's head sharply against the window before unseating her. The contents of her stomach, only recently settled, lurched wildly, before the coach shuddered and came to a stop.

Petra lifted her head from the windowpane with a wince, gingerly touching a finger to her temple. *Bollocks, that hurt.*

"Dear *Lord*. Petra, are you all right?" Her mother's worried face swam before her. "I hope that doesn't bruise. Goodness, whatever is Jenkins thinking, shaking us about in such a manner?"

"I'm fine, Mother."

Satisfied, Mother sat back and clasped her gloved hands in her lap in expectation, waiting for the coach to begin moving once more.

"Perhaps an animal ran out in front of the coach," Petra surmised. The lovely bonnet, created especially to accompany her new traveling dress, had been knocked sideways. One of the tiny blue flowers decorating the brim had fallen off. Petra discreetly picked up the flower and tucked it into the pocket of her dress, hoping her mother wouldn't notice. Mother wished Petra to look her best for her first introduction to Lady Pendleton, and the dress had been made especially for the occasion.

Petra straightened the bonnet, making sure the remainder of the flowers gracing the crown were still intact. Satisfied all was well, the bonnet once more perched fetchingly on her head, Petra moved to stand. Unfortunately, she could not. Looking down, she saw the skirts of her dress were caught between the edge of the leather seat and the coach wall, possibly on a wayward nail. Giving a gentle tug, she tried to free herself.

Mother's eyes bugged and her hands waved frantically at the tearing sound. "Don't you *dare* rip your dress, Petra. We spent hours choosing *exactly* the right fabric and trim for the dress in which you would meet your future in-laws. The color is perfection. Your father nearly had a fit of apoplexy at the cost. We are *not* going to appear on their doorstep in torn clothing as if we are *beggars*. First our servants appear unsupervised at the door of Brushbriar, and now you wish your future mother-in-law's first impression of you to be one of you in rags? Whatever are you thinking?"

"I was thinking I should like to return to my seat. What do you suggest I do, Mother? Spend our visit in the coach? Won't such a thing be much more ill-mannered?" Petra tried to make herself more comfortable without tearing her skirt further.

A rap on the door silenced her mother's retort. "My lady?" It was Jenkins, the driver. "We've a problem with the coach."

"Well, fix it," her mother ordered. "It can be repaired, can it not? We don't wish to be late."

Jenkins made an odd sound as if something were stuck in his throat. More likely he didn't know what to say to her mother, who expected the world to bow to her dictates. Everyone in the Marsh household, including Father, certainly did.

Because of James. Petra thought guiltily of her long-dead brother, Mother's favorite and the heir. He'd been gone for many years but his death still left such a pall over the family that Petra and Rowan had been raised to never displease Mother.

"Of course, my lady." Jenkins' lips drew taut as he tipped his hat. He caught sight of her on the floor of the coach. "Are you injured, Lady Petra?"

"I'm fine, Jenkins. Thank you." Nausea was slowly making its way back through her mid-section, followed by a vague cramping sensation.

An hour later, the coach still sat in the road while Jenkins and the two grooms attempted to fix whatever had caused them to stop. Sounds of banging and masculine grumbling came from the back of the coach, although Jenkins assured her mother all was well.

Petra slumped against the seat of the coach, still stuck in place. Every time she attempted to move, Mother shot her a look of pure murder. After the third such admonishment, Petra asked, "What *is* your plan, Mother, concerning my dress? I assume you have one."

"Oh, I can't worry about such a thing now. I'm quite concerned we shall have to stay the night out here in the open." Her hands flapped around tragically. "Whatever shall we do? Lord Pendleton will think some great ill has befallen us. Kidnapped by highwaymen or eaten by wild animals."

It was a struggle to keep from laughing out loud at her mother's dramatics. The slightest inconvenience could be a cause for concern. A broken heel on one's shoe, a missing earring, serving fish instead of chicken, tearing an expensive traveling dress. Another painful cramp tightened Petra's stomach. Her daughter becoming ill upon catching sight of the man who'd offered for her and his family.

"Petra, cease moving this instant." Mother's chin quivered. "I cannot think with such a distraction."

"Ho, there."

A deep baritone sounded from outside the coach, and the greeting was returned in kind by Jenkins. Someone had miraculously found the Marsh coach on this road in the middle of nowhere. Petra hadn't heard another coach or even the sound of a horse approaching. The newcomer must be on foot.

Boots crunched outside. The coach swayed, followed by a male grunt as the visitor examined the wheel. "You've broken the axle. See there. A tiny fracture but enough to dislodge the wheel."

The raspy, low voice sent a ripple over Petra's skin,

temporarily dislodging the awful cramping in her stomach. Though faintly familiar, Petra had no idea who the visitor could be.

"We haven't the means to repair it," Jenkins answered. "We are on our way to Brushbriar, the estate of Lord Pendleton. Do you know of it?"

A snort answered Jenkins's question. "You're going the wrong way, my good man. Brushbriar is due west of here. You took the right fork in the road, not the left."

A deep sigh of exasperation followed the information.

Poor Jenkins.

"Don't worry. Happens all the time. The road isn't well marked, and if you aren't familiar with the area, it's quite easy to get lost. And I've a man who can fix the axle."

"Thank you." Jenkins was overjoyed at having a solution to the broken axle. "I'll inform Lady Marsh."

"Lady Marsh?" The visitor seemed to contemplate the presence of Petra's mother. "I'm acquainted."

Mother gave Petra an odd look and shrugged. She didn't know who their rescuer was, either.

The door to the coach flew open to reveal a broad set of shoulders followed by a mop of dark curls.

Bloody hell. Could the journey to Pendleton's become any worse? If Petra hadn't been ill before, she most certainly was *now*.

The Earl of Morwick invaded the small space of the coach, the slightly battered coat he wore dripping moisture on the floor. A leaf was stuck in the unruly tangle of his hair, and the stain of a beard darkened his jaw. He looked savage and wild, much like the landscape outside. His beautiful eyes flashed with mild annoyance at seeing Petra and her mother.

A delicious trickle of awareness suffused Petra's skin. She allowed the feeling to sink into her bones before remembering how horrible Morwick was.

"Lord Morwick," Mother said in a surprised tone, clearly unsettled by his unexpected appearance. "My goodness, you are the last person I thought to see."

"I could say the same, Lady Marsh. You are quite far from your usual habitat of London." His tone was polite though Petra could have sworn she detected a hint of sarcasm. It was difficult to tell since everything he said sounded mildly sarcastic.

"I happen to live here," he continued. "My estate is close by, or relatively close." He pointed over his shoulder to a spot in the distance. "I've been out fishing and caught nothing. Except for the two of you." This time when he looked at Petra, the gold flecks in his marvelous eyes caught the light in the coach.

Petra suddenly felt quite warm despite the chill in the air.

"What a lucky occurrence, Lord Morwick." Mother wasn't pleased. Even though she'd chosen to accept her son's marriage to Arabella, as she'd had no other choice, Mother was not enamored of anyone related to the Duke of Dunbar, though Mother liked the duke well enough. "Will you be able to assist us with our coach?"

"I've a man in my employ who'll be able to fix your wheel, but you'll not get to Brushbriar tonight. Besides the broken axle, Pendleton's estate is at least a three-hour ride in the opposite direction."

Mother's face collapsed. "But we are *expected* at Brushbriar today. Lord Pendleton will be most concerned. You are acquainted with Lord Pendleton, I assume?"

"We are well acquainted, Lady Marsh." He didn't elaborate, but Petra thought his tone sounded dismissive. He looked down the road then back at the horizon. "The sun is beginning to set. It would be best if you and your daughter," he finally gave Petra some acknowledgement, "come to Somerton with me."

Mother's lip quivered at the thought of spending the night under Morwick's roof. She was eyeing him as if he were some wild animal. "I hate to inconvenience you. Perhaps there is an inn nearby?" Her mother sounded so hopeful.

"There is not." The response was clipped as if Morwick were already tired of dealing with Lady Marsh. "My mother is in residence and will be thrilled for your company."

Petra's stomach cramped again. The last thing she wished was to accept the hospitality of Lord Morwick under *any* circumstances, but especially when she felt so dreadfully ill. At least she wouldn't have to greet Simon in such a state.

"Thank you, Lord Morwick. We gratefully accept your offer. If you are certain we aren't an inconvenience."

"Perish the thought." A tiny bit of derision colored his reply as the left side of his mouth ticked upward.

Petra found her gaze focused on his mouth. Hastily, she looked away. It seemed strange those lips had once been on hers.

"I *do* look forward to renewing my acquaintance with Lady Cupps-Foster." Mother bestowed a genuine smile on Morwick while plucking at her skirts.

"She often tells me I am poor company. She'll be most pleased to see you regardless of the circumstances." Again, there was a hint of mockery. "I've already sent one of your grooms to my home to retrieve a carriage. He should return within the hour."

"Then this is a happy accident," Mother replied, accepting Morwick's assistance as he took her hand and helped her out of the coach. "Isn't it?"

Petra didn't think so. She found this a most *unhappy* occurrence. She was ill, not at her best, and must now spend the evening in the company of a man who had insulted and...*ravaged* her.

The ebony curls came back through the door, flicking

drops of moisture on Petra and looming over her like a villain in a lurid novel. Did he have to be so *bloody* intimidating?

"Are you injured?" Could he sound any less concerned with her well-being?

"No, my lord. At least no more so than our last meeting." The last bit slipped out before Petra could think better of it.

A tiny grimace flitted about the full lips. "I barely *recall* our last meeting. Your brother's wedding, was it?"

The very nerve of him. My God, he'd *kissed* her. Why hadn't she slapped him? Perhaps he would have remembered *that*. "Stop looking at me as if I were spoiled pudding," she said back to him. "It's rude and impolite."

Heat slid over her arms and across her chest. Another disturbing development, and one which infuriated Petra. "Have I done something to annoy you, my lord? Besides my mere presence, of course."

The gold strands in his eyes sparked. "A rather spirited retort. How out of character for a *well-mannered* young lady such as yourself. Perhaps you've hit your head." His lips twitched again.

He was enjoying her discomfort. "I'm *quite* spirited," she snapped. "Terribly so."

"So I've noticed." He leaned closer, the heat of his body chasing away the last of the chill clinging to the inside of the coach. Not that Petra was cold; on the contrary, she felt hot all over. Dear Lord, she hoped she hadn't caught a fever of some sort.

"You smell very piney," she said. He smelled of the moors and the fresh air, an incredibly intoxicating scent. "Like a giant tree."

"I've been outdoors. Fishing. And it isn't the insult you perceive it to be."

His lashes were unusually long and lush for a man. And a small scar bisected his left eyebrow. She hadn't noticed a scar at Rowan's wedding, so perhaps it was recent. According to gossip, he was famous for fist fights and brawling in taverns. He was probably loaded with scars and cuts...all over.

Heat rushed across her chest.

"Are you sure you haven't hit your head?" His gaze lingered on the knot swelling on her temple. "You've a small lump." He touched her forehead. "Just there."

"I was wondering about the scar." Against her will, Petra's gaze was drawn to the stretch of his coat across the breadth of his shoulders. Many gentlemen in London actually padded their coats to unnaturally give the appearance of a more manly form. An acquaintance of hers, Betina Willingsworth, had told a story of one of her suitors whose right shoulder slowly slid down to form a lump on his upper arm while she and the gentleman in question had been dancing. Much to the gentleman's horror.

Morwick tilted his head, peering closely at her eyes. Their lips were mere inches away. She almost thought he meant to kiss her. The words he said next were like a bucket of cold water.

"You look a bit addled."

"Addled?" Thankfully, he'd reminded her what a complete ass he was. *Addled*. *Pea-wit*. He thought her little better than a stuffed dress wearing a bonnet. Not even memorable enough to recall their kiss.

"Well, if you aren't hurt, what are you waiting for?" His lips tightened and he pulled back to the opening of the coach. "Expecting me to carry you out? Come along."

Expecting him to— "If you must know, I'm trapped." Petra nodded toward the bunched pile of her skirts. "I realize behaving politely is beyond you, but I beg you to find a spark of manners."

Morwick's tightening of the lips turned into a full-blown frown.

"My skirt is caught," she hissed.

"Well, pull it out." He spoke in the tone one uses for an idiot. Or a *pea-wit*. The frown deepened.

"Mother doesn't wish me to tear the fabric. The traveling dress is new and quite expensive." Good Lord, she did sound like an insipid twit obsessed with her clothing, but she was striving to regain her usual decorum, which was difficult given she couldn't seem to avert her gaze from his mouth. "I know you probably don't carry a pair of scissors with you, that would be ridiculous. But perhaps a small knife? Some gentlemen carry a—"

A large hand reached behind her and grabbed a handful of her skirts.

Petra squeaked in alarm and tried to get away. "No. Absolutely do not—"

One sharp jerk and the sound of her skirt tearing, as well as her underskirt, echoed in the coach. Now untethered, Petra toppled over in a graceless manner, exposing her calves and ankles.

"You—" Her mouth gaped open in shock. "Why—"

Her beautiful traveling dress, the one made especially for this journey, was utterly *ruined*. The skirt was torn beyond any repair a skilled seamstress could make. Mother would be furious about the destruction of the dress.

And possibly also at Morwick for seeing Petra's ankles. Thank goodness Mother had left the coach.

"Stop gaping at me like a fish and hurry along before the sun descends completely and we must pluck our way back to Somerton as if we are blind."

Morwick was an *utter* cad. And he had a dimple in his cheek.

"You are no gentleman," she huffed.

The dimple deepened. "I never claimed to be. And it's only a dress, *Perfect* Petra." Morwick took her elbow, ignoring her hiss of outrage. He practically pulled her from the coach. His hand stayed on her elbow, brushing against her hand as his fingers fell away.

Petra was sure he'd done such to unnerve her. *Cad.*

"I'm sure you've hundreds of dresses. At the minimum, dozens. Far more than you could wear in a lifetime."

"Thousands." She said with determination as he turned his back to her. "They can barely be contained in my wardrobe." Petra would have said more but a lightheaded feeling came over her, and the ground felt unsteady. She blinked as her stomach lurched painfully again. Mother was sitting on a large tree stump, across which Jenkins had draped his cloak.

Mother seemed to be very far away from where Petra stood.

Clenching her fists in resolve, Petra made her way forward, the nausea rolling through her stomach in waves. She refused to be humiliated further by becoming ill in front of Morwick. Her temple was throbbing, and she was sure she'd have a large bruise when she arrived at Brushbriar.

"He is insufferable," she muttered, determined to hang onto her anger. A horrible gurgling sound came from her stomach as Petra struggled to hold the end of her dress together. She was so utterly, completely miserable that for a brief moment, Petra wished fervently she'd just married Dunning.

BRENDAN LORNE, 11TH EARL OF MORWICK WAS IN AN incredibly foul mood caused in no small part by the appearance of Lady Marsh and her daughter on his doorstep. Perfect Petra was far more beautiful than he remembered and his attraction to her had not lessened one bit, as evidenced by the hardening of his cock the moment he set eyes on her.

Desire punched him in the gut as he discovered her, glaring defiantly at him from the floor of the Marsh coach. It was the same desire that had led him to inappropriately kiss her in the shadowed hall of her own home. Worse, she'd not resisted him in any way; instead, the little nitwit had grabbed the lapels of his coat and pressed herself against him with a tiny whimper.

Christ.

Brendan had been unsettled from the moment he'd seen her at Arabella's wedding. Upon being introduced he'd behaved badly, pressing his lips against her gloved hand for far too long. Petra had worn a gown the color of spring grass, the pale tops of her delicate breasts pushing up against the silk with every breath. He'd had to rein in the urge to pounce on her and disrupt the entire wedding. Worse, she'd been seated next to him at the brunch, smelling of roses and oddly, sugar cookies.

Brendan adored sugar cookies.

Petra, to her credit, had attempted to engage him in polite conversation. In return, he had treated her with barely concealed disdain, the only weapon against her he possessed. When she had confronted him, calling him a monster, Brendan had only wanted her more. Perfect, ladylike Petra, fists balled at her sides, calling him a monster, had been incredibly arousing. Brendan had come very close to lifting her skirts and taking her against the wall. Instead, he'd merely kissed her senseless.

Nothing good could come from involvement with a woman like Petra.

Although at the moment, his cock begged to differ.

Brendan had ruined her gown deliberately today, behaving in the most ungentlemanly way he could imagine. Rude, callous behavior was guaranteed to push Petra away. Ladies hated poor manners. It would be better for all concerned if she detested the sight of him.

Which was *why* inviting Petra and the pompous Lady Marsh to stay the night was absolute idiocy on his part. But there hadn't been an alternative. He could hardly leave them sitting in the road. Even Brendan wasn't that much of a cad. Besides, keeping the Marsh ladies under his roof for the night was bound to make Pendleton livid. The prig needed to show a tad of emotion once in a while.

"I must thank you again, Lord Morwick, for coming to our rescue," Lady Marsh repeated. The woman seemed completely unsure of how to converse with Brendan. She tried to hide her dismay at his rumpled appearance, the only sign of her distaste the small lines forming around her lips as she struggled not to frown. Did she expect him to go tramping about the woods in a tailored coat and trousers? She stared with muted horror at the sight of his bare throat. Lady Marsh was an excellent example of why he didn't involve himself with young, vapid ladies of the *ton*; they grew up into fussy, vapid matrons of the *ton*. A horrible vicious cycle.

"The pleasure is entirely mine, I assure you." He glanced at the top of the disabled Marsh coach. "I see no trunks, Lady Marsh." He was sure she had a change of clothes for every hour of the day. Had her trunks fallen off?

"Our trunks, along with our maids were sent on to Brushbriar early this morning ahead of our arrival. Petra needed her rest." Lady Marsh spared a glance for her daughter. "Nerves, you see. Meeting your future husband's family can be rather trying."

"I suppose it must be." He ignored the sudden tightening of his chest at her announcement, even though he'd assumed such when Lady Marsh had announced their destination.

"So, you see, our things are at Brushbriar and we

are...*here*." Her mouth quivered in distress. "We've nothing but the clothes on our backs." Lady Marsh managed to make the lack of clothing for one night akin to dying of the plague. She really was a ridiculous woman.

"Pray, don't distress yourself, Lady Marsh. I'll send a note to Brushbriar. I've a groom who rides incredibly fast and will carry word to Pendleton of your delay. I can instruct him to have a valise packed for your stay this evening. And I'm sure my mother will be happy to lend you her lady's maid for the night."

A choking noise came from behind Brendan. Petra had been unusually quiet while he conversed with Lady Marsh, though he'd been keenly aware of her, seething with anger, standing behind him.

Brendan turned, about to toss a veiled insult in her direction, one guaranteed to ruffle her perfect little feathers. The words died in his throat at the sight of her.

Petra was trembling and deathly pale. One slender hand was pushed flush against her lips, the other pressed against her stomach. A horrified look had entered her eyes.

"Petra, dear Lord!" Lady Marsh gasped, making no move to come to her daughter's aid, and turned away. "You've torn your skirt."

Brendan had no such reservations about approaching Petra in such a state, and he didn't give a damn about her skirt since he was the one who'd torn it. She was going to be ill; Brendan had worn the same expression on his own face once or twice.

Damn. I knew I should have walked the other way home today.

Petra's eyes widened at his approach. "No. Don't you *dare* help me," she sputtered before placing the hand back across her mouth. She loped in the direction of a thicket of bramble off the road behind the coach.

Brendan ignored her entreaty to be left in peace. She looked close to collapse.

Petra looked up at him as he took her arm. "I insist you release me." Then she cast up her accounts. All over his boots.

3

My God. I was wrong. This journey can get worse.

Petra had done several embarrassing things in her life. She'd once tripped while dancing with Lord Rhys, and her slipper had come flying off, skittering across the ballroom floor. When she was barely twelve, she'd written a mushy note of affection to the brother of one of her friends who'd just returned from Eton. She'd been teased endlessly for months.

But never, had she *ever*, cast up her accounts on an earl.

A strong hand wrapped around her waist and firmly propelled her to a spray of bushes hidden from Jenkins, her mother and the remaining groom. Morwick grabbed her skirts in one large hand, hauling them up, exposing her stockinged legs rather improperly.

Petra twisted, trying to pull down her skirts even as she felt the remainder of her tea and toast from breakfast rise in her throat. "My God, you would take advantage of me when I'm ill?"

"Stop fussing. You don't want to get any on your dress, do you? I've seen plenty of ankles, Lady Petra, and yours are quite average. And you are ill and not appealing in the least. I think I'll be able to control myself."

"You are *horrible*," she whispered, becoming ill again.

"I never claimed to be anything else." His hands held her firmly about the waist.

Petra had never been so miserable in her life. Her stomach heaved and rolled. She was shaking and coughing. Of all the people she could have been sick in front of, Morwick would have been her last choice. But he said nothing more as he held her until the last of the heaves subsided, merely producing a handkerchief hastily from somewhere in his coat. He pressed the square of cloth to her lips.

The handkerchief smelled of Morwick and dust.

"Better?"

"Your handkerchief smells of dirt. But yes. Thank you." She tried to straighten, but another stomach cramp caused her to double over.

"I'm sorry it's not the delicate, monogrammed bits of silk you're used to, but this isn't London." His voice lowered. "Deep breaths, Petra. You've eaten something spoiled, I imagine. Lady Marsh seems to think you've nerves, but you don't strike me as especially nervous. What did you eat last before becoming ill?"

"Lamb stew," she whispered. "I believe it was the lamb stew." Her stomach turned again. "Are you going to call me Puking Petra now?"

"I hadn't thought of that," he murmured. "What a grand idea."

Morwick tightened his hold, supporting her body with his. He was warm and solid, a port in a storm.

"I shall not apologize for ruining your boots." She choked as the stomach cramps momentarily subsided. "I still find you reprehensible."

"I would expect nothing less." His words were brusque,

but his arm stayed around her waist. "Are you ready to go to your mother?"

Petra nodded dully. "Yes. Thank you."

"Petra!" Lady Marsh stood several feet away, waving her hands. "Oh, my dear one." A startled squeak popped from her lips. "Lord Morwick. Your boots!"

Morwick did not release his hold on Petra even though Mother had noticed. Her lips formed that tiny hill of displeasure. "I see your mother," he said with a trace of humor, "is ready to offer her assistance."

"Oh, she won't be able to help." Petra kept her voice low least her mother hear. "Mother positively faints at the sight of blood or...other things. She will be quite useless and I should hate for you to contend with a fainting countess as well as Puking Petra." She tried to pull away from him but wobbled; he held on tighter.

This time Mother made an odd cluck, the sound of an outraged hen.

"They are just boots, Lady Marsh," Morwick said smoothly. "And old ones at that. Not much of a loss. If you'll excuse me for a moment, I'll clean them off." Morwick's sapphire gaze turned to Petra. "I hear the carriage approaching. Will you be able to make the short ride? Somerton isn't very far." There was concern in his eyes, though he still sounded annoyed at her condition.

"Yes, thank you. I will need to rest before dinner, I think."

"I insist you rest *during* dinner and a physician will be summoned."

"I'm sure that isn't necessary, Lord Morwick." Mother wrung her hands. "It's only nerves and exhaustion from the journey. A good lie-down before dinner and she'll be right as rain, won't you, Petra?"

Morwick stared her mother down, not intimidated by Lady Marsh in the least. "Nevertheless, my lady, Dr. Stubbins will be called." At her mother's protest, he said, "I insist." He walked Petra to the stump her mother rapidly vacated upon their approach and settled her gently before stomping off into the underbrush.

Mother turned to Petra. "How kind," she said over her shoulder to Morwick, clearly resenting his interference. She took Petra's arm. "I'm sure you aren't *really* ill dearest, but nonetheless, I'm happy this didn't happen at Brushbriar. Imagine what Lady Pendleton would have thought had you arrived with a ripped dress and then been unwell in her presence. Thank goodness something positive has come from our little mishap."

Another cramp twisted Petra's stomach. She was too miserable to care what Lady Pendleton would have thought about her being ill.

"A good night's sleep will restore you, I have no doubt. We'll be at Brushbriar well before tea."

As usual, Mother was wrong.

❦ 4 ❦

"Here now, my lady." Tessie, her lady's maid, held the cup of tea to Petra's lips. "Would you like a hot bath?"

"That would be lovely, Tessie. Thank you."

"Afterwards, should you feel well enough, Lady Cupps-Foster is in her private parlor and asks you to join her for tea."

"I should like that." Petra took the cup from her maid's hands with a nod and sipped, thankful the cramps in her stomach had begun to subside. She was by no means well, but at least she'd started the day without a chamber pot in her lap. "Thank you for your care of me yesterday, Tessie. Whatever would I do without you?"

The maid, buxom and red-haired, gave her a gap-toothed smile. "I am so happy you are better. Your mother has been beside herself with worry about you."

Once Dr. Stubbins had pronounced Petra not be moved for several days, Mother had had to capitulate. She sent for Tessie and her own maid, Agnes, who were awaiting their arrival at Brushbriar. Mother had been forced to write a letter

39

of apology to Simon and his mother for their unexpected delay. Dr. Stubbins had declared Petra very ill from spoiled stew, refuting Mother's constant claims Petra was only suffering from nerves. He prescribed bed rest, broth and tea.

Illness aside, Petra was thrilled with the reprieve.

Putting the tea aside, Petra stretched her arms, and gingerly rolled over to leave the bed. The room wobbled and she grabbed the bedpost. Petra shut her eyes firmly until the feeling passed. She needed to drink more fluids. Dr. Stubbins had declared that plenty of water and tea would assist in her recovery. Broth as well if she could tolerate it.

The carriage ride to Somerton had been blessedly brief and passed in a blur of trees and grass. Petra had curled up against her mother's shoulder for the duration of the journey, focusing only on not becoming ill again and ruining Lord Morwick's carriage in addition to his boots. She had barely glanced at the large stone edifice, covered in a thick growth of ivy, rising up from the moors.

Lady Cupps-Foster, face warm in greeting, had grown concerned at the sight of Petra. She'd marched about like a general, issuing orders to a group of servants who had all scurried to do her bidding. Before Petra had known what was happening, she had been changed into a borrowed nightgown of soft cotton and settled on a comfortable bed beneath a down comforter, Mother's concerned face swimming above her. She remembered very little after that except for the chamber pot on her lap.

Once her bath was finished, Petra felt better than she had in days.

She made her way downstairs, pausing to ask a servant for directions to Lady Cupps-Foster's private sitting room and strolled down the hall, admiring the soft blue color of the walls and the polished tile of the floor. A footman standing guard outside of a door at the end of the hall announced her.

While she tried to stop herself, Petra listened for the sound of Morwick's low rasp.

"My dear!" Lady Cupps-Foster looked up as Petra came forward. She put aside the book she'd been reading. "Come in, come in." She patted a spot on the couch to her right. "I'm so glad you felt well enough to come down."

"Thank you for the invitation, my lady." The room was warm and welcoming, much like Lady Cupps-Foster. A fireplace, expertly fitted into a corner, crackled merrily with a fire. An oriental rug, the fibers plush and full, cushioned Petra's steps as she came forward. The colors of the rug, deep blue and burgundy, were accented by curtains of the same colors, framing a large rectangular window with a view of the moors. The furniture was slightly worn, comfortable and well-used. She took a seat and Lady Cupps-Foster placed a pillow behind Petra's back with a smile. The pillow was missing a tassel.

A massive portrait of a young man dominated one of the walls. He was tall and dark-haired, with a signet ring on his pinky finger. At first glance, Petra thought the man was Lord Morwick.

"They look very much alike, do they not?" Lady Cupps-Foster tilted her head toward the portrait, a wistful look on her face. "My late husband." Lady Cupps-Foster spoke. "Reginald—Reggie, I called him."

Petra knew the story of Lady Cupps-Foster; everyone in London did. Widowed three times, all three husbands expiring under mysterious circumstances. Reggie had disappeared on the moors right outside this very window, never to be heard from again.

"Handsome, isn't he?"

The man staring down at Petra had the same mop of ebony curls as Morwick, but his eyes were dark and his build lean, unlike his son's big, broad form. The twist of the lips was the same, a combination between amusement and annoyance. Petra was beginning to know it well. "Very."

"Reggie swept me off my feet. I was widowed less than a year with a son barely out of swaddling clothes when I met him." A small laugh escaped her. "He was relentless in his pursuit. My father was furious. But I found Reggie to be the most fascinating human being I'd ever met. He brought me here to the moors, with Spence. My elder son," she added.

A tingle ran through Petra. She feared Morwick held the same fascination for her as Reggie had for Lady Cupps-Foster. She almost wished he hadn't been so gentle with her. It was easier to dislike him if he remained scornful of her.

"I see Reggie whenever I catch a glimpse of the mop of hair my son refuses to cut properly. And the set of his chin. Goodness, I do tend to rattle on. Come and sit. Timmons has just brought tea and some biscuits."

Petra took the cup of tea and nibbled at a biscuit, careful to gauge her stomach's response to something other than broth.

"Slowly, my dear. Should you feel ill," Lady Cupps-Foster nodded toward a small potted plant near the window with drooping brown leaves, "I'm not fond of that particular lily." Winking at Petra she picked up her own cup and sipped. "I'm told you ruined my son's boots."

Petra's face grew warm. "I'm afraid to tell you I did." She put down the unappealing biscuit. *Maybe tomorrow.*

"I must thank you as the boots needed to go. Woods, that's Brendan's valet, was likely overjoyed. My son has never cared about clothing and is the farthest thing from fashionable you can imagine. Poor Woods." She laughed. "Now my eldest son, Spencer, is much more of a clothes horse. I would hate to see his tailor bill. But not Brendan. He's been mistaken for one of the miners he so enjoys conversing with more than once. I do think he wishes to actually be a miner, for he has a love of going underground. Caves, specifically, though he is just as often seen climbing about." A graceful hand waved in the air. "He will give me a fit of apoplexy one day, I'm sure, with his antics."

"What is he looking for? In the caves?" Petra wondered what would prompt a person to find interest in descending into the earth.

"Fossils, minerals, bits of rock and earth to study. He pursued mineralogy and geology while attending Oxford." A rueful smile graced her lips. "Though his fists and temper got him thrown out. Brendan loves nothing so much as a brawl. My father was so angry with him." Her hair, nearly the same dark shade as her son's, gleamed in the light streaming through the window. She leaned back against the cushions, holding the cup of tea to her lap. "Your mother told me last night you are visiting Brushbriar and Lord Pendleton."

Lady Cupps-Foster had the same indigo eyes as Morwick and was just as direct.

Disconcerted by the question, Petra put down her tea, hands crawling toward each other to clasp together in her habitual ladylike manner. "Lord Pendleton has offered for me."

Lady Cupps-Foster cocked her head. She nodded, her eyes knowing. "Your mother's conversation led me to believe you've accepted."

A rush of frustrated anger rose up in Petra. "I'm sure my mother did not intentionally misinform you, my lady."

"I see." Her eyes were knowing. Before Lady Cupps-Foster could say more, the door to the small sitting room swung open in a great whoosh, the startled footman stepping back with a bow.

Morwick strode in, bits of dirt falling from his boots and pants as he moved forward. He looked down at the mess he had created and sent his mother an apologetic look.

"Can you not wait to be announced?" She didn't sound upset, but instead pleasantly surprised. "How lovely of you, and the cloud of dust you constantly wear, to visit me."

Petra clutched her hands tighter. A wave of awareness washed over her skin, so acute it was nearly painful. She lowered her eyes as the prickling sensation tickled the skin of her neck and arms. He was studying her.

"It's my house, Mother. I shouldn't have to be announced," was his curt reply. Morwick's heavy tread moved closer to finally settle in a chair across from them, stretching out his long legs to cross at the ankle, bumping the small tea table as he did so. With a careless flick, he took the tattered hat he wore off his head, tossing it carelessly onto a neighboring chair. The ebony curls had been flattened from the hat, sticking to his sweat-dampened neck and cheeks. He wore a cambric work shirt, faded from age, and a pair of equally worn leather breeches. Every bit of his large form was covered with a thin layer of dust.

Lady Cupps-Foster made a face and gave a delicate sneeze. "Could you not have refreshed yourself before visiting? Were you digging something up?"

Morwick didn't answer his mother; instead his sapphire gaze turned to Petra. "Hello, Lady Petra." The rasp of his voice was low and deep.

"My lord," Petra greeted him, the familiar heat rushing down her body.

"Feeling better? If not, Mother doesn't care for the lily over there." He nodded toward the pot Lady Cupps-Foster had indicated only moments before. "Brought it home from Castleton one day as a gift."

Lady Cupps-Foster gave him a faintly annoyed look.

"My mother lacks a green thumb." He winked at Lady Cupps-Foster, ignoring the look she shot him. "I fear the poor thing is begging to be put out of its misery, should you require assistance."

"Your mother has kindly already offered the use of her lily, should I need it." Petra answered with a tilt of her head. "You need not worry for your boots again. I can't say the same for your hat."

The gold flecks in his sapphire eyes sparkled back at her. "I stand warned." He stretched his palms over his thighs.

Calluses stood out on the sides of his hands and the tips of his fingers. How had he come by so many? Lady Cupps-Foster was correct. Looking at him now, she would never guess Morwick to be an earl.

Except for his arrogance and manner—that of a person who answers to no one.

Looking at Morwick's hands, Petra thought of Simon's and realized she'd never actually seen them. He always wore gloves in her presence.

He caught her looking. The split eyebrow raised in question. The fingers on his thigh drummed.

"Tea, Brendan? Or perhaps a biscuit?"

"No, thank you." He held Petra's gaze. "I'm headed in the direction of Brushbriar later this afternoon, should you wish to write to Lord Pendleton." A genuine grin split his face. "I'm happy to relay any message."

"How kind of you." Petra picked up her discarded biscuit, determined to try a bite, anything to turn her attention away from Morwick. She took a tiny nibble, felt her stomach rebel, and hastily put the biscuit back down.

Morwick picked up his hat, moving it purposefully out of her reach. "I've many pairs of boots but I am partial to this hat." The corners of his eyes crinkled in amusement at her discomfort.

Maybe Petra didn't care if her stomach settled or not. Meeting his eye once more, she defiantly bit into the biscuit.

IMPUDENT LITTLE THING.

She had a lovely neck of delicate porcelain skin. He wished to feast on the tender expanse, possibly nibbling a line to just beneath her ear. Once there he would suck and nibble until Petra made the delicious noise she'd made when he'd kissed her so long ago. He'd not forgotten.

I'm mad. Completely mad.

Lust aside, Brendan was pleased to see her up and about. His mind screamed to stay away from her, but every other part of his body, especially his cock, didn't wish to listen. But he should listen. *Especially* in this room, of all places.

When he was younger, Brendan had referred to the favorite room of his mother's as the *Mourning* Room, a subtle play on words which no one but his brother Spence had seemed to take note of. This was where Mother had grieved for Reggie. How many times had he seen her here, reading one of his letters, sobbing as she looked up at his portrait?

Too many times to count.

Though time had tempered the wound, Brendan had seen the pain his mother experienced at the loss of Reggie. The price one paid for loving so deeply. He shied away from any meaningful commitment to a woman, determined to only enjoy the physical delights of the opposite sex. Brendan had mostly been successful, except for Katherine. His affair with Pendleton's sister had been fiery and combustible, and he'd felt a great deal of affection for her. They'd grown up together after all, and he'd known her his whole life. Thankfully, when she had married, Brendan's heart had remained surprisingly intact. So many years later, he wasn't even sure he was capable of such emotion. Nor did he seek love.

Perfect Petra should not have inspired the least interest in him. Proper, well-bred and so self-contained, Brendan found her enticing beyond words. Why, he wasn't sure. Lust should have fled as she had become ill and puked on his boots; instead, he'd wanted to cradle her smaller form close to his chest and care for her. Petra was a beautiful, *dangerous* thing.

Mother started chattering away to Petra about London and some improvement his cousin Arabella was making to her town house. Once the discussion turned to the decoration of the nursery, Brendan stopped listening. He was too taken by the sight of Petra's graceful hands as they held her cup of tea. What would those fingers feel like as they touched him?

Jesus. He needed to stop thinking such things least he burst the seams of his pants.

At last, Petra discarded what remained of her biscuit and excused herself to return to her room, claiming fatigue. In truth she was still pale and exhausted, with dark shadows beneath her eyes.

He stood, watching her leave, the desire for her coursing through his veins.

When he turned back to his mother, he found her calmly sipping her tea, a tiny smile tugging at her lips.

P etra declined another tray in her room and ventured down the stairs to breakfast. If she had to spend yet another day in her room, Petra would go mad. She had just slathered butter onto a piece of toast when Lady Cupps-Foster bustled in, her lovely face distressed and worried.

For a moment, the toast hovered above Petra's lips. Honey dripped onto the table. Her first thought was something had happened to Morwick. He'd fallen climbing or disappeared much like his father had, into the earth never to be found again. Her chest tightened painfully at the thought of his loss.

But Lady Cupps-Foster was *distressed*, not...anguished.

Petra lowered her toast. Dear God, had Simon come from Brushbriar to fetch her? Was he waiting in the foyer? Petra sincerely hoped not. He'd not written her since their arrival, and, truthfully, Petra hadn't longed for him to do so. The lack of his regard should have bothered her more, she supposed.

"Oh my dear, I'm sorry to tell you your mother has taken ill." She placed a hand on Petra's shoulder. "I don't want you to worry. You shall stay here as long as need be until she is well. I've already summoned Dr. Stubbins. I am afraid your departure to Brushbriar will be delayed yet again. It is unfortunate, but one cannot predict illness."

Mother was ill. Stricken by the very same stomach distress Petra experienced. She couldn't help gloating just a tiny bit over the fact Mother was abed with a chamber pot in her lap. Even after Dr. Stubbins pronouncement, Mother had continued to insist a fuss had been made for nothing. Petra was only the victim of nerves.

It appeared Mother was nervous as well.

That was a terribly unkind thought, but Petra was so relieved. The trip to Brushbriar, already ominous as she had left London, had grown more so with each passing day. "Thank you, my lady. You are kindness itself." She took Lady Cupps-Foster's hand. "I'll go up and check on her."

"I'll direct Dr. Stubbins up as soon as he arrives," Lady Cupps-Foster assured Petra. "He should be along soon."

Petra thanked her again and moved up the stairs toward the bedchamber her mother occupied, halting as she heard the sound of retching coming from within. The door cracked open to reveal a long beak of a nose situated between eyes dark like bits of onyx.

"Good morning, Agnes," Petra greeted her.

"Lady Petra," Agnes sniffed, "I am happy to see you up and about."

The maid's tone led Petra to think otherwise. "How is mother? Lady Cupps-Foster informed me she'd fallen ill?" She'd never liked Agnes, though the woman certainly took excellent care of Lady Marsh. Bitter and unpleasant, Agnes delighted in reporting infractions by the other Marsh servants to Lady Marsh. The rest of the household staff detested Agnes, who seemed to care little for their opinion.

"The stew, I'm sure, at that *horrible* inn we stayed, though why she didn't fall ill earlier is a mystery." Her tone was slightly accusatory, as if Petra had done something to purposefully make her mother ill. "We've only that Dr. Stubbins to rely on instead of my lady's physician in London." Her opinion of Dr. Stubbins was obvious. "I'll take excellent care of your mother, my lady."

"Agnes!" Mother wailed from behind the door. "Is that Petra?"

"Yes, Mother." Petra tried to peek into the room.

Agnes pulled the door closed. "You'll not want to become ill again, Lady Petra. Your mother wishes nothing more to delay our arrival at Brushbriar. Perhaps it would be best if you return later."

"Of course. Please fetch me once Dr. Stubbins has examined her." Petra gratefully retreated. Maybe her mother would be more sympathetic the next time Petra became ill. She sailed back down the stairs whistling a jaunty tune.

With Mother ensconced in her room, unable to leave her bed, Petra was free of her dubious supervision for the day. Or possibly longer. Petra had been ill for a couple of days; perhaps Mother's stomach distress would be lengthy as well. The thought made her giddy.

She spent the next hour or so exploring Morwick's home. Somerton was old, in a way the Marsh town house and estate were not. Many of the walls were constructed of limestone from the nearby countryside, and Petra suspected what she was seeing were the original castle walls. The manor house, though far from modern, had been built around a large, ancient tower, spiraling out in a jumble of stone and brick. As Petra became lost for the fifth time, she decided Somerton's architect had designed a maze and not a house. She half expected to find the bones of some former guest who'd gotten lost and expired without ever finding the main hall again.

"*Bollocks*," Petra whispered under her breath, staring at yet another dead end. Morwick really should post signs on the walls or pass out breadcrumbs. However would one find their way around Somerton on a consistent basis? She wondered if Morwick was even at home today, or was he busy exploring caves?

"I find him very intriguing," she said in passing as she stopped before a group of portraits lining the wall.

Petra studied a painting of a sad looking matron seated with a dog on her lap. The dog was an ugly looking little beast, more closely resembling a pig. The woman's head was overly large and her body, in relation to the dog's, was drawn all out of proportion. A terrible work of art to be sure. She hoped the artist was not richly compensated. Next she perused a gruff, elderly man with a shock of white hair.

Another hour later, finally bored with her study of the portraits, Petra stopped a passing servant to ask the direction of the library. The Somerton gardens were wild and over-grown, but she'd spied a stone bench from her bedroom window. A perfect spot to read.

BRENDAN STRETCHED THE MUSCLES OF HIS NECK, TURNING his head back and forth. He threw the weather-beaten ruck-sack on the table. He was pleasantly tired and sore.

After an early breakfast with his mother, Brendan had made his way back to the cave he'd visited the day before. The cave was nothing special. Not even so much as a fossilized leaf or fern. He had looked for the telltale line of blue and yellow, but there had been no sign of Blue John in the cavern. Brendan wasn't surprised. His father's obsession with finding the mineral on their estate hadn't produced fruit thirty years ago and was unlikely to do so now. Still, Brendan was compelled to look.

Blue John, or calcium fluorite as Brendan had been taught when studying at Oxford, was the reason behind his father's disappearance. Mother insisted Reggie had been searching for the rare mineral when he'd gone missing. Maybe Reggie had found a deposit and before he could return to share the news, he'd fallen into a hole in the limestone and broken his neck. He wouldn't be the first person, nor the last, to fall prey to the numerous holes littering the moors.

Reggie's body had never been recovered nor a trace of him found, even though half the county had gone looking for him. Mother still teared up when she thought of that day. Knowing the area as he did, Brendan thought it likely his father's body lay at the base of a ravine or in a cave somewhere, swallowed by the earth. Brendan preferred his version of his father's disappearance to the gossip.

Brendan reached up with his forefinger to touch the scar bisecting his eyebrow, remembering the punch he'd thrown at one of the taverns in Buxton. The drunken son of one of the mine owners had felt it necessary to relate the tragic events of the disappearance of the former earl, not realizing the man's son had sat at the bar next to him. When the man stated Reggie had had a secret mistress and had fled to America with her, Brendan had gone a bit wild.

Stretching again and pulling a chair over, Brendan decided, no matter his aching arms, it had been best to be away from Somerton today. He'd left the estate at first light, determined to put Petra out of his mind. She was only a girl and a rather prim one at that. Brendan was reckless by nature and the thought of Petra lying upstairs in a guest room was far too tempting.

Thankfully, the object of his lust hadn't come down for

dinner last night, although he had not been spared the presence of Lady Marsh. Brendan found Petra's mother to be the most frivolous, annoying woman he'd ever met. She had chattered incessantly throughout the meal, pausing only to take a breath, or take a forkful of roast before launching into another overly long story about Lady Upton's ball, or dissecting the gown another lady had worn to the opera. Questions had flown from her lips about Pendleton and his family. Shooting a look Brendan's way, Lady Marsh had made sure to give Brendan and his mother a glowing rendition of Simon's courtship of Petra, as if she suspected Morwick wanted to ravish her daughter. By the end of the meal, Brendan had wished to strangle himself with the cravat his valet had carefully tied around his neck despite his protests. Finally, Lady Marsh seemed to have exhausted herself, and had bid him and his mother good night. He wondered if Mother also had had a headache for he certainly had.

Brendan returned his attention to the matter at hand. Picking up the rucksack, he untied the flaps and spilled the day's gatherings across the table. He hadn't expected much from the cave as it was too far from Pendleton land to have any Blue John. Still, there might be something equally as valuable. Copper or tin. Possibly lead. Brendan did not mine on his own land but he was a partner in several mining enterprises, most north of Buxton. A geologist by trade, though he'd not finished his schooling, Brendan's knowledge and skills made him much sought after by the consortiums who ran the majority of the mines in the area. He surveyed. Studied. Told them where to start digging. Sometimes when a group of paleontologists or fellow geologists came up from London, Brendan would act as a guide through the miles of caves and moors surrounding Somerton.

Brendan walked over to the windows, throwing open the

heavy drapes to allow the late afternoon light into the study. This had been Reggie's space, and Brendan never felt closer to his father than when he was here. Books and surveys crowded every available space. Equipment for testing samples along with an assortment of ropes and tools for climbing were littered across the floor. The walls were hung with sketches and watercolors, all done by Reggie. In addition to his interests in geology and nature, Brendan's father had been a gifted artist.

Dumping out the contents of the pack, Brendan pushed up his sleeves. A beautiful nut-colored stone laced through with bits of green rolled out and across the table. The rock wasn't valuable or particularly interesting, but it had reminded Brendan of Petra's eyes.

Frustrated at having her invade his thoughts again, Brendan shoved the stone to the side.

He was treading a dangerous path. One had only to look at his mother and see the damage love had done to her. Katherine had been the only woman who'd stirred his affections so strongly, and in the end, he'd let her go rather than marry her as her father had wished. Besides, Katherine had wanted London and Brendan still did not. He couldn't live his life trapped in and amongst the filth of the city, teeming with people. Brendan hadn't been Katherine's first lover, so he hadn't been compelled to do the right or honorable thing. In the end, Katherine chose Whitfield. Whitfield had died six months ago, right about the time Arabella had married, and Katherine had returned to her mother at Brushbriar. She'd made a point of letting him know of her availability and the lack of impediment her widowhood presented should he wish to strike up their previous relationship.

But after his return from London, Brendan had no interest in Katherine, nor any woman. That bothered him far more than anything else.

He looked toward the edge of the desk. The stone resembling the hazel of Petra's eyes winked at him as it caught the sunlight.

Damn.

❧ 6 ❧

Petra *finally* found the library. Even after seeking directions, it had taken her a solid fifteen minutes to reach her destination. She didn't hold out much hope Morwick would actually have anything of interest in his library, but his mother *had* spent a portion of her life at Somerton. Perhaps there was something to draw her interest.

Rows of books lined the walls and stacked in rows behind a well-used leather couch. Tiptoeing around the books, afraid the least bit of movement would cause them to topple, Petra approached the bookcases first.

A dull scratching sounded.

"I'm sure there are mice living in the walls," she said out loud. "Poor things made their way down a hallway and can't figure out how to leave." Petra ran a finger over the row of books facing her, grimacing at the dust coating the bindings.

Cluttered and disorganized, the library was much like Somerton itself. There seemed no rhyme or reason to the way the books had been placed on the shelves, other than utter chaos. Moving to another bookcase, Petra found this section to be less dusty and the books grouped together.

She saw dozens of books on the same topic. Geology. Another grouping was all on paleontology. She wasn't quite certain what that was, though she'd heard of geology. Lady Cupps-Foster had said something about Morwick studying geology.

"I've no idea exactly what that means," she whispered to the books.

There was an entire section on gritstone. Several books in German. Another section on mineralogy. Nothing remotely tempted her. Or would tempt anyone. Petra turned away with a sigh and turned toward a smaller stack leaning against the arm of the couch. *Novels.* Some looked quite lurid. These books could only belong Lady Cupps-Foster. Morwick's mother apparently had a particular interest in the adventures of Lord Thurston. Petra was thrilled. She'd always wanted to read Lord Thurston but hadn't been afforded the opportunity.

Lord Thurston was the hero of a series of somewhat shocking novels deemed too risqué for proper young ladies. The books detailed the adventures of a nobleman who becomes a pirate after his father disinherits him. Mother forbade Petra from even *mentioning* Lord Thurston, let alone reading his adventures.

"But she's ill." Petra picked up "Lord Thurston's Revenge" and stuck it under her arm.

Scrape. Scrape. Scrape

Petra wrinkled her nose and tried to keep from sneezing at the dust. The sound appeared to be coming from behind the bookcase. Petra pictured a score of mice, all sharpening their tiny claws on the stone walls. Vermin were known to inhabit old, drafty castles and certainly at least part of Somerton qualified. She sincerely hoped not to meet any of the home's furry residents. Exiting the library, she tapped one finger against her lips, struggling to remember the shortest way back toward the stairs when the scraping came again, a bit louder. The rhythm was steady and purposeful.

Not a mouse, then. The sound was coming from the room next door to the library.

She looked down the dimly lit hall and saw no sign of a footman or maid, nor anyone at all lingering about. Her stomach gave a grumble. She'd missed lunch and should find something to eat. Maybe check on her mother.

Another scratch, this time long and drawn out.

Curiosity got the better of her and she really didn't want to check on Mother anyway. Tucking the book beneath her arm Petra walked down the hall. The scraping sound immediately became louder.

A door stood open.

Scrape. Scrape.

Petra peered around the open door.

Morwick was bent over a massive desk, the top of which was littered with rocks and pebbles. His shirtsleeves were rolled up, exposing muscular forearms dusted with dark hair. Ebony curls hung over his forehead, one falling over his eye. Holding up a rock, he batted away the offending curl and squinted, turning the piece of stone over in his hand. Setting the rock back on the table he picked up a small pick and began scraping until he had a pile of shavings. Spreading the shavings across a snowy white cloth, he picked up a magnifying glass and looked down, moving the shavings around with the tip of a small metal stick. His worn cotton shirt stretched taut across his shoulders as he worked, doing... something. Perhaps she should have chosen one of the books on geology, for she hadn't a clue what Morwick was up to.

He shifted his face into the light coming from the window. The line of his jaw was dark with the shadow of a beard above the swath of tanned skin at his neck. Petra couldn't take her eyes from that small triangle of flesh.

"Are you going to continue to just stare at me, or are you actually going to enter?" he growled, not taking his eyes from the rock in his hands. "Always sneaking about, aren't you, Petra? One would think you'd learned your lesson about eavesdropping."

"I heard scratching noises, reminiscent of a *giant* rodent." She gave him a pointed look so he would not mistake her meaning. Her heart was thumping like a drum in her chest. His comment led her to believe he did remember kissing her after all, though she doubted he'd ever admit such to her.

"How would you know what a loud rodent sounds like? Do you have many opportunities to socialize with rats? Oh wait," he snorted. "I forgot the *ton* in London. A bigger nest of rodents I've yet to see." He turned from the rock and sat back in his chair to look at her. The left side of his mouth tipped up just enough for the dimple to deepen in his cheek.

Petra's stomach fluttered. She hoped her illness wasn't returning.

"I see you've found the library. I applaud your accomplishment." He looked at her with intent.

"You do? For finding the library?"

"The few guests who've stayed at Somerton invariably get lost in the warren of halls, rooms and back staircases. One of my ancestors evidently had a misguided sense of humor. Or a very poor architect. Probably both. Did you leave yourself a trail of breadcrumbs?"

Petra's stomach grumbled as it was reminded of food.

Morwick eyed her midsection and leaned forward, stating curtly, "Don't puke on my samples."

"I'm quite well, my lord. Only hungry. I've not eaten since breakfast. Your pebbles and rocks are safe. The same cannot be said for my mother, who has become ill, I'm afraid."

"Pity. Must be nerves. *Certainly* not lamb stew."

Petra shot him a look of chastisement. "That was unkind." Though she was guilty of thinking the same.

"I am often unkind. I thought we had established such."

His intense gaze burned across Petra and the pulse leapt in her throat. She imagined the depths of the ocean were the same color as his eyes.

"Tell me, how did you meet Pendleton? He's not the frivolous type, so I can't imagine him putting his name on your dance card." There was a rough quality to his question.

The question surprised her, she hadn't thought he'd ask about Simon. "At a charitable event. One which your cousin, Arabella, organized, as a matter of fact. He spoke to us on a bill he was working on. Reforms for workhouses." Petra moved further into the room. "I attended as a favor to my new sister-in-law."

"Oh, yes. Arabella does adore her charitable work. I believe she is atoning for something—or, rather, a great many things. Still, I am glad she is happy. But back to Pendleton."

"You don't like Simon, do you?" Petra said.

His gaze lingered on her mouth before coming back to her face.

"Not in the least," he admitted. "But I've known him longer than you have. It's possible after some time you may feel the same way."

The statement struck Petra as far too close to her actual feelings for Simon, or rather the absence of them. Morwick was handsome even when he frowned, but smiling brilliantly at her as he was now?

Breathtaking. Beautiful.

Her heart thudded so loudly she could barely hear herself think. Eager to change the subject from her relationship with Simon, she cleared her throat and asked, "What are you doing?"

His lips resumed their usual semi-frown. "Do you know anything about geology?"

"I'm afraid I don't, pea-wit that I am."

"I should apologize for saying such a thing. Incredibly unfair of me."

"Yes, you should. Apologize, that is."

"I was upset about something else and you, Perfect Petra, got in the way. If I do apologize, will you decide I'm not a monster?"

She cocked her head as if considering his request. "I suppose that's fair. Go on."

A mischievous look entered his eyes, offering Petra a glimpse into the boy he had once been. "I'll let you know when I'm ready." He turned back to the table. "Back to geology. Not the most interesting or popular of subjects, I suppose. Puts most people to sleep. And certainly not something taught to proper young ladies such as yourself."

"I assure you I will attempt to grasp the basic points."

"Geology is the study of the earth. Rocks. Minerals. Tin. Lead. My father adored anything to do with minerals and became quite a student of the science, though he never studied the subject formally."

"But you did," Petra said as she walked toward the samples, pretending interest. She was so aware of Morwick, big and vital, in the room with her, she could hardly think, even if she really *had* felt true interest in the rocks spread across his table.

"I did. But then I had a disagreement with several of my fellow students. Oxford declared they no longer wished me to remain at their institution."

Petra lifted a brow. "Brawling, no doubt."

His eyes narrowed. "What would you know of that?"

"A bit more than I know of geology," she replied. "So you are looking for minerals? In the cave?"

"Surely you know the story of the Pendleton fortune? The entire family brags about the source of their wealth on a consistent basis. The current Lord Pendleton's father became quite famous when he found the third largest deposit of calcium fluorite in England. It's very rare."

"Fluorite?" Petra stepped closer and the edge of her skirts brushed against his boots—shocking behavior for a demure young lady such as herself. Mother always told her allowing your skirts to swirl around a gentleman's legs was brazen.

Yes, but Mother is ill today.

"Blue John. Used for jewelry. Vases. Other frivolous but expensive bits and pieces to litter a proper gentleman's home. I don't care for the stuff myself."

"I'm familiar. I didn't realize Blue John had another more proper name. Your cousin, the duke, has a mantle made from Blue John in his drawing room. It's quite beautiful." The fireplace in the Dunbar townhouse was oversized and took up a vast portion of one wall. The mantle probably cost a small fortune.

"Nick is a snob. My cousin likes others to know how obscenely wealthy he is."

Surprised at him saying such a thing, she looked up to see there was no malice in his words. "Are you always so full of mockery?"

The lopsided tilt to his lips appeared again. "Nearly always."

"Simon," she ignored the look he shot her at the use of the name, "did mention his father found Blue John and what a shock it was to all concerned."

"Indeed. Brushbriar and Somerton share a border. The Blue John was found very close to the boundary, barely a quarter mile from our property. My father was convinced there must be fluorite on our land as well. He searched for such a discovery nearly every day during the last year of his life. I'm sure the search for fluorite indirectly caused his death. At any rate, Pendleton's Blue John will keep you in silks and satins for the rest of your life."

"Silks and satins can become rather tiresome," Petra said lightly as she moved toward the wall where a drawing of a large peak, drawn in charcoal, hung. The detail was exquisite down to the sprays of heather and the curve of the gritstone. A tiny signature in the lower right-hand corner read '*Morwick*'.

"This is beautiful. Is it your work?"

"No, I've not an artistic bone in my body. Father was the artist. He didn't do portraits or people at all, only the outdoors. Sometimes animals, but not often. That drawing is of Mam Tor, the largest peak in the area."

"I'm happy to know he didn't do portraits," she said thinking of the painting of the woman and the dog she'd seen earlier. "What does Mam Tor mean?"

A deep masculine laugh came from him. "You've been to the portrait gallery and seen the atrocious painting of great auntie Barbara. I've tried to find out what breed of dog she's holding but there isn't a record. I'm convinced my ancestor had a pet piglet. Mam Tor means 'mother hill'. The land often slides beneath the peak and forms multiple, small hills. As if Mam Tor were constantly giving birth to more peaks." He looked back at the drawing.

"The detail is amazing. He was incredibly talented."

"He disappeared around the time I was born." Morwick's eyes held a faraway look. "Somewhere out on the moors. I'm sure you've heard the tale; everyone in London knows it. I was reminded of such when I visited for Arabella's wedding."

"Actually, Arabella told me when I informed her we were traveling to the area."

"Oddly enough, Reggie didn't take this." Morwick nodded

to the battered pack sitting on the table. "Nor any of his tools."

"Perhaps he went to meet someone," Petra mused, her finger rubbing over the signature on the drawing. The glass was dirty and in terrible need of a good dusting.

Morwick's gaze on her was suddenly frigid; Petra had the sense she'd said something wrong.

"Did Pendleton mention something to you?" Morwick questioned.

"No, of course not. I only meant if your father left to do his usual exploring, why wouldn't he take his backpack or any tools? Surely you've thought the same thing."

"I have." His large body relaxed, the tension easing out of him at her reply. "The entire area is rife with holes, caves, underground rivers. He could have easily taken a wrong step and fallen into the ground or into a crevice. Men came from Castleton and Buxton to search for him. Brushbriar's staff as well as Somerton's scoured the moors. Nothing was ever found. Not even so much as his hat. Vanished into thin air as if he'd never been."

What an incredibly sad story. Arabella's eyes had watered when she had told Petra, though she had blamed it on her delicate condition. A rush of sympathy filled Petra for Morwick, but especially for Lady Cupps-Foster. To have her husband disappear while she was with child and never know what became of him? It was horrible. "I'm sorry." She had the urge to comfort him. Stroke the dark curls back from his forehead and press a kiss to his temple. The idea was ludicrous, of course. Morwick didn't strike her as the type of man who required such comfort.

"Mother still grieves for him, but I never knew Reggie. Though growing up with your mother in a constant state of mourning was rather unsettling. I didn't realize she had gowns in any other colors until after I left the nursery. I couldn't imagine caring so deeply for someone or worse allowing their loss to devastate you in such a way."

Petra stilled, momentarily puzzled by the lack of emotion in his tone. She thought he could imagine and didn't wish to. It was a subtle warning, she realized.

"But my mother and Reggie would not be denied. Theirs was a great love-match, though my grandfather, His Grace the Duke of Dunbar, didn't wish them to marry, saying prophetically the relationship would end in tragedy for my Mother. Henry," his eyes twinkled with affection as he mentioned the old man's name, "was quite vocal in his opinion. My grandmother changed his mind, I'm told. But Henry was right. The marriage was cursed. Love, in the end, almost destroyed my mother."

Morwick looked at her intently, his gaze lingering on her mouth before moving to the top of her bodice.

"I disagree," Petra said softly, warmth spiraling down her chest at his perusal.

"I would expect you to, proper young lady that you are. Your head's been filled with romantic fluff."

She looked him in the eye, returning his assessment of her in a very unladylike manner. Something about Morwick invited the most brazen thoughts and actions. "Romantic fluff?"

"You should leave, Perfect Petra." His voice was raspy and low, stirring the hair along her forearms. "I've work to do."

The air between them sparked as if lit by dozens of fireflies. Petra closed her eyes for a moment, breathing in his scent, allowing the delicious sensation to seep into her bones. The attraction between them was real. It drifted and flowed in a continuous ebb around them both.

"Why did you kiss me?" Brazen. A proper lady would never ask such a thing.

Morwick's hands fell from the small stone he was

worrying between his fingers. The lopsided smile tightened with annoyance at her question until it more resembled his usual frown.

Petra moved toward the table holding his samples as his eyes followed her movement like a large, savage animal, waiting for an opportunity to pounce on its unsuspecting prey.

"I found it the only way to stop your tirade," he murmured. "You'd become quite hostile. I was concerned for my personal safety."

"Of course. I may have attacked you with a hair pin." Petra came around until she stood before Morwick, knowing she was deliberately provoking him. To what end, she wasn't entirely sure, except that his declaration earlier on the matter of love bothered her. "But I don't believe you."

The small square of skin exposed at the base of his throat was incredibly distracting, even if he was covered with dust. Dark hair sprinkled across the tanned skin. Perhaps Morwick's entire torso was sun-kissed in such a way. She wondered what he would taste like—

"Jesus, Petra. *Leave.*" The husky whisper rippled down her spine.

"You haven't answered my question." Petra looked at him boldly, well aware of her unladylike behavior and not caring what madness possessed her.

Morwick stood abruptly, leaning over her to place both his palms on the table, one on either side of her. When he had kissed her before, he'd made the same attempt to keep from touching her.

Petra arched toward him, fascinated at the way his dark lashes fell against the top of his cheeks as he lowered his eyes. The soft brush of his breath caressed her neck, disturbing the fine hairs below her ear. "I've work to do. You're distracting me."

An exquisite longing shot down from between Petra's breasts, swirling across her stomach to linger and feed the ache starting between her thighs. "You haven't answered my question, my lord." She wondered at the seductive quality of her own voice.

"Because I wanted to." Morwick's lips brushed the curve of her ear.

The book fell from Petra's hands, tumbling to the floor.

"I'm very busy." Morwick said as he leaned back, breaking the spell and making Petra feel like an idiot. The handsome features were once more contorted into irritation. "You should go, Lady Petra." Bending down, his hand brushed her skirts as he picked up the fallen book. He glanced at the title and smirked. "Your book. Lord Thurston."

Petra likened the change in his mood to someone snuffing out a candle, suddenly leaving the room in darkness. Disappointed and embarrassed, Petra could think of nothing but escaping his presence. "Of course. My apologies for the intrusion. Thank you for the lesson in geography, Lord Morwick."

"Geology," he snapped, shooing her out with a wave of his hands.

She turned and strode from the room, anger flaring at being dismissed. "Cantankerous, ill-mannered—" she muttered under her breath.

"I can hear you."

Petra did not shut the door quietly.

ALL MEN HAVE MOMENTS OF MADNESS. BRENDAN'S MADNESS was far beyond such a time constraint.

Women, particularly attractive, demure young ladies in possession of a surprisingly saucy tongue, shouldn't be permitted to go about smelling like roses and sugar cookies.

Brendan hadn't quite figured out how Petra managed such a thing. She should also not be permitted to visit him, unchaperoned, when he was filled with lust at the mere sight of her.

Even being rude to her wasn't driving Petra away. She kept coming back for more of his ill-mannered behavior. Why she tolerated his insults, Brendan had no idea. And worse, she didn't seem to be frightened by him.

I want her.

That was the rub. He didn't wish to lust after Petra. Didn't wish to dream of her beneath him moaning his name. His desire for her was unwelcome. Unwanted. The entire endeavor was fraught with disaster. Soon, she'd leave Somerton for Brushbriar and the comforting arms of Pendleton. After leaving Brushbriar, Petra would return to London and marry Pendleton. As she should.

Brendan glanced at the stone he'd picked up earlier in the day, the one which reminded him of Petra's hazel eyes. Grabbing up the stone, he threw open the drawer to his desk and tossed it into the depths to be lost amongst the collected junk of his wanderings, never to see the light of day again.

❧ 7 ❧

Brendan waved away his valet with an angry flip of his wrist. "I'm headed out to the moors, Woods. No need to dress me." He scratched his chin. "And I'm in no need of a shave just yet. It can wait."

"You *are* in desperate need of a shave, as you are every morning. I beg you, my lord, either grow a beard and mustache and save us both this tedious conversation, or allow me to shave you." Brendan's much shorter valet brandished shaving soap and a razor in his gloved hands. A towel was flung over one forearm.

"What difference could it possibly make whether I am clean shaven or not? I doubt anyone I might encounter on the moors will care what I look like. You're being ridiculous. I order you to put that away."

Woods gave a long-suffering sigh of defeat, knowing he'd lost the current skirmish. Woods had been Brendan's valet for nearly fifteen years and undoubtedly suffered quite a bit in his employ. Serving as Brendan's valet had to be a thankless endeavor.

"Lady Cupps-Foster will assume I'm not doing my job. At the very *least* allow me to help you dress."

Brendan threw up his hands. "Very well. Dress me as if I'm a doll."

He found the entire need for a valet to be silly. The thought a grown man couldn't dress himself without assistance because he bore a title was ridiculous.

Woods cocked a brow at him. "Yes, my lord. I've never known an earl as delicate and fine boned as you. Very much like a doll."

"I should send you packing for your insolence." Brendan fired Woods on a near weekly basis, all well-deserved, of course.

"OF COURSE, MY LORD. I'LL GATHER MY THINGS AS SOON AS you're dressed."

"My buckskins and one of my old shirts. Something I can ruin without you feeling as if you need to mend it."

The valet strode to the armoire, bringing forth Brendan's worn buckskins, holding them between his fingers as if the clothing were a poisonous snake. "Will I be leaving Somerton immediately, my lord? I do hope I'll have an opportunity to pack."

"You are to leave this instant." Brendan snapped back as the valet next produced one of Brendan's oldest shirts.

"May I at least inquire as to the direction you'll be taking today, my lord, in case Lady Cupps-Foster wonders? She does worry." He held up the shirt, his lips curled in distaste. "This will be cut into rags for the maids to use as soon as you return. I won't waste soap to have this shirt laundered, let alone mended."

"You won't be here; I'm sacking you." Brendan allowed the valet to place the shirt over his shoulders. "The path from the gate and down to the moors. I'll be back at tea-time. Can you ask Cook to make sure the sandwiches are a bit more substantial today? I don't care for watercress and cucumber. I keep mentioning I would like something a bit heartier. Meat of some kind. No one seems to listen. And some berry tarts."

"Of course, though your mother adores watercress." Woods made a small sniffling noise as he eyed the wild mane of Brendan's hair. "Forgive me, my lord. Perhaps you'd allow me to trim your hair before I vacate the premises? Lady Cupps-Foster has expressed to me she'd prefer you not resemble a wild Celt as you roam around. You could frighten someone. And we have guests."

"I doubt Lady Marsh will have a fit of vapors should she spot an errant curl."

The ghost of a smile hovered over the valet's lips. He looked incredibly smug. "I was thinking of Lady Petra."

Brendan had thought of nothing *but* Petra all night, and he didn't need to be reminded of her presence by Woods. Naked Petra, crawling over him on all fours with her glorious hair draping over them both. He'd awoken in the middle of the night with a groan, his hand gripping his shaft.

"My lord, if I may offer an opinion?" Woods took a look at Brendan's attire and shook his head in disgust.

"Do I have a choice?" Woods had an opinion on every aspect of Brendan's life. He was worse than an elderly aunt. Brendan was convinced Woods and his mother were conspiring against him.

"Lady Petra is quite lovely."

"I've not noticed her appearance." *I'm too busy imagining her naked.* "Besides, the lady is on her way to Brushbriar at the invitation of Lord Pendleton. I expect an engagement announcement to follow Lady Petra back to London."

"Poor girl." Woods snorted. "You tore her clothing like some barbarian."

"Is that the theme for today, Woods? I'm a barbarian? Or is it a savage Celt? Make up your mind." At the valet's pointed look, Brendan said, "She was stuck. What else was I to do?" He ran a hand through his hair, not meeting the valet's eyes. "Who told you I tore her skirt?"

The valet gave a mysterious shrug.

"Timmons, I suppose?" Brendan asked.

Somerton's butler and Woods had a close relationship. Brendan suspected there was more to their friendship. Once, Brendan had awoken in the middle of the night, starving. Rather than rouse a servant, he'd gone down to see if there was any chicken in the larder left from dinner, and possibly some tarts. He'd seen Timmons and Woods sitting together before the fire in the kitchen, a single candle lit between them. Just as he was about to announce himself, Timmons had leaned over and kissed Woods rather passionately. Shocked though he was, Brendan had silently backed out of the kitchen, returning to his bedchamber, hunger forgotten. Even servants deserved their privacy and he didn't particularly care who Woods tupped as long as the valet was discreet, which he was.

"Possibly Timmons relayed the news to me." Woods began putting away the unused shaving kit. "I'm not sure. The footmen like to gossip."

Brendan snorted, not believing it was one of the Somerton footmen for one moment. "All the footmen are afraid of me, as you well know. I suppose I'll have to dismiss Timmons for his insolence as well. Gossiping about me like two old women. Besides, she's utterly boring," he lied.

"Who?" Woods pretended ignorance.

"Lady Petra. Talks of nothing but fripperies."

"Pendleton must not find her so," Woods said smoothly. "I should point out, my lord, a tic appears in your cheek when you lie." He carried the shaving kit into the dressing room and a flurry of noises commenced.

"You are quite insolent, Woods." Brendan headed to the door and lay his hand on the knob.

"Yes, my lord. You've mentioned this to me many times." Woods strode back out and bowed. "I'll warn Timmons of your displeasure and we'll collect our things."

Brendan sighed in frustration and left the room.

"The half-boots, Tessie," Petra instructed her maid. She'd had enough of being inside and this may be her last chance to be free without being hovered over by her mother. Dr. Stubbins had pronounced Mother well enough for the ride to Brushbriar. They would leave Somerton in the morning.

An unusual ache filled her heart at the thought of leaving Somerton. In the short time she'd been here, Petra had grown to love the sprawling, unwieldy mass of stone. Somerton was beautiful in a wild, unkept way, reminiscent of the estate's owner. Petra liked the silence to be found here, so different from the constant rattling of coaches and people on the streets outside her window in London. The only sound here was that of the wind crossing the moors.

"My lady?" Tessie gave Petra a look. "Your mother said you were to rest today in preparation for your journey tomorrow to Brushbriar."

Petra shrugged. "I need fresh air and the sun is shining. I'm positive Dr. Stubbins mentioned something to that affect. I'm only going to take a turn about the gardens and then I promise to come rest. Goodness, I didn't even go down to dinner last night."

She'd *wanted* to go down to dinner, but Mother, sitting up in bed and looking pale and tired, had begged Petra to dine with her. After a light supper, Petra had read out loud from a book of poetry at her mother's request, her reading interrupted every few minutes as Mother reminded Petra of how she must comport herself with Lady Pendleton. Finally, Mother's eyes had drooped, and Petra had been able to seek her own bed.

She had dreamt of Morwick.

They were once again in his study, but this time Petra had boldly pressed her lips to the tanned swathe of skin at the base of his throat. She'd reached up to allow the ebony locks to curl around her fingers. When she had awoken, her nightgown had been wrapped around her thighs, her body throbbing with the need for something she couldn't describe.

Simon never invaded her thoughts in such a way.

"I'll be back before tea," she informed Tessie. "Best get us packed for Brushbriar."

After donning her boots and the oldest, plainest dress she had with her, Petra waved at Tessie and headed down the stairs, wondering exactly where she would go. The moors beckoned to Petra, as did the patch of trees visible from the window of her guest room. She was ready for an adventure.

I don't miss Simon.

Shouldn't she miss him? Not so much as a note had come to her from Brushbriar, nor had she felt compelled to send one herself. Mother, between retching into the chamber pot, had chastised Petra for her oversight and insisted she pen something to Simon immediately.

Petra, defiance filling her, had not.

A dapper, well-dressed servant passed the stairs as Petra reached the bottom step. He was no footman, for he wasn't much taller than Petra and most of the Somerton footmen were burly looking lads. Tessie had mentioned she'd met Woods, Morwick's valet, as she ate in the kitchen with the other servants the night before. Her description of the valet had been spot on, for surely this was he.

"Excuse me." She caught Woods as he was about to turn the corner. "Mr. Woods?"

Woods bowed formally. "Just Woods, my lady." The valet had a pencil thin mustache, neatly shaped above his upper lip, which wiggled as he spoke. His dark hair was styled to perfection and laced with silver. "How may I assist you? Should I fetch Timmons for you?"

"No, that won't be necessary. I was only wondering...do you know where Mam Tor is?" she asked, in a burst of inspiration. The drawing of the peak had stayed in her mind since seeing the charcoal drawing the day before in Morwick's study. "I thought I'd walk in that direction. I fear I'm in need of some fresh air and exercise."

"Unfortunately, Mam Tor is some distance from here and can't be reached easily on foot, my lady. But if you venture out through the gardens behind the house, there is a small gate leading to the moors beyond. A path leaving the gate will take you along the outer edge of a patch of gritstone, the dark rock. Once you cross the gritstone you'll see the tree line, along with a lovely view of the moors *and* Mam Tor. The scenery is quite magnificent. But stay on the path, my lady," he cautioned. "You don't wish to get lost, especially since you are departing for Brushbriar tomorrow."

"No, of course not. If my mother —"

"I shall make sure she is informed you are walking through the gardens." He gave her a conspiratorial wink.

"Thank you, Woods." She smiled gratefully. "And may I say," Petra said a bit impishly, "I do not envy you your job."

"You may, my lady." The valet bowed, his lips twitching.

Leaving the house, Petra whistled as she strolled through the gardens and past the bench where she'd spent the day reading Lord Thurston yesterday. The gate soon came into view, rusted and hanging by the hinges. It swung open easily with a gentle push of her hand. Obviously, the gate was well-used and oiled, despite looking as if it were to fall apart.

Keeping a brisk pace, Petra stayed on the path made up of a series of stones. The moors stretched out before her, covered with sprays of heather. Just as Woods had said, the path soon evolved into large patches of gritstone. Ahead was a patch of trees, where the moors ebbed away and forest took over. As she came closer to the tree line, Petra caught her first real glimpse of Mam Tor, rising to tower over the moors.

"Oh, my." She'd never seen anything half so beautiful, though the rise and dip of the land obscured her view.

Every few steps Petra would jump, in an effort to catch a better glimpse. Petra had never given much thought to her smaller stature, but just now, wanting to see Mam Tor, she wished for longer legs. If only she was higher, she may be able to see better. The tip of her boot caught on something on the ground, tripping her, and Petra caught herself.

A large tree root, twisted and rough, stuck out of the ground attached to a massive oak tree.

"I've never seen one so large."

The oak towered above all the others, the gnarled bark and width of the immense trunk telling the story of a long life. The branches above her head created a thick canopy, stretching out as far as Petra could see. How old could an oak tree be? She made a mental note to find out. Surely Morwick had a book on trees in the chaos of his library.

Then Petra remembered she was leaving early tomorrow for Brushbriar. She wouldn't have time to seek out such a book.

She glanced toward Mam Tor and then back at the tree,

considering her options. Once upon a time, before Mother had decided to focus her energies on her daughter, Petra had been a bit of a tree climber. She had never been as quick as Rowan, but she had spent many summers at the Marsh family estate in Essex learning how to climb a tree in order to escape her governess. Miss Persimmon had been a dour spinster who, along with teaching proper French, a language Petra still hadn't mastered, also sucked the joy out of any room she entered.

Petra had climbed a lot of trees that summer.

"I shouldn't." Her words fell into the summer breeze. A young lady, especially the daughter of an earl, didn't climb trees.

If she married Simon, there would likely be little time for such outlandish behavior. He did not strike her as the type of man who wished his wife to go round climbing trees in Hyde Park. Simon expected her to preside over his dinner table exchanging polite conversation with his political cronies and their wives, none of whom spent their time considering how best to scale an oak tree. This may be her last chance.

"Just once more." She ran her fingers over the bark, looking for natural footholds, trying to remember how it was done. A small limb hung over her head. If she could get herself up off the ground, she could take hold of the branch and pull herself up. At least, that's what she surmised. She hadn't actually done such a thing since she was ten. "All right then."

Lifting her skirts she tucked them up at the sides, which felt incredibly scandalous, though there wasn't anyone around for miles. She raised her right leg, moving her ankle back and forth until she felt secure in putting her weight into it. Cautiously, she moved up into the canopy, the bark scraping and tearing at the front of her dress. Thank goodness the dress was old and beneath the notice of her mother. If Petra never wore the flowered muslin again, it was doubtful Mother would remark on it. Gritting her teeth, Petra managed to pull herself up and lodged her left foot into another groove in the trunk.

Lightness filled Petra the further she climbed. There was something so incredibly...*free* about doing something purely because she *wished* to. A young lady's life, and indeed most women's, was structured from start to finish. What to wear, how to behave. Decorum. Manners. Mother constantly hovering over her.

Whom she should marry.

It had all become exhausting. The last few months, even before Simon offered for her, Petra had started to feel as if she were drowning under the weight of her mother's expectations.

She'd always loved being outside, something she'd forgotten until this journey. Young ladies took quiet walks through gardens with their maids trailing behind, or carriage rides in Hyde Park to show off a new bonnet. When she was younger, Petra had run after frogs and collected twigs and sticks to make castles. She'd strung together daisies and worn them in her hair. Then she'd had to become a young lady. No longer could she roam about; instead she was confined to the schoolroom learning how to dance and embroider. Mother was a relentless taskmaster, demanding perfection from both Rowan and Petra.

Good God; Mother has turned me into her version of me. An obedient, well-mannered dressmaker's dummy she can trot out to ensnare a proper son-in-law.

The bark bit into her fingers. Morwick was correct. Climbing did clear one's mind.

Petra reached for the low hanging branch and with much effort and straining of her arms, managed to pull herself up. Dr. Stubbins, she was certain, would not approve of tree climbing as a method of recuperation from her stomach ailment. Resting for a moment to catch her breath, Petra was filled with a sense of achievement. She'd done it. And she was free and unencumbered looking out at the beauty of Mam Tor.

As Petra sat drinking in the color of the peak set against the moors, contentment filled her. There were no calls to pay. No guests for tea for whom she had to pretend interest. No need for her to sit demurely, hands firmly clasped in her lap, while Mother gossiped. No amount of lessons would teach her to speak French properly because she didn't care to. Embroidery bored her. Her entire life was pretense. Petra grabbed tighter to the branch to keep from falling off.

Mam Tor beckoned, shining like a beacon in the distance. The smell of damp earth, leaves and pine filled her nostrils. If she went higher, the view would be better. She reached up again, pulling herself close to the trunk of the tree and kept going, unmindful of anything but the task before her.

BRENDAN WHISTLED, BOOTS CRUNCHING AGAINST THE stones as he took the path leading back to Somerton. Lady Marsh, according to his mother, was much better this morning. Petra and her mother were scheduled to leave for Brushbriar today. By the time Brendan returned for tea, Petra would be gone. Before long, she would be reading a tome of poetry in Brushbriar's garden while Pendleton hung on her every word. Simon might even take her hand, which would be something. Simon was a cold fish.

Brendan hiked the rucksack up higher on his shoulder, ignoring the pain as the leather strap bit into his flesh. His pack was full of samples today, many more than he needed, but Brendan was trying to keep his mind from Petra. He didn't care to think of Petra in the garden with Pendleton, nor the jealousy the image invoked. Petra wasn't his, nor would she ever be. His was a life meant to live alone. Solitary. Having Petra would mean *caring* for Petra—something that could not be allowed.

I still want her.

Brendan forced himself to summon up a painful memory. His mother, dressed all in black, talking to the portrait of Reggie. Weeping, she had pled with his father to return to her. He'd been five or six at the time and he'd run to her, wrapping himself inside her skirts, begging her to stop being sad.

He didn't wish such a future for himself. Digging through caves was a far safer option.

"Damn."

The unladylike curse sprung from the giant oak tree to the right. He'd been by this very tree hundreds of times and had never heard the oak swear at him.

"Damn and blast." A tearing of fabric sounded. Bits of bark and leaves fell from somewhere above him. "Bollocks."

Brendan craned his neck back, searching upward, delighted to see a pair of slim, stocking clad legs dangling above him. A tree nymph.

Another burst of leaves rained down on him followed by a gasp of utter horror. The tree nymph had spotted him.

A smile pulled at his lips. "Petra?" Desire bloomed in him, his fears of not a moment ago evaporating. It wasn't only the sight of her legs, which were spectacular, but the knowledge she'd climbed a *tree*. What on earth would have possessed her to do such a thing? And she was cursing up a storm, something well-bred young ladies weren't supposed to do. He doubted she'd learned those words from Lady Marsh.

"I didn't know tree climbing to be practiced amongst the *ton*." Brendan spoke to the pair of legs.

"As it happens, I am one of several young ladies who believe in challenging ourselves with physical feats of strength. We gather every Thursday in Hyde Park. In addition to tree climbing we are known to run foot races, sail boats and compete in other competitions." Her voice floated down to him. "Obviously we don't go around speaking of our...*conditioning*."

"I'd no idea the ladies of the *ton* were so interesting." What a sassy little minx Petra was. A slow ache stretched across his heart, adding to the slow throb in his breeches. "And the cursing? Where you did you gain such a vocabulary? A governess?"

A bit of bark and several acorns bounced off his shoulder. "Surely you are acquainted with your cousin's wife? Her Grace would put a sailor to shame. Jemma's profanities are quite colorful."

Brendan had never actually heard the Duchess of Dunbar curse, but considering her other eccentricities, he didn't doubt Petra's explanation.

"I do hope you won't mention my language to Mother. She'd be most distressed." A feminine grunt sounded from above.

"Perish the thought. I've no desire to give your mother a fit of apoplexy." He looked up into the branches, admiring Petra's calves and ankles. "Are you coming down?" She had lovely calves. Too bad she was wearing stockings. He would so adore pressing a kiss to the hollow behind her knee.

"Of course I am," she snapped. "I'm only working on how best to make my way, and I find it difficult to do so when you are distracting me. Feel free to be on your way."

Brendan had climbed all his life. Rocks, peaks, trees. The roof of the tavern in Buxton. It was no secret why Petra hadn't yet come down. Climbing up something seemed a wonderful idea until you realized you must come down at some point. "Petra, don't look down."

"How should I make my way to the ground unless I look down?" she growled in frustration. "Now you'll refer to me as the climbing pea-wit." Petra lowered her voice in an imitation of his deep rasp. "She's like a cat in a tree that can't come down. I can just hear you now."

"I told you." He struggled to keep from laughing. "I was angry about something else at the time. I don't truly think you to be a pea-wit."

"You have yet to apologize. You also said my only purpose in life was to marry well, which isn't at all true. I *have* a purpose."

"Your purpose?" He would have to climb up to her. "Now you've piqued my interest."

"I'm not going to discuss my purpose with you, of all people."

"Of course not. I wouldn't expect such a thing." He *was* curious, though.

"It's of no import." Another shower of leaves came down.

He thought it might be, but now was not the time to ask her to explain. "I'll come to you." Brendan looked up at the stockinged legs above him. "Don't move."

"You can't come up here." He heard a rustle of clothing. "I'm—" He heard her gasp as she realized her legs were exposed. Shrieking with panic, Petra swung precariously above him as she tried unsuccessfully to cover her exposed limbs.

"Petra, I've already seen your legs. Stop moving about or you could fall."

"You are being overly familiar by remarking on my legs. A gentleman would turn away and ignore the sight completely. Nor would a gentlemen mention...them by name."

Another delicious ache fluttered across his chest. "I am

climbing a bloody tree to rescue you. If I wish to look at your *legs,* I will."

"You are horrible. Truly. Very ill-mannered."

"I suppose so." Brendan threw down his pack and started up the tree, finding the hand and footholds naturally to pull himself up through the branches. A few minutes later, he reached the thick branch Petra was holding onto for dear life. Her skirts were rucked up on either side and in addition to her calves she was showing a good bit of her knees and thighs. Slinging one leg over, he straddled the limb and faced her.

Petra caught the direction of his gaze. "A gentleman wouldn't look. Avert your eyes."

"I thought we'd established I am not a gentleman. Why haven't you left for Brushbriar?"

She was so fucking beautiful with a smudge of dirt on her cheek, and a twig sticking out of her hair, just above her right ear. Her bonnet was long gone and probably laying amongst the leaves below them. Thick strands of honey-gold hair fell over the tops of her shoulders. He wanted to kiss her sense-less. But first he needed to get her down from the tree.

"Mother had a bit of a relapse this morning. Though she is eager to continue our journey, she's more concerned about appearing ill as she meets Lady Pendleton for the first time." He didn't miss the slight bit of satisfaction in her words. "We will leave for Brushbriar in the morning."

Brendan suppressed the surge of happiness that swelled inside him. He shouldn't be happy, but the idea of Petra under his roof for another night did strange things to his heart, as well as other parts of his anatomy.

Petra had stopped trying to cover her legs. She shot a wistful glance at Mam Tor and whispered, "Simon is expecting us."

Pendleton would *never* allow a tree climbing viscountess. He was too much of a prig, as were most any gentleman of his station. Thankfully, Brendan wasn't of that ilk. He was delighted to discover Petra's reckless streak.

"The view of Mam Tor is amazing from this high up." Petra's hair blew across her face as a breeze took the long, golden strands. She looked wild and scandalous with her skirts hiked up and her legs dangling on either side of the branch.

Brendan had never been so aroused in his life. He clutched the limb he sat on so tight the bark dug into his skin. "Are you ready to climb down?"

"If I answered no, would you leave me here?" She kept her face pointed toward Mam Tor. Sunlight filtered through the leaves, sparking the bits of gold in the honey of her hair. He saw sadness in her lovely features. "Perhaps I could build a tree house."

A fierce rush of protectiveness filled him. He sensed her melancholy and wondered at her feelings for Simon. He'd been under the assumption she wanted to marry Pendleton. After all, he was a most suitable match. But now, hearing the wistfulness in her voice, Brendan wasn't so certain. He held out his hand, stretching out the fingers. "Take my hand."

Petra finally turned to him, fear in her eyes. Cautiously she inched toward him and reached out her hand, the slender length of her fingers intertwining with his. "Don't let go."

The words echoed across his heart even though he didn't wish it. He saw the trust for him shining in her face, despite her fear. Despite all he'd done to ensure her dislike for him.

Damn it.

Slowly, she moved forward. "Don't let go," she whispered again.

"Never." The word resonated with certainty, despite Brendan's best attempts to discard the feeling. He wasn't sure who was more afraid in that moment, him or Petra. "I won't."

After several tense minutes, Petra closed the distance

between them, shifting until their knees were mere inches from each other. Carefully, without letting go of her hand, Brendan wrapped his free arm around her waist, pulling her gently toward him. He held Petra much closer than he should have, though she didn't protest. She was looking up at him, the color of the leaves around them bringing out the green in her eyes. Her gaze was focused on his mouth.

Christ. Absolutely not a shred of self-preservation.

The delicate palms of her hands reached out to flatten against his chest. "How are we getting down?"

Could she feel the hammering of his heart against her palms? He inhaled her scent, wanting to bury his nose against her shoulder. "Very slowly." His words were rougher than he'd intended. "I will inch down and then you will follow."

"No. I—"

"Petra, listen to me. You are not to look down, keep your eyes focused on the bark of the tree before you. I will not let you fall. I promise. If anything, you'll land on my head." A vision of Petra's stocking-clad legs hiked over his shoulders as he— *Christ.*

"Trust me." The words choked out as he struggled to control his breathing.

"Right." She lifted her chin with determination. "I'm ready."

Disengaging her fingers with care, Brendan turned and crawled to the trunk and secured a foothold in the bark. Motioning with his hand, he beckoned Petra to move toward him.

She took a deep breath, as if preparing herself and then cautiously made her way to him, her fingers notched into the bark of the tree. She was poised above Brendan but still too far away. He moved up a few inches.

"Don't you dare look up my skirts."

"Petra, I'm much more concerned with getting you down

safely then I am with your undergarments." It was only a small lie. His interest in her undergarments was limited to imagining taking them off of her.

Brendan moved up the trunk until Petra was between him and the tree. He tried to focus on getting her down safely, but if she so much as twitched, her rounded buttocks brushed against a certain part of his anatomy. Having her so close was pure torture, with her body so close and her scent filling the air. He had to restrain himself from nipping at her ear. "Now we move down together. My left foot moves down and so does yours."

"Yes," she said. "You don't have to sound so irritated with me."

Brendan was *incredibly* irritated—at her, *because of her.* He needed to control his craving for this slim young woman who smelled of roses and sugar cookies and he couldn't seem to.

Fifteen minutes later, his boots landed on the ground.

Petra still hung onto the bark for dear life. "Where are you going?" She didn't take her eyes from the tree trunk."

"Relax, Petra. We've made it down." Brendan's hands wrapped around her waist and lowered her the rest of the way until her feet brushed against the leaves covering the ground.

Petra closed her eyes in relief as her feet made contact with the forest floor. Then she smiled brilliantly, her eyes opening with reverence at the oak before them.

"I shall never forget this day." She looked over her shoulder at him.

Brendan doubted he would either.

☙❧

ELATION FILLED PETRA AS SHE LOOKED UP AT THE OAK tree. For the first time in a very long time, she'd done something *she* wished. Not a *proper* something. Or a *polite* something. And Morwick had her neatly trapped against the trunk of the oak.

He seemed in no hurry to release her.

Morwick smelled so good, like the moors around them. His larger body, strong and vital, hovered over Petra, the breadth of his shoulders blocking the sun filtering through the trees. She felt safe and protected within the circle of Morwick's arms. He'd been so gentle with her, both today and when she'd become so horribly ill all over his boots. Few gentlemen on such a short, antagonistic relationship as she and Morwick had, would have done the same.

Had. Petra reminded herself. What she felt now was the furthest thing from dislike.

Acting on impulse, Petra stood on her tiptoes, the rough scrape of his unshaven jaw chafing her lips as she pressed a kiss to his cheek. "Thank you, my lord," she whispered against the tanned skin, holding herself up for a moment, before standing down. It was an incredibly brazen thing to do.

Morwick's body vibrated like a tuning fork at her touch, tightening sinuously, like a large snake stretching itself. His gaze burned into her, the sapphire orbs flaming, like the embers of a fire stoked to flame. No other man had ever looked at Petra the way Morwick did, and certainly not with such wicked intent gleaming in his eyes. He was going to kiss her, knew he shouldn't, and didn't much care.

Petra didn't blush or stammer, nor turn away from the look in those blazing eyes. A truly demure young woman would make a polite excuse and escape to the safety of her chaperone. Or perhaps run all the way back to Somerton as if the devil were at her heels. But Petra had no such inclination. A part of her had been locked away, lying dormant until Morwick stormed into her life, like a whirlwind, to overwhelm her.

Simon didn't once enter her thoughts as Morwick's lips brushed gently against hers. He was tentative at first, as if making sure Petra wouldn't scream and run away.

Nothing could have been further from her mind.

Petra's hands slid up Morwick's torso absorbing the warmth of the skin beneath the rough work shirt. Her fingers found the hills of his ribs, ran along the ridges of hard muscles sculpting his chest. Morwick was strong and solid. Vibrant like the leaves in the tree above them.

Beautiful.

"Petra." He murmured against her lips as he moved closer, effectively pinning her against the tree. "You should run as fast as you can and as far away from me as possible."

"No," she murmured, allowing her fingers to sink into the folds of his shirt. "Stop warning me. I already know how horrible you are. There's no need to go on and on about it."

An amused chuckle came from deep in his chest even as his mouth slanted over hers. The press of his lips became more insistent, pulling Petra's very soul from her. This was not the hard, almost angry kiss he'd bestowed upon her at Rowan's wedding. This kiss spoke of longing. And hunger.

She moved into him, like a tiny vine wrapping around a much stronger, sturdier tree to survive. A spool of desire slowly made its way down between Petra's breasts, her nipples peaking to chafe against his chest. A dull ache, demanding and pleasurable coursed between her thighs. Petra arched against him, grasping the rough cambric of his shirt. She rubbed herself against him like a cat, begging for his touch.

Morwick complied, moving his big hands from the curve of her waist to wind around her back.

Petra could feel the hard length of him even through her skirts, thick and heavy. He wanted her. Desired her. As Morwick's arms tightened and the kiss deepened, a tiny whimper came from her lips.

One hand moved down to cup her backside, lifting her and pushing her more firmly against his arousal. His other hand wound through Petra's hair, keeping her mouth captive. Nipping at her bottom lip, he coaxed her mouth open, his tongue flitting out to touch hers.

Petra trembled at the unexpected invasion, clinging to his shirt as her knees buckled. Unsure what to do, she moved her tongue in unison with his, matching his movements.

A low growl erupted from Brendan at her response. He kissed her with a lazy sensuality, drawing out her surrender to him until Petra sagged against him. Her hands moved up to touch the silken curls tangled against his collar, sinking her fingers through the strands to trace the curve of his skull. Petra had never felt so...intoxicated in her life.

When he pulled back, Petra bit out a low sound of disappointment. He pressed a small kiss to the corner of her mouth before dropping his arms and releasing her. Lust, irritation and resignation were all stamped across his handsome features. His passion was swiftly replaced by his usual annoyance—Morwick's way of dismissing her.

Petra didn't consider herself to be particularly intuitive or experienced, but even she surmised this was his way of shutting her out.

"Morwick—"

"Come along, then," he demanded, voice curt, cutting through the haze of desire she'd felt only moments before. "The sky is darkening, and I've no desire to be caught in a storm." Morwick stooped to pick up his discarded leather rucksack. The stomp of his boots kicked up leaves as he took several steps in the direction of Somerton.

Stunned by his mercurial change in mood, Petra stared at his back. "That's it?" she stammered. How could he kiss her senseless and then calmly walk away? Hadn't he *felt* anything? Didn't he have the decency to at least pretend...*something*?

"Can you not at *least* slow down?" Her voice raised an octave. "Your legs are quite a bit longer than mine."

His steps slowed but did not stop.

Leaves churned up beneath her feet, as she struggled to keep up with his longer strides. It was no use. He was moving too fast in his haste to get away from her. It hurt that he could dismiss her so easily. Finally, out of breath and angry, Petra came to a dead stop. "I do hope you aren't going to apologize for kissing me."

"I won't apologize. I wanted to kiss you." Morwick stopped to glare back at her. "Does that please you?"

"What?" Good Lord, he could be snide. Right now she didn't like him at all.

"Hearing me admit that I wished to kiss you." A slight curl appeared on his lips. "Now, come along."

"I've a pebble in my boot," she lied. Actually, his admission would make her happy if he weren't busy scowling at her.

He slung the rucksack higher. "You don't. You were walking fine a moment ago. Must you always play the damsel in distress to gain my attention?"

Petra was so flummoxed by his words it took her a moment to make sure she'd heard him correctly. *Played a damsel*— "I've *never* intentionally garnered *your* attention. You *kissed* me. Both times, as I recall. I've never so much as flirted with you. Don't you dare pretend I've acted improperly."

"Haven't you?" The accusation was thick with sarcasm. "What about Pendleton? Haven't you *promised* yourself to him?"

"I *haven't*," she spat. What a perfectly awful thing for him to say.

"I suppose you want to muck around a bit before marrying the illustrious Simon. Something for comparison purposes, I'm sure."

Petra sucked in her breath at his insinuation. "How *dare*

you imply such a thing? I'm only a *pea-wit,* of course, Perfect Petra and all of that." Her chest heaved with anger at him and herself, maybe because there had been a hint of truth to his accusation. "Except I'm not *perfect*. I never have been." She blinked back a tear. "I'm only a dressmaker's dummy Mother clothes in proper gowns and flounces to be dangled out to gentlemen seeking a suitable match. Rather like fishing, I suppose. She seeks to catch a fat trout. I suppose that makes me a worm." Tears gathered in her eyes. He'd no idea how horrible it felt to be paraded around like a prize sow at a country market, knowing your only value was in whom you married. She'd been foolish to assume he might actually like her.

"Petra—" He set down the rucksack, all smug mockery gone.

"No." She held up a hand to silence him. "I may not be as bloody *brilliant* as your cousin Arabella, or as daring as my own cousin, Jemma. I am not interesting and I lack a proper purpose. I've no special talents." She shook her head. "I can't even poor tea without spilling a little. But I can climb a tree." She shook as the painful words left her.

"You couldn't climb down. I had to fetch you." The corner of his mouth ticked up.

"Don't you dare mock me. Ordinarily, I find your sarcasm tolerable; just now, I do not." She stepped around him, determined to return to Somerton and the relative safety of her room. He saw her as a joke. A pea-wit. All the joy at climbing and looking at Mam Tor had been crushed. "You are a horrible person to accuse me of such a thing."

"I see your pebble is no longer bothering you."

"Leave me alone." Petra turned and strode off in the direction of Somerton, not trusting herself to say more. He'd succeeded in making her hate him, at least for the moment, which she suspected was his ultimate goal. He had kissed her and now regretted it. Well, that was his problem. Guilt filled her over her own behavior. While she hadn't agreed to marry Simon, and wasn't certain she would, Petra owed him the courtesy of not kissing another man behind his back. His offer deserved honest consideration. An ugly thought occurred to her. What if Morwick was only toying with her because she was involved with Simon? While he'd not said so, Morwick's dislike of Simon was evident. Maybe this kiss had nothing to do with Petra at all.

The thought sobered her enough so that she stopped. It was bad enough to have her mother manipulate her life. She'd not stand to be used in such a way by Morwick.

Taking a deep breath, Petra turned, prepared to meet his annoyed smile, but the moors at her back were quiet except for the chattering of the birds flitting about the heather. She could see nearly all the way back to the oak and there was no sign of him. She should have known he'd gone, as not one sarcastic remark had been hurled in her direction for at least the last ten minutes. She'd been so angry, so absorbed in her thoughts, she hadn't realized she was alone.

Good.

Straightening her shoulders, Petra brushed off her skirts, frowned at the small tear she found in the muslin, and began walking again down the path. Hopefully Tessie had packed the remainder of her things so there would be nothing to delay their departure tomorrow. She hadn't thought she'd feel quite so relieved to leave Somerton.

BRENDAN WATCHED PETRA'S SLENDER FORM, STIFF WITH anger, until she reached the gate leading into the gardens. Her little tirade had been more than justified. The remark about Simon had been particularly cruel, given *he* had kissed *her*.

And he'd practically accused her of being a lightskirt, a woman who flirts with one man while involved with another.

Not nearly as bad as having Petra compare herself to a worm.

The words, choked and bitter, pained Brendan as if someone had taken a fist to his chest.

He'd hurt her, terribly. The worst was, Brendan had meant to. His emotions, once buried so deep as to be nonexistent, had bubbled up while Petra was in his arms, feelings he'd sworn never to entertain for any woman. Worse, she was promised to Simon, a man who Brendan loathed since they were children. The last time he and Pendleton had been involved with the same woman had ended with Brendan's expulsion from Oxford.

I have to stay away from her.

Brendan needed to think and he simply couldn't when the scent of roses and sugar cookies crept into every part of Somerton. He couldn't seem to keep from touching her, which inevitably ended in hurting her in some way. It would be best for them both if he didn't see her again. There was a man in Buxton who had asked after Brendan's services and written to him several times. Mr. Wilcox had found a small cave on his property and was convinced the glittering streaks through the rock were copper. Brendan hiked the rucksack up higher on his shoulder.

Now would be a good time to visit Buxton and Mr. Wilcox.

❧ 9 ❧

The sun shone brightly as the newly repaired Marsh coach lumbered toward Brushbriar. The moors were filled with waves of flowering rowan and heather. Small patches of brush stood out against the rolling hills and the stark outline of Dark Peak. Simon's home, Brushbriar, lay to the west of Somerton, closer to the area known as White Peak. Dark Peak and the moors circled the White Peak, which was strewn with limestone and dotted with farms. From this angle, Petra couldn't see Mam Tor; it almost felt as if the mystical peak had deserted her.

"Goodness, but I am pleased to not have my stomach in such disarray. I am feeling right as rain today. After several days of broth, I believe my dresses may have to be taken in."

Petra gave her mother's purple dress a curious look, thinking the need for a seamstress to be premature. "I'm happy you are feeling well, Mother."

"Can you imagine if we had landed at Brushbriar in such a state? Both of us ill and casting up our accounts in front of Lord Pendleton and his mother? I believe it was divine intervention that caused our axle to break."

"Yes. It was most fortuitous," Petra murmured. She wished to still be climbing a tree and, if she were being honest, she'd like to be kissed senseless again by Morwick. It was a terrible thing to admit, given how unkind he'd been.

"I do hope we will see Lady Cupps-Foster upon our return to London. Possibly we shall see her again during our visit. She *is* neighbor to Lord Pendleton, after all. I mentioned to her that I've always wished to make the acquaintance of Lady Canfeld, and she has promised an introduction."

Lady Canfeld was Her Grace the Duchess of Canfeld. Mother was socially ambitious and always on the lookout for a way to ingratiate herself within the *ton*. Poor Lady Canfeld had no idea what was headed her way. After meeting Petra's mother, the duchess may decide to retire to the country.

"I was rather surprised our host did not appear for dinner last night. One could see how embarrassed Lady Cupps-Foster was for his absence. A previous engagement in Buxton he couldn't delay, apparently. Terrible breach of etiquette to leave your guests without even a polite goodbye."

So that's where Morwick had fled to after their encounter in the woods yesterday. Petra found riding all the way to Buxton in an effort to avoid her a cowardly act. Upon her return to Somerton yesterday Petra had ventured into Lady Cupps-Foster's small sitting room again. She'd walked over and stared at the portrait of the previous Earl of Morwick, wondering at the pain Lady Cupps-Foster endured at his loss and the damage her grief wrought on her youngest son.

No matter his reasons for kissing her, Petra understood that much about Morwick.

A week ago, when Petra had climbed in her coach for the journey to Brushbriar, she had been uncertain whether she had a future with Simon. Now she was doubly so. She'd seen Mam Tor and discovered a piece of herself she hadn't even known was missing. Kissing Morwick only muddied the waters further.

"He's rather odd, isn't he?" Mother cocked her head, eyes boring into Petra. "Wild. Involved in dirt and rocks. His clothing certainly leaves much to be desired."

"Who, Mother?" Petra's irritation was growing by leaps and bounds. Patience for her mother was stretched thin and she was in no mood to play guessing games when Mother obviously had something on her mind. Besides, there was no doubt of whom Mother was speaking.

An exasperated sigh came from the seat across from her. "Your mind is constantly wandering, Petra. I'm referring to Lord Morwick. Consorting with miners and common day laborers rather than coming to London and taking his place in society. Poor Lady Cupps-Foster must be in a constant state of disappointment while he roams the moors picking up stones with his tiny hammer."

"Geology, Mother. He is a geologist. It's a science. The hammer is his rock pick." Before Petra left Somerton, she'd filched another book from Morwick's library, in addition to Lord Thurston which lay tucked inside her trunk. The book had been taken on impulse. She'd only read the first few chapters of '*Principles of Geology*' by Sir Charles Lydell, but already Petra thought herself more informed on the topic.

"How would you know about such a thing, Petra?" Mother clasped her hands, her eyes narrowed and accusatory.

Petra knew she must choose her words carefully, for Mother had a nose for indiscretion. "While you were ill, I visited the library at Somerton." Technically *not* a lie as she did visit the library, she just happened to visit Morwick at the same time. "It was full of books on geology and minerals. Rocks. Lead. Mining. The structure of gritstone. There was very little else to choose from." She didn't dare mention the Lord Thurston book to Mother, who would most likely confiscate the novel immediately. "Since this is Simon's home, I thought becoming more familiar with the subject of geology, I could be of greater assistance to him if we were to marry. I believe one of his bills before Parliament relates to the welfare of miners."

Mother clapped her hands, pleased as punch and more than satisfied with Petra's answer. "Brilliant, Petra. Now you are thinking like the politician's wife you are meant to be."

Petra felt more like a trained monkey than a future politician's wife but she smiled back at her mother.

"At any rate, I pity Lady Cupps-Foster, for she's constantly excusing Morwick's behavior. It must be tiresome. I'm sure his manner is directly related to being raised without a proper male influence."

Petra kept her tone polite and her expression bland. "I'm quite sure Lady Cupps-Foster would not care to have you pity her, Mother. And Morwick's grandsire, the late Duke of Dunbar, would disagree with your assessment of Morwick's upbringing. I understand he was involved."

"His Grace fell short of the mark, in my opinion." Mother straightened her purple skirts, puffing slightly, looking like an overfed orchid about to explode, regardless of having lived on broth for all of two days. "I understand Morwick's brother is little better."

"That's rather unkind." Mother was such a terrible gossip. "I don't know Baron Kelso, and to the best of my knowledge, you don't either. I'm not sure Lady Cupps-Foster, who has been so kind to us, would appreciate you disparaging her father, the duke, or her children. You may wish to recall the previous Duke of Dunbar also raised the current duke, whom you are related to by marriage. Do you think His Grace suffers from a proper male influence?"

Mother's mouth pursed, the tiny hill forming at the top of her upper lip. "Your impudence has only gotten worse and I find such a manner intolerable. What has gotten into you? Questioning me in such a way?"

"Perhaps I've always been impudent, and you haven't noticed. Imagine your disappointment were you to find out I am not as demure and obedient as you assume."

Mother's eyes blinked, shocked at Petra's statement. She searched every line of Petra's face, then her eyes ran over the bodice of her daughter's dress, before flitting down her form, as if looking for something improper. Finding nothing, her lips slowly eased into a smile. Relaxing back into the squabs she tapped Petra playfully on the knee. "Shame on you for teasing me. I know you better than anyone. You've always been the most obedient of daughters and know what is expected of you, unlike others." Mother's eyes clouded and Petra surmised she was thinking of Rowan's marriage to Arabella. "You are malleable."

Petra bristled. What a horrible description. "Malleable? Do you see me as clay which you can form into whatever you wish?"

"A poor choice of words, my dear. Of course that isn't what I meant. You are open to direction and guidance. Your willingness to further your future husband's career is a perfect example. Reading books on a boring topic you can't possibly hope to understand all in an effort to assist Simon speaks well of your character. The true hallmark of a good wife is her ability to be a helpmate to her husband and a mother to their children."

Though she knew Mother meant her words as a compliment, it was difficult to be told her value only depended on her ability to support someone else.

"Lady Cupps-Foster was not in the least biddable and look where it has landed her," Mother continued. "Her first marriage to Baron Kelso was to spite her father, the duke. And before you tell me I am gossiping, the good lady told me so herself." Mother's face took on a wistful gleam. "I remember Kelso quite well. I had just married your father and Kelso was known as one of the biggest rakes in the *ton*. Handsome. Dashing. Possessed of incredible wit. The barony is one of the oldest in England and *very* wealthy. Kelso died mysteriously while out and about in London with his cronies. Some speculated the old duke had had his son-in-law killed, for Kelso made no secret of being unfaithful to his wife. Lady Cupps-Foster was with child at the time. I'm told the current Baron Kelso, Lord Morwick's brother, is cut from the same cloth as his sire."

Mother clutched the squabs as the coach hit a pothole. "Dear me, I do hope we don't break another axle, although I suppose Lord Pendleton would come to our rescue this time. Lady Cupps-Foster's second husband, the Earl of Morwick, was handsome as well, but possessed little more than his title and several struggling mines. The old duke disapproved of that marriage too, though Lady Cupps-Foster would not be dissuaded. Theirs was a *love-match*. Unfortunately the mines proved more profitable than the marriage. He disappeared rather suddenly."

"You make it sound as if he left her by choice, Mother, which you know is not the case."

Mother puffed her cheeks. "They have never found his body and there is some...*gossip*." At Petra's look, she swallowed. "Very well. Death by misadventure, we shall call it. While Lady Cupps-Foster felt terrible at Kelso's death, Morwick's devastated her. She wore black and didn't appear in public for *years*. Everyone was surprised when she finally remarried. Lord Cupps-Foster was another husband cut from the same mold as Kelso. Handsome, wealthy, but known for his rash temper. He died in a duel six months after they were wed."

"You seem to know an awful lot about Lady Cupps-Foster, and most of it's conjecture and gossip."

"I'll have you know, *Marissa* told me these things herself. And yes, she asked me to call her by her Christian name. I had quite a bit of time on my hands while you were upstairs recovering. When I experienced the same stomach distress, she was beyond kind to me. *Marissa*," Mother emphasized the name, "read to me and kept me company. *You* were nowhere to be found. Where had you gotten off to?"

I was climbing trees and getting kissed. Becoming impudent.

"The garden, Mother. I found a quiet bench where I could read." Knowing she was destined to be subjected to her mother's dramatics and possibly further suspicion, Petra said quickly, "I'm so sorry I wasn't there when you needed me." She lowered her eyes, playing at contrition. "I only walked in the gardens and to the library. I'm sorry you weren't informed."

"I would have thought you'd spend your time writing to Simon. You've not sent him one note."

He's not written me either. "By the time I was well enough to do so, we were ready to leave, so I saw no reason. I'm sure he'll understand."

"I sincerely hope so. I know after our long coach ride and illness, you probably needed the fresh air and a walk. But a young, unwed girl should not be wandering about unchaperoned. What if you'd been accosted?"

"Who would accost me on the grounds of Somerton?" Petra gave a weak laugh. *Except for Morwick.* Had her mother always been so overbearing? She thought back to the way Mother had tried to force Rowan to rid himself of his wife and found the answer. She wondered why Father tolerated Mother's behavior and knew it was because of James, her much adored older brother. Mother hadn't ever recovered from his death. No wonder she'd formed a bond of sorts with Lady Cupps-Foster. Both women were well-versed in grief.

Understanding Mother's behavior did little to stop Petra's irritation at being trotted about like a prize pig. Or a *worm*.

And Simon is a large trout my mother wishes to catch.

Brushbriar appeared over the rise of the hill surrounded by gardens, filling Petra with dread. Nerves. There was no spoiled stew now to blame for her stomach's distress. She shrank back from the sight of Simon's estate, trying to tamp down her rising alarm.

"Oh, Petra, how lovely." Mother clasped her hands in awe. "It's almost a shame you shall spend most of your time in London. Thankfully, of course. I know some appreciate the isolation but I'm certain you would not. There's barely any society to speak of. No one to pay calls upon. You are made to grace a table or dance at a ball."

Once again, Mother was incorrect. The moors and Mam Tor called to Petra in a way the ballrooms of London never had.

And Morwick. Let's not forget him.

Simon's home looked nothing like the heap of stone that was Somerton. The design of the manor house was elegant and modern. Two wings jutted out from either side of the gray brick structure, to curve around the main entrance. Graceful flowering vines, unlike the wild mass of greenery covering Somerton, had been coaxed up the stone columns at the front to spill color against the windows. The drive was wide and circular, the gravel perfectly raked and the grounds manicured to perfection. A bevy of liveried footmen stood at attention prepared to assist Petra and her mother. The occupants of Brushbriar stood just outside the massive, black door graced with a golden knocker.

Simon stood tall, confident and impeccably dressed. Petra had been attracted to Simon's strong sense of decency when they'd first met, his strong scruples and principled manner. She glanced out the window at his ramrod posture and perfectly tailored clothes. His manner now struck her as more rigid than anything.

He was flanked by two women.

The voluptuous brunette on his left was certainly his sister Katherine, the widowed Lady Whitfield. Petra had never met Katherine, only seen her from across ballrooms or at the opera. Simon's courtship of Petra had begun shortly after the death of Lord Whitfield and his sister had already left for Brushbriar. Lady Whitfield was known in London for her beauty, her fashion, and her lovers, with whom she was not particularly discreet, something Petra knew did not sit well with Simon. Conscious of his sterling reputation in Parliament and with his own stiff sense of propriety, Katherine was probably lucky Simon hadn't shipped her off to a convent.

Whitfield's heir had certainly wanted Katherine gone from London, as he'd forcibly removed her from the Whitfield townhouse. She'd not provided an heir nor had Whitfield provided for *her*, according to his nephew who had inherited. Dressed in a dark pewter dress, even though Whitfield had only been dead six months, Katherine looked nothing like a grieving widow.

An older, less voluptuous version of Katherine stood on Simon's right, her hand placed firmly on the arm of his coat. Dressed in a stylish day dress of evergreen, Lady Pendleton looked as fashionable as any grande dame of the ton. She could have been preparing to pay calls in London rather than welcoming guests to her country home. Slender to the point of emaciation, Simon's mother surveyed Petra with the smile one usually reserves when served day old scones at tea. Her fingers absently plucked at the sleeve of Simon's coat.

Simon had spoken of his mother fondly and with much

affection. His description had been of a loving, generous woman who was quick to laugh and enjoyed a brandy before dinner. The woman regarding Petra and her mother with forced welcome didn't seem to have much in common with Simon's description. Brittle, was the first word that came to Petra's mind.

Mother noticed Lady Pendleton's coldness, taking Petra's hand firmly and squeezing her fingers. "Do not worry, dearest. You will dazzle her. *You* are the daughter of the Earl of Marsh and the *perfect* match for her son. She is only being territorial. Once she comes to know you better, she will adore you as Simon does."

Petra nodded and squeezed her mother's hand back. She was beginning to detest the word perfect. Nothing about marrying Simon or Brushbriar was perfect. After the chaos of Somerton, Brushbriar, at first glance, appeared polished and mannered. It should have brought Petra comfort, but had quite the opposite effect.

"I'll be fine, Mother," she said quietly.

"We will handle Lady Pendleton together, dearest." Mother straightened her plump shoulders as if preparing for battle.

Mother was many things, Petra mused. But she would never allow any disparagement of her children for any reason. Only she was allotted such a privilege.

The Marsh coach rolled to a stop, wheels crackling against the gravel of the drive. A brace of footmen sprang into action, hurrying forward to assist Jenkins and the Marsh grooms who had ridden with them.

Simon released his mother's hand with a pat and came forward to greet the Marsh coach with a smile on his face. A rush of relief filled Petra. She'd been concerned Simon may have had time to regret his decision to invite them all the way to Brushbriar.

Simon was not unappealing. Indeed, Lord Pendleton, ambitious politician, was a very attractive man. His hair shone a rich chestnut in the morning sun, perfectly framing his refined, patrician features. The coat of nut brown was expensive and expertly tailored to fit his lean, energetic form. He didn't have Morwick's height, nor his build; instead Simon was lean and aristocratic, looking as if he'd just stepped out of his gentleman's club.

Lord Pendleton had been one of the Season's most eligible bachelors and was highly sought after. He'd been in the sights of several young ladies before meeting Petra at the charity luncheon she'd attended. Simon was well-spoken and unfailingly polite. After avoiding Lord Dunning's groping hands for much of the Season, Simon's manner toward Petra had been a welcome relief. Mother hadn't given Dunning a second thought once Simon began to direct his attention to her daughter. At the time, Petra enjoyed the envy of nearly every woman in London for snatching up such a catch as Viscount Pendleton.

As she returned his smile of greeting, Petra considered Mother could be right. Maybe with a bit more effort on her part, she and Simon might find passion between them.

Morwick flashed before her eyes. She could still feel his mouth on hers. The way the heat flew up her body at the merest touch.

Petra's smile faltered. Why didn't she have that with Simon? The man everyone wished her to marry? Simon was a gentleman, a shining example of everything Morwick wasn't.

Yet he never wrote nor came from Brushbriar to check on you.

She had a difficult time imagining Simon holding her if she'd made the mistake of puking on his boots. But Morwick had.

"Lady Petra." Simon helped her from the coach. "It is my

great pleasure to finally welcome you to Brushbriar." His lips brushed her knuckles.

"My lord." Petra curtsied in a fluid motion. "We are delighted to accept your hospitality."

"Lady Marsh." Simon greeted her mother. "Welcome to Brushbriar." He bowed.

Mother inclined her head, looking expectantly toward Lady Pendleton and Katherine as she waited for Simon to lead them over.

It was all *perfectly* polite. Well-mannered. Petra was certain she'd have no trouble at all finding the library as Brushbriar was bound to be as well-ordered as Simon.

Stop it, Petra.

"Lady Marsh, Lady Petra, may I present my mother, Lady Pendleton, and my sister, Lady Whitfield."

Again Petra dipped, this time a bit lower, her back ramrod straight, her eyes down. As she straightened, she looked Lady Pendleton in the eye, something Petra wouldn't have done even a few months ago, but Petra wasn't feeling demure at the moment. She'd spent enough of her life being intimidated. "It is a pleasure to meet you, Lady Pendleton, Lady Whitfield."

Mother made a small sound of displeasure at Petra's show of spirit, but mercifully restrained from offering comment. "Lady Pendleton, I am thrilled to finally make your acquaintance. Brushbriar is stunning. Lady Whitfield, a pleasure to see you again."

Petra lifted an eyebrow at her mother's words. She'd no idea Mother was acquainted with the notorious Lady Whitfield.

Lady Pendleton inclined her head, looking down the length of her aristocratic nose. "The pleasure is ours, Lady Marsh. I was distressed to learn of your difficulties. I fear you are not the first guest of ours whose coach was not up to the rigors of the journey. I understand the Earl of Morwick offered his assistance and hospitality."

A pretty speech, except for the evident distaste at the mention of Morwick.

"Indeed, we were incredibly fortunate to have him come upon us," Mother stated. "The axle of our coach snapped, and our driver took a wrong turn, sending us much too far out of our way. Had he not come upon us, we may have slept in the road until help came."

Lady Pendleton's eyebrows fluttered at Mother's rather dramatic recitation of their rescue. "And I understand you also experienced a stomach ailment?"

"Lady Cupps-Foster was kind enough to offer us shelter until we were well enough to travel. Lord Morwick made sure to summon a physician and we continued our journey as soon as we were well again."

"How terribly kind of Lord Morwick. He has our thanks, doesn't he, Simon?" Tiny teeth shone between her thin lips as she spoke. Her regal head tilted in her son's direction as she addressed him.

"Terribly kind," Simon said, ice dripping from his words.

Petra had been mistaken. The animosity between Simon and Morwick seemed more than a case of mere dislike, if Simon's manner were any indication. She'd never seen such a look of utter contempt on his face before. He made no effort to comment further.

Is that why he hadn't sent word or visited her at Somerton?

Lady Pendleton reached out to take Mother's arm. "Why, you have experienced the trials of Job, have you not? You poor thing. I'm sure you are exhausted by your travails."

Mother's cheeks pinked. "You've no idea, my lady." She allowed herself to be led into the house by Lady Pendleton.

Lady Pendleton clucked sympathetically. "You'll never wish to venture so far from London again, I fear."

"Perish the thought," Mother replied. "However, I shall not be recommending the Duck & Crow to anyone traveling in this direction. A terrible place, but it was the only remotely reputable inn on the main road."

"Ah yes, spoiled stew." Katherine's voice was silky. "Lamb, was it?" She waved Petra through the massive oak door. "After you, Lady Petra."

"Yes," Petra murmured, assuming Morwick must have said as much in his note to Brushbriar.

Simon fell into step beside Petra as their mothers chattered away. "I'm so relieved you're feeling better. Imagine, coming all this way only to have spoiled stew. I plan on speaking to the proprietor of the Duck and Crow on your behalf. I'll see such a thing doesn't happen again. At the very least he'll mind his kitchen better."

"That's not necessary, my lord," Petra said, wondering at his willingness to confront the innkeeper on her behalf when his feelings evidently didn't extend to at least sending her a note while at the home of a man he didn't care for.

Petra's eyes widened at the entryway of Brushbriar, somewhat taken aback by the extravagant display. Simon hadn't struck her in London as a gentleman who flaunted his wealth and influence but looking around, Petra thought perhaps she'd been mistaken about that facet of his personality as well.

The floor beneath her feet was crafted of expensive marble of a type usually reserved for ballrooms, not a foyer. The stairs stretching up to the second floor were wide, curving up to an enormous landing graced with a small table laden with a profusion of colorful blooms. But it was the balustrade Petra could not look away from. The spindles had all been individually carved in an array of leaves and acorns.

Blue John decorated the entire balustrade. The mineral took the form of leaves, flowers and clusters of berries. A circular table sat at the base of the stairs holding an immense, intricately sculpted horse made entirely of Blue John. The amount of the mineral needed to create such a thing must have cost a small fortune. If anyone had doubted the immense wealth of Viscount Pendleton, that wealth was showcased for all to see.

What an incredibly vulgar display.

Petra looked at her mother whose eyes had widened at the decoration of the foyer.

"Your rooms are prepared and waiting for you. I know the ride from Somerton wasn't terribly long, but given all you've been through, I thought you may like to refresh yourselves or have a lie down before tea." Lady Pendleton bestowed her thin-lipped smile on them.

"My servants—" Lady Marsh started, looking upward at the immense staircase.

"I instructed our housekeeper, Mrs. Leonard, to show them to your chambers so they can begin unpacking. Luckily, only a small trunk was packed for your unexpected stay at Somerton, so most of your things have already been aired out and await your pleasure. Your rooms face the moors and I'm sure you'll find them much more comfortable than those at Somerton." Lady Pendleton gave a delicate shiver of her boney shoulders. "Renovation is quite costly."

Mother's smile froze into place on her plump lips at her host's insinuation that the stay at Somerton had been uncomfortable. "Lady Cupps-Foster was very kind and Somerton very pleasant. I found the estate to be lovely."

Petra wasn't surprised at Mother's defense. She could be surprisingly loyal to those who captured her affection, as Lady Cupps-Foster apparently had.

Lady Pendleton's eyes grew a bit dark and much less

welcoming at being rebuked by her guest, no matter how politely. "Yes, Marissa is a lovely hostess," she conceded.

"How odd, Lady Petra, we've not been introduced before today," Katherine interjected, clearly attempting to diffuse the sudden tension between her mother and Petra's. "I'm sure we've seen each other across a ballroom dozens of times, not knowing one day we would become family."

Petra wanted to politely correct Katherine's assumption that Petra and Simon would marry but didn't, not with Mother standing next to her. "I'm sure you're correct."

"You left London shortly after Lady Petra and I met at a charitable event," Simon reminded her. "There wasn't the opportunity."

Katherine's eyes were deep, black pools. "Of course, with the death of my beloved husband I immediately retired from society."

"My condolences on your loss," Petra murmured noting that the pewter dress Katherine wore was trimmed with the finest Brussels lace and clung to Katherine's numerous curves. It was hardly the type of dress a grieving widow would typically choose to wear. The neckline in particular offered an expansive view of the tops of Katherine's breasts.

Petra looked down at her own small bosom. Barely a valley between them could be formed. Next to Katherine, Petra thought her figure to be rather childish.

"I miss him dreadfully." Katherine said, blinking as if she would burst into tears.

"How terrible for you." Petra suppressed a snort of disbelief. Katherine and her affairs were often the talk of the Season; even young, virginal ladies of Petra's ilk had heard the rumors. Nonetheless, Petra kept her features schooled into the serene mask she'd worn for so long.

"I miss London. Castleton, though nearby, doesn't offer much excitement. Thankfully, we are to have a diversion now that you and your mother have arrived." The lips of her full mouth pulled back into an approximation of her mother's condescending smile.

A woman appeared silently from the depths of the shadowed hallway. As broad as she was tall, her form was clothed in a severe dress of indigo, so dark Petra mistook the color for black. Silver hair had been twisted back from her forehead and formed into a tight braid wound around the top of her head like a small crown. Her eyes, though not friendly, sparkled with intelligence. A large circle of keys jangled from the belt at her waist.

"Ah, Mrs. Leonard." Lady Pendleton waved the woman closer. "Lady Marsh, this is our housekeeper, Mrs. Leonard. She'll see you up to your rooms and ensure you have everything you require."

"What type of diversion?" Petra was curious. She looked to Simon who had remained mostly silent since greeting them outside, and who appeared to be slowly drifting away from the group of women as if he couldn't wait to make his escape. As she watched, he pulled out a pocket watch, consulted the time and frowned, declining to look up at her.

Katherine clapped her hands, eyes glittering like bits of jet. "A house party."

"A house party?" Lady Marsh stammered in surprise, discomfort clear as her eyes shot to Simon and then his mother. "I didn't realize—"

"Nothing like what you are used to in London, of course." Katherine's excitement was evident. "A small gathering of what little society can be found around Castleton. We'll have dancing and other diversions. I believe I've even found a fortune teller from Buxton to entertain us. It's been great fun to plan and has helped take my mind off of poor Lord Whitfield."

Petra and her mother hadn't been informed of such plans.

Her opinion of Lady Pendleton, already not high, dropped another notch. Simon continued to study his watch to avoid catching Petra's eye.

"House party is a bit of an exaggeration," Lady Pendleton cautioned her daughter. "It's only the Divets, Baron Haddon, and perhaps a few others who will be staying the week. Barely enough to fill up our guest wing. I believe Haddon is bringing one of his daughters," her voice grew thick with displeasure, "though I can't for the life of me recall exactly which one. They are quite close in age and their faces all blur together in one's mind."

"Thank goodness we came prepared." Though she smiled politely, Mother was furious at being ambushed in such a way. Her plump form quivered like a plate of aspic. "I made sure to instruct my maid to include a choice of ballgowns for both myself and Petra," Mother said with satisfaction, "in case such a situation should arise."

Katherine's slender hand flew up to her throat. "Oh dear, I worried I would need to send for the seamstress in Castleton to assist with an appropriate gown to wear. With your delay in arriving I did worry there wouldn't be time. I'm happy that won't be necessary."

Bullocks. The house party had clearly been in the works for some time. Lady Pendleton and Mother had been corresponding about the trip to Brushbriar on a regular basis. Nothing about a ball and dancing had ever been mentioned. Nor had news of the house party reached them at Somerton. If Lady Pendleton meant to unsettle them, she was sadly mistaken. Mother's skills at overpacking and being prepared for any occasion were legendary in the Marsh household.

"Yes, how fortuitous." Lady Pendleton echoed her daughter's false sentiment.

Katherine gave her mother a sideways glance. "And given their assistance to our guests, I thought it appropriate we extend an invitation to Lord Morwick and Lady Cupps-Foster to attend our little party as well. I'm sure they'll only stay a night or two." Katherine appeared incredibly pleased with herself.

A flutter passed across Petra's heart at the thought of Morwick here, at Brushbriar.

Simon, who had nearly managed to escape the foyer, turned at his sister's news, an ugly pinched look on his handsome face. "I beg your pardon?"

"I've invited the Earl of Morwick and his mother to join us." Katherine spoke each word with determination. "They've accepted."

"Darling," Lady Pendleton's voice was curt with her own surprise. "You *neglected* to tell me you'd invited Morwick. And you say he's accepted? He so rarely leaves Somerton. And I haven't seen Marissa in ages." Lady Pendleton managed with only a small curl of her upper lip. "What a delightful surprise."

"I think given the aid offered to Lady Marsh and her daughter, an invitation to our little party is the very least we can do. It will give Simon the opportunity to thank Lord Morwick personally."

"Of course. I'd not thought to include them in our original plans, as Marissa rarely socializes when in residence at Somerton. How wonderful they will be joining us."

Petra's glance shot from Katherine's smug assurance to Lady Pendleton and Simon, who were both trying to hide their displeasure at the news of Morwick invading Brushbriar.

Lady Pendleton nodded to the housekeeper. "Please show our guests up, Mrs. Leonard, and have two additional rooms prepared for the Earl of Morwick and his mother."

"Of course, Lady Pendleton." Mrs. Leonard, keys jingling, bowed before Mother. "This way, my lady."

"Consider our home yours for the duration of your stay. Mrs. Leonard will see you have everything you need," Lady Pendleton added. "If you'll excuse me, I've a mountain of correspondence that requires my attention, as well as the final preparations for our little house party."

"Of course." Mother inclined her head. "Mrs. Leonard, please proceed."

"I must take my leave, Lady Marsh, Lady Petra." Simon made a short bow. "I will see you both later at dinner. If you'll excuse me?" Simon bestowed a charming smile on them, though there was no warmth in his eyes. "Shall I collect you for a walk about the gardens before dinner, Lady Petra? With your permission of course, Lady Marsh."

Petra automatically looked to her mother, who nodded her acceptance. She found it frustrating to ask her mother to approve something as mundane as a turn about the gardens. It had been so nice not to have a chaperone while Mother was ill. Her brief stretch of freedom was over.

"That would be lovely," Petra replied.

"Until then." Simon turned and strode down the hallway toward the back of the house. Almost as if on cue, a pair of spaniels, tails wagging, appeared from the depths of the house to trail at his heels.

"My lady," Mrs. Leonard repeated, before starting up the stairs. "If you will follow me."

Petra stayed a step behind her mother and the beefy housekeeper and Katherine stuck to her side. Apparently Simon's sister had more to say.

"I'd forgotten how much my brother dislikes Morwick." Her tone was unapologetic. "I'd thought Simon had outgrown such a thing."

Conveniently forgotten, Petra thought. The invitation to Morwick and Lady Cupps-Foster was probably in retaliation for Simon forcing Katherine to return to Brushbriar.

"We all grew up together, Simon, me, and Morwick. We played hide and seek on the moors and went exploring. I've missed seeing him." She pressed her hand to Petra's arm.

A *look* had entered Katherine's eyes as she spoke of Morwick. A look that spoke of more than childhood friendship.

"Mother likes to have a sherry in the large drawing room before dinner. It would be best if you weren't late." She glided back toward the stairs, pewter skirts wafting around her ankles gracefully.

Petra was trying very hard not to dislike her. She'd have to be an idiot not to hear the meaning in Katherine's words. The house party wasn't Katherine's distraction, Morwick was.

It's none of my business. But the jealousy leaked into her chest all the same.

As she watched the other woman make her way down the stairs like a beautiful, tragic swan, Petra had the unkind, uncharacteristic inclination to push Katherine down them.

P etra took a deep breath as she was ushered into the drawing room before dinner, mentally preparing herself for the evening. After a nap, she'd indulged in a long, hot bath and requested tea in her room. Now better fortified, she prepared to acquaint herself with Simon's family.

Simon himself would be missing from the drawing room. He'd sent a curt note explaining business matters required his attention until dinner and their walk in the gardens would have to be postponed.

Petra was hardly surprised. Her discomfort with Simon and Brushbriar had increased tenfold since the Marsh coach had arrived earlier in the day.

The drawing room was even more garishly decorated than the foyer of Brushbriar. Blue John had been tucked into each available nook of the large room. Four floor-to-ceiling windows faced the moors, each possessing a windowpane of Blue John. A fire crackled in the immense fireplace, large enough for Petra to walk in to. The mantle and hearth were made of the rare mineral. A small table to Lady Pendleton's right held an enormous egg carved of Blue John, held aloft by a gilt stand.

Petra found the entire room overdone and bordering on vulgar.

Mother was already here, seated to Lady Pendleton's right. The girlish curls she sometimes affected were bouncing to and fro as she nodded in agreement to a story her hostess related. Mother appeared absolutely fascinated by Lady Pendleton's conversation and barely blinked when her daughter was announced.

"There you are, dearest." Mother looked up as she entered the room. "I do hope you're well rested." Her eyes ran over Petra's attire searching for anything warranting her disapproval; apparently finding nothing, a satisfied smile crossed her lips.

"I'm quite refreshed, thank you." Petra dipped to both Lady Pendleton and her daughter. "Good evening, Lady Pendleton, Lady Whitfield."

Both ladies inclined their heads in acknowledgement.

"Come, sit next to me." Katherine patted a nearby chair, dark eyes gleaming. "So that we may become better acquainted."

Petra settled herself in the chair indicated. She perched on the cushion, posture so ram-rod straight one could put a plate of food on her head and not a drop would spill. Indeed, that had been a game of Mother's years ago. A plate of peas, rolling about a small saucer would be placed upon her head while tea was served. If even one pea left the plate, Petra was denied anything to eat and had to wait until dinner. "What a lovely gown." Petra nodded to Katherine.

The dress, cut in the latest fashion, was of shimmering dove-gray silk. An underskirt shot through with deep indigo thread, brushed her matching slippers. The neckline, decorated with ribbon matching the underskirt, was rather dramatic and Katherine's very ample assets were on full display. Hardly appropriate widow's weeds. The cloud of Katherine's dark sable hair was pulled away from her face and piled atop her head in a spill of curls. The hairstyle emphasized her delicate bone structure and the swanlike length of her neck. Small diamonds dangled from her ears and a pear-shaped diamond hung between the deep valley of her breasts.

Katherine was stunningly beautiful, Petra acknowledged, looking down at her own pale yellow dress. She had never felt more like a child playing dress up than she did next to Katherine's sophistication and style.

Katherine's full lips pulled into a smile as she noted Petra's assessment.

She's trying to intimidate me. And thus far succeeding brilliantly.

"I was growing concerned your previous ailment had returned." Petra's mother looked up from her conversation, plump fingers clutching the glass of sherry, eyes systematically checking her daughter's posture for any deficit.

"I'm quite well, Mother." Petra's hands slid together and locked atop her lap. Her mother's gown was the color of a blackberry and coupled with her generous form, invited all sorts of unwelcome comparisons.

"I trust you find your rooms acceptable?" Katherine asked.

"Yes, thank you. They're lovely. How kind of you to inquire," Petra said automatically, knowing she was doomed to another evening of polite conversation about nothing.

"I must thank you," Lady Pendleton said from her place on the couch as she took a generous sip of sherry. "I have been looking forward to your visit for weeks, not only because it gives us all a chance to know one another better, but also because it has given me an opportunity to entertain. I don't think we've had guests at Brushbriar since dear

Katherine was to marry Whitfield." Her eyes grew wistful. "The engagement party was the stuff of legends."

"I'm sure it will be a *marvelous* time," Mother said.

Petra didn't think Mother had yet gotten over the fact they'd been surprised by the news of the house party. Her fingers toyed with the folds of her skirt, a sure sign of annoyance. "We are looking forward to meeting your neighbors."

"All of our friends are lovely, of course, but I'm especially looking forward to seeing Lord Haddon. He's a widower." Lady Pendleton gave her daughter a pointed look. "And a handsome, wealthy one at that. The poor man has four daughters and each of them a trial. I read again his reply to our invitation and Haddon will be bringing his eldest daughter, Jordana, to Brushbriar. He finds our little party to be a perfect opportunity for the girl to practice her dancing and social skills. She'll have her first Season soon."

"I do hope he's had more luck with her manners. Haddon has lost yet another dancing instructor for the Haddon Hellions," Katherine interjected. "This one, Mr. Gatwick, recommended by the Countess of Suffolk no less, ran from the house without taking his belongings. He took the first coach to London and sent for his things rather than stay at Bronsby Abbey one more night."

Mother's sherry was poised at her bottom lip. "Dear me."

"The girls are only in dire need of a strong, feminine hand." Lady Pendleton shot another warning glance at Katherine. "Haddon is looking for a wife. His has been dead for over five years. High time he remarried."

"He will need to look elsewhere," Katherine murmured in a low tone.

"I confess, Katherine was right to correct my error and invite Lord Morwick and his mother. We were once quite close, you know. Before..." Her words trailed off. "Poor, dear Marissa. She's had her share of tragedy, hasn't she? Widowed three times, each time under mysterious, tragic circum-stances. My husband and the late earl, Reginald, were friends and often went hunting together." She shook her head. "When he disappeared..." Lady Pendleton allowed the words to hang in the air, "we never found any sign of him even though every man in the county searched for days. He had vanished without a trace and no one has seen him since."

Petra immediately stiffened at Lady Pendleton's recounting of the tragedy of Morwick's father. *Gossiping old harpy.*

"So I've been told," Mother agreed. "Even in London, his disappearance is still discussed. Lady Cupps-Foster has endured much."

"Indeed, I'm sure you've noticed how eccentric Morwick is. Katherine, Simon and Morwick all ran about the moors together, the greatest of friends. But, Morwick." She shook her head sadly as if it pained her to impart such information. "He and Simon were often at odds. One well-mannered, one rather savage."

There was no doubt who she thought the savage.

"Not to mention Morwick's elder brother, Baron Kelso. A brute and a bully. He was constantly picking fights with Simon. Between the brawling and the Gypsies—"

"Gypsies?" Mother set down her empty glass.

"Yes. I forbade Simon to associate with Morwick after that." She glanced at Katherine. "And Katherine as well. Morwick would disappear, much like his father, for days at a time. Marissa often worried her son would run away with the tribe for he adored the colored wagons they drove. Katherine did not heed my warning about associating with such...people."

"The Gypsies were interesting." Katherine lifted her chin in defiance. "I could hardly blame him for chasing after them or their wagons. The women wore the most gorgeous scarves and dresses, all in bright yellows, reds, and purple. And they danced barefoot around the fire. I declare I could not look away."

"Katherine," Lady Pendleton warned. "Your childish observations are in no way based in reality. The Gypsies were dirty, ill-mannered thieves who stole sheep and picked pockets when no one was looking."

Katherine's lips tightened at the rebuke.

"Regardless," Lady Pendleton said, "Morwick didn't care to be a gentleman. When the old duke of Dunbar finally took a firm hand with his grandson, it was too late, in my opinion. Morwick had been overindulged by his mother, who was too busy mourning her late husband to raise him properly."

Petra's hands clasped so forcefully she thought her knuckles would snap. While the information was identical to the stories Lady Cupps-Foster and Morwick had imparted to her, the retelling by Lady Pendleton was far different.

"Morwick's brother, Spencer," Lady Pendleton continued, "is a horse of a different color altogether, isn't he Katherine? The bully turned into a rogue." Mother and daughter exchanged looks. "A bigger rake I've never seen, except for his father, of course. Kelso is likely terrorizing society in India as we speak. He's not been back to England in years." She tapped her upper lip. "Mayhap he'll never return. Look at me." Her eyes widened at Mother. "Gossiping away. Pray forgive me. I've not had the opportunity to converse with another lady in quite some time."

Petra struggled not to roll her eyes. Simon's mother knew exactly what she was doing. Mother was practically salivating, both at the gossip as well as Lady Pendleton's appreciation of her company. She would repeat Lady Pendleton's version of the events which painted Morwick and Lady Cupps-Foster's tragic past with less sympathy. Which, she supposed, was exactly Lady Pendleton's intent.

"And of course, Lady Cupps-Foster's family is as infamous as they come. The old duke struck terror into the hearts of London and I'm told his nephew, the current duke is no better. I understand you are now related to the Devils of Dunbar through marriage?"

Mother's throat worked. "My niece, Jemma, married His Grace some time ago."

A calculated look entered Lady Pendleton's eyes. "I must know how such a thing came about." She patted Mother's hands. "I've heard from my friends in London, of course, but that is only gossip and conjecture."

MOTHER'S CHEEKS PINKED. "OH, I'M SURE YOU WOULDN'T be interested in such a tale."

"But I am." Lady Pendleton said. "We are *family*, dear Lady Marsh, after all."

Lady Pendleton knew her audience well. Mother's eyes glistened with the compliment that Lady Pendleton considered them family. "My niece, Jane Emily, and the duke met..." Mother's voice lowered as she related the tale to their hostess.

Petra had to admit. It was a rather juicy story.

Katherine turned sideways in her chair, uninterested in Mother's tale. She regarded Petra with no small amount of boredom, which she didn't bother hiding. "Well, I suppose you must tell me about your journey."

Petra found Katherine to be a most interesting creature. She'd been at turns pleasant, condescending, and intimidating. She seemed determined to keep Petra unsettled. Petra's hope she might find an ally at Brushbriar was rapidly fading. "Must I? The journey was uneventful until the coach axle broke. Shall I relate the contents of the spoiled stew I ate?"

Katherine's eyes widened for a moment in surprise at

Petra's retort but was soon replaced with a grudging gleam of admiration. "I'm sure we both know I've no interest in your tedious journey. I'm far more interested in the occupants of Somerton, particularly Lord Morwick." Dark eyes flashed with interest. "I haven't seen him since I first returned to Brushbriar, and, as my mother has related, we were once great *friends.*" Her voice lowered to a purr. "Is he still in need of a haircut?"

"I'm ashamed to say," Petra kept her voice light, "that I didn't notice his hair. I was more concerned with the contents of my stomach."

"So you spent no time with Morwick at all?" Katherine said.

"I'm afraid I didn't." *Except for the kissing under a tree and a spirited discussion on geology. Oh, and I puked on his boots.*

"I'm not surprised." A throaty laugh came from her. "I can't *imagine* you and Morwick in the same room, let alone engaging in conversation."

"You can't?" *Well, that was rather insulting.*

"Well, no." Katherine laughed softly again. "I meant no offense."

Petra somehow doubted that.

"What on earth would the two of you possibly find to talk about? I suppose the weather, possibly. Or maybe you could have discussed the spoiled stew. But once the pleasantries were over, I can't imagine..." Her shoulders moved in a delicate shrug. "Morwick is obsessed with rocks and fossils, things most of us know nothing about. He's a scientist. An explorer of caves and such. I've known him practically my entire life and *I* barely understand a word."

Petra didn't know which she disliked more, Katherine's implication Petra was too unintelligent to understand anything Morwick said, or the idea he wouldn't care to speak to her at all. Her hands tightened once more in her lap.

"Oh, dear me, that didn't sound correct either. It's only you are so proper and ladylike, you must find a man like Morwick to be beyond the pale. He doesn't care for society as a whole, nor any of its trappings. And he can be very blunt in his opinions. I only meant you would not tolerate him for long. You are too much like my brother."

"Appearances can sometimes be deceiving, Lady Whit-field." Petra shook off the shield of decorum wound around her and fixed her stare on Katherine, uncaring if Mother noticed. She refused to allow Katherine to assume her no more than a bland bit of fluff from London incapable of attracting a man like Morwick. "Take for instance, Lady Whitfield, your dress."

"My dress?" Katherine's dark brow knit in confusion.

"It's beautiful, of course, and as I said, the color suits you much more so than black."

The barb struck home, politely said though it was. Katherine's eyes hardened into bits of onyx. "How kind of you to say."

She gave Katherine a perfect, ladylike smile. Petra already possessed the most difficult sister-in-law in all of London, and didn't feel the need for a second, should things come to that.

Before Katherine could offer a rebuttal, her brother was announced.

Simon strolled into the drawing room like a king, resplen-dent in formal evening wear, his dark hair brushed back from his temples and gleaming in the candlelight. The light aroma of his soap wafted from his freshly shaved cheeks, scenting the air. His waistcoat sparkled with silver thread and his cravat had been tied into an expert knot. Every inch of Simon was burnished and shiny, like a newly minted coin. Not a curl out of place, nor a wrinkle in his clothing.

Altogether and entirely...*too perfect.*

Not a skip of her heart greeted his appearance, but

Petra smiled brightly at him all the same. He *was* terribly handsome. Simon had none of Morwick's rough, wild beauty, but he was still a very attractive man. The first time they'd danced together at Lady Upton's ball, Petra had floated on a cloud of happiness and barely remembered if they spoke.

"I am the luckiest man alive." Simon bowed. "I'm to sup surrounded by the loveliest ladies in all of England."

"Ever the charmer." Lady Pendleton offered a genuine smile to her son. It was clear she adored him.

With an incline of his head, Simon took his mother's arm then took Petra's and tucked her fingers into his elbow. "You look lovely tonight," he said, taking in the pale yellow of her gown, the modest neckline and simply styled hair. "Perfect, in fact."

"Thank you, my lord." Perfection, she was rapidly beginning to understand, was overrated. Mother had chosen the gown with its incredibly modest neckline. And though her breasts were small, Petra had a sudden notion that they should be *seen*. Simon had barely glanced in the direction of her bodice. She cast a sideways look at Simon wondering why he'd never noticed her breasts. Or ogled them.

Morwick had done both.

As Simon led her forward, Katherine and Mother conversed quietly, falling in line behind them. It was all perfectly pleasant. Ordered. Polite. *Boring*.

Dinner, something overcooked and not to Petra's liking, passed in exactly the same tedious, intolerable manner.

Everyone at the dinner table took Petra's engagement to Simon for granted, including Mother. No one seemed concerned with whether Petra had accepted him or not. Petra's two Seasons were dissected in excruciating detail, down to her dancing partners at various functions. Lady Pendleton seemed determined to ensure Petra had done nothing remotely scandalous or inflammatory to eventually infect her brilliant son.

Mother, in her effort to reassure Lady Pendleton of Petra's innocence, recounted every bit of the last two years, discussing Petra as if she weren't even at the table.

Petra had never been so horrified.

Katherine listened to the conversation swirling about the table with mild interest, interjecting a comment or two only when necessary. Her dark eyes glanced every so often at Petra with something akin to pity.

Petra ate sparingly, almost wishing her stomach ailment would return so she could excuse herself from the table, but she wasn't that lucky. Her resentment grew, along with her hatred of the mashed turnips on her plate.

"Tell me, my lord," she spoke up, startling the entire table into silence with her words. "What has occupied you since our arrival?"

His nostrils flared slightly at her questioning of his whereabouts. "This and that," Simon answered, his nod to her indulgent, as if she were a small child asking after the existence of fairies. "I've an important bill I must finish to present to Parliament. I don't wish to bore you with the details." He smiled at the table. "I'm sure you ladies would prefer to discuss other things far more interesting."

"But, I *am* interested, my lord," Petra challenged. "I should like to know more. You must have been quite busy while I was ill at Somerton." She deliberately left the unvoiced question lingering in the air.

Simon took her meaning as evidenced by the slight reddening of his puffed cheeks. "It's fairly complicated and the subject is not fit discussion with such charming company."

"Hear, hear." Lady Pendleton agreed with her son. "The theater is what I miss most about not being in London. I was privileged to see the great Edmund Kean in Macbeth years ago."

"Magnificent," Mother agreed. "I, too, was privileged to see him on stage."

Petra gritted her teeth as Lady Pendleton deftly steered the discussion into theater, Covent Garden, Edmund Kean and his son. What Simon meant in his pretty speech was the women present couldn't *possibly* understand the principles of his *important* work or his bloody bill. She turned to Simon. "I am fairly up to date on many of the issues facing the reform of —"

"Later, perhaps." Simon stabbed his roast, pulling the chunk of meat from his fork with relish.

"Petra," Mother announced from her place at the table as their plates were taken up and fruit and cheese was brought out. "We should relate to Lady Pendleton your experience visiting Gray Covington." At Lady Pendleton's exclamation of delight, Mother continued, "we are friends of Lord Cambourne, you see. I cannot begin to tell you of the gardens. The Dowager Marchioness planned them out herself. Simply divine, though there are no more midnight roses in any of the beds."

"Oh, for shame," Lady Pendleton remarked. "Midnight roses were once the most sought after blooms in all of England. What happened to destroy such a treasure?"

"Aphids." Mother lowered her voice. "I'm told Lady Cambourne was most distraught at the infestation. Expert gardeners were brought in, but to no avail. The bushes all had to be destroyed lest the entire garden be ruined. Even without the roses, the stories told of the sweeping gardens do not do Gray Covington justice. Am I right, Petra?"

Petra nodded dully, shaking her head at a footman's offer of berries. After her mother's recitation of the magnificence of Gray Covington, Petra's dinner companions took it upon themselves to plan out her future with Simon. Each time Petra tried to say something, Mother answered for her until eventually, Petra ceased trying. No one seemed to care that Petra hadn't yet said *yes* to Simon's offer, *especially* Simon. He directed none of his conversation at her, probably in a fit of pique for her earlier insinuation he'd been too busy to check on her when she'd been ill.

As the dinner dragged on, the conversation continued about her. Petra, still like the perfectly demure lady she no longer was, with her hands clasped in her lap, came to a startling conclusion about the evening. Any of the other young ladies of Petra's circle could be sitting in this same chair, dressed in a similar dress and no one, *especially* not Simon, would note the difference.

I am virtually interchangeable with half of the girls in London.

The irony, thought Petra, was though Morwick had called her a pea-wit, he'd never actually treated her as if she were a mindless ninny. Simon, for all his posturing and respectful treatment of her, assumed Petra's intelligence to be that of the mashed turnips served for dinner. She didn't blame Simon, necessarily. Petra had been so in awe of Simon and so careful to do as Mother had instructed, she had difficulty recalling if she and Simon had ever been alone together let alone engaged in an honest conversation.

Pleading exhaustion after dinner, much to the dismay of her mother, Petra retired to her rooms. Her reservations about marrying Simon had multiplied tenfold during dinner. She'd been right to insist on a visit to Brushbriar, and asking her father to delay signing a betrothal agreement. How could she marry a man who wouldn't even discuss his interests with her? She thought many women probably did, but until lately Petra hadn't realized how such a thing would matter. Simon must cease treating her as if she were a child.

When she finally sought her bed, after much pacing and

wringing of hands, Petra didn't rest well. She tossed and turned, dreaming of the giant oak tree and Mam Tor. She scaled the oak up to the top in her dreams, and dangled from a branch, but she wasn't afraid.

Morwick stood below waiting to catch her.

❧ 11 ❧

"**W**ell, where have you been?" Mother barely looked up as Brendan entered the breakfast room. Taking a seat at the head of the table he tried without success to hide the wince as he sat. His ribs hurt like the blazes. Possibly at least one was broken or cracked. Danvers could throw a mean punch when he'd had too much ale. The man's fists were like fleshy sledgehammers.

"Buxton, Mother. I told you. I needed to go to Buxton. A meeting with a gentleman who wished to discuss the methods for surveying his property on the other side of Castleton. Mr. Wilcox."

"Hmm." Mother looked up, her eyes shrewd and knowing. "The discussion took the form of a beating? You've a cut on your lower lip and a bruise beginning to bloom on your cheek. You look like a prizefighter who's lost his last match. Please tell me the other man looks far worse?"

The beating had taken the form of a fight at the Whistling Pig tavern which Brendan, were he being honest, had instigated. "One of the miners took exception to the way I played cards."

"You were accused of cheating? Brendan, please remember you are an earl."

"Not exactly. Danvers simply didn't care for the fact that I beat him fair and square." There was also the small matter of the barmaid who had draped herself over Brendan's shoulders like a well-used cloak, though he'd tried, unsuccessfully, to shoo the woman away. Danvers was sweet on the barmaid, and had objected strenuously to his woman flirting with Brendan.

"Well, I suppose that's something." She took the small, circular pair of glasses from her nose and laid them down along with the letter she'd been reading. "The heir to Dunbar has been born. Henry, they've named him. Nick is beside himself with happiness. His duchess is well and healthy, as is the babe."

"I'm glad. Nick deserves every happiness, after all he's endured." Brendan and his cousin Nick were good friends. Brendan was pleased to know Nick had found peace and contentment. "And grandfather would be pleased to have the young lad named for him, I think."

"Yes, he would." Mother sipped at her tea and gave him a hard look. "You know, no amount of beating is going to help your situation."

"I'm not sure what you mean." He knew exactly what she meant. He detested Mother's Dunbar intuition for it showed itself at the most inopportune times. Brendan raised a cup of tea to his mouth, ignoring the stinging of the hot tea on his cut lip.

"Psh." Mother waved a hand. "Petra," she said firmly.

"Don't be ridiculous." His heart thudded dully. The last person he wished to discuss Petra with was Mother. "I merely offered her and Lady Marsh our assistance and hospitality, nothing more. I've met her exactly twice in my life. I barely know the girl and what I do know of her is not favorable." Unless you liked sassy young ladies who could climb trees.

"Brendan." Mother reached out and took his hand, frowning at the scraped knuckles. "I am sorry." She squeezed his fingers. "I am the one to blame for the mess you find yourself in."

The words surprised him. "What are you sorry for?"

"My grief over the loss of your father." She looked away and cleared her throat. "I've known for some time my unhappiness did something to you and Spence. Perhaps, altered your view of affection between a man and a woman. You must understand, I was young and twice widowed, with one young son clinging to my skirts and another in my arms." A sad laugh escaped her. "I found myself somewhat tragic. I was scared."

"Mother —"

"It pains me that I have given you both an unfavorable impression of love. Had I ever anticipated such a thing..." She shrugged. "Perhaps I would have been a bit more careful to keep my grief hidden from you."

"I've no idea what you're talking about, Mother," he lied. "I'm perfectly fine, as I'm sure Spence is. My little spat in Buxton had nothing to do with Petra. I merely ran afoul of a very hostile miner. Petra is destined to marry the illustrious Pendleton and live in a whirl of social activity in London. Besides, she'd shrivel and die in the Peaks." He thought of Petra, dangling from the tree and knew he was at least partially incorrect. But Brendan had spent the better part of a week getting into fights, digging in the earth, and drinking until dawn in order to forget the feel of Petra in his arms. And he'd done a decent job, until Mother and her intuition had begun sniffing about.

"Don't be too sure." Mother patted his hand. "I've a feeling there is more to Petra than meets the eye. At any rate, you should go and get cleaned up." She placed the glasses back on her nose and picked up the letter again. "I've already instructed Woods to pack your things."

"Am I going somewhere, Mother? I've only just returned from Buxton."

"No." She laughed. "*We* are going somewhere. An invitation has come from Brushbriar. A small house party. Dinner and dancing."

Brendan waved over the footman holding a rasher of bacon, gesturing for the man to load up his plate. "No. Absolutely not." He detested the way his pulse quickened at the thought of Petra. Apparently, not even a decent brawl was going to help his affliction.

"I've already accepted for the *both* of us, Brendan." Her eyes glinted like steel, before they softened. "I ask you for very little, my love, and I don't wish to attend alone without escort. Do this small thing for me. I find I am in the mood to socialize. And think how much your presence will annoy Simon."

Damn.

"I dislike house parties."

A trill of laughter escaped his mother. "We all do, dear. Best hurry and wash up. I'd like to be there in time for tea."

Petra urged her horse forward, enjoying the feel of the wind blowing through her hair. Several pins holding together the carefully constructed bun at the back of her neck loosened and bounced off her shoulder. A tendril of hair, now free, bounced jauntily against her upper back. Air rushed past her ears, muffling the sound of the horse behind her. The smart little hat decorated with a spray of violets flew off the top of her head and went sailing out over the moors.

Mother would be quite upset. Hysterical, maybe. The hat had been designed to accompany the deeper lavender riding habit, and the ensemble had cost a small fortune. While Petra wasn't overly fond of the color, as anything with a hint of purple was usually reserved for Lady Marsh, the riding habit did set off Petra's slender form to perfection and managed to make her bosom appear more generous, an amazing feat.

Would Simon notice?

Morwick would.

Petra hastily pushed all thoughts of the dark and alluring Morwick out of her mind. She was not at Brushbriar to dwell on him but to decide if Simon would make her a good husband. At the moment, things didn't look too promising.

The sour look on Simon's face as she galloped past him should have made her pause in her mad gallop through the heather. In London, Petra had appreciated Simon's manner toward her, thinking his treatment meant he held her in high esteem. Respected her. Now Petra suspected his aloof manner was more dismissive than respectful. He still laughed easily enough at her observations, when he deigned to have an actual conversation with her. But his amusement was more indulgent, like that of a parent's toward a child. A mere six weeks had passed since Simon had left London to return to Brushbriar, but his earlier courtship felt like a lifetime ago. The Petra he'd said goodbye to was not the woman who now rode crazily across the moors.

Outside of dinner every evening, and one brief turn around the gardens where they spoke of nothing but the types of flowers blooming, Simon avoided her. He cited a variety of reasons for not being available—business at the mines, an errand in Castleton, the very important bill he was drafting. But this morning, he'd finally sought her out. Petra had been seated in the drawing room with a book on her lap when Simon had suggested a ride, explaining he'd been remiss in his attentions. Petra had been more than happy to comply and escape the company of the rest of Brushbriar's occupants. She had left the drawing room before Mother could pepper her with questions or admonishments.

"Petra! Slow *down!*" Simon yelled as his horse, a gelding with a coat like mahogany, came up alongside her mount. Deep grooves of disapproval bracketed his mouth. "A more sedate pace would be preferable."

Joy at riding with the wind in her hair quickly faded at his tone. Simon was spoiling her first bit of freedom in days. Dutifully, she slowed, pulling back gently on the reins. She sensed again his unyielding nature, though she'd not been so averse to his manner in London.

Of course not. I was too busy enjoying the thrill of being courted by the brilliant Lord Simon Pendleton and congratulating myself I'd gotten rid of Dunning.

"Preferable to whom?" Petra snapped a bit more sharply than intended as she walked her horse back toward him. "Certainly not myself, my lord."

Only the slight flare of the nostrils of Simon's perfect patrician nose warned Petra he hadn't cared for her retort. "I specifically instructed the groom to saddle a *gentle* horse for your use."

"The horse you chose for me was better suited to someone like my mother, should she care to ride, and not myself. I prefer a bit more spirit. I overruled you." She fluttered her lashes in a fetching manner, professing a contriteness she didn't feel in the least.

Pretending. I'm always pretending.

"You shall not do so again," he uttered, lips tight and hard. "I have a duty to ensure your safety. Decisions I make for you have your best interests at heart."

Petra lowered her eyes and looked out at the vastness of the moors. Simon had a very clearly defined set of rules for every aspect of his life. Breakfast at exactly the same time every day. Always bacon, tea and one piece of toast with fresh butter. The meal was followed by a walk with his two spaniels for approximately thirty minutes, after which Simon then went to his study to work.

When Petra had first visited the Brushbriar library, she had found that Simon had kindly selected several tomes for her, none of which she cared to read for they were all poetry. Certainly no lurid gothic novels, like the Lord Thurston book tucked safely away upstairs. She dared not read Lord

Thurston outside the safety of her room, for her mother would confiscate the book in an instant.

When Petra had returned to the library the following day, she had ignored Simon's selected reading pile and snuck out with a tome on the study of fossils tucked discreetly under her arm. It was a mild act of defiance.

"You could have injured yourself." Simon was glaring at her.

Petra looked up, ready to refute him, but saw he was truly concerned. Instantly contrite, she took a deep conflicted breath. "Simon," she began gently, "I have ridden almost from the moment I could walk. While we've never gone riding together in London, I did so often before I met you. I'm an excellent rider. You have nothing to fear."

"What would I tell your mother if you fell from your horse? You can be terribly headstrong sometimes. From now on, we ride at the pace I set."

Irritation flashed. "I'm perfectly capable of—"

"You don't know the terrain." His lips grew tighter. "And I expect a bit more decorum from my wife. Racing about in such a way will be frowned upon. Your behavior is a reflection on me. Pray remember such."

The comment stung though she wasn't sure how galloping across the moors could possibly injure Simon's political aspirations in any way. She wished to tell him she'd not officially accepted his offer but decided this was not the time. Petra was on a mission to ensure their suitability, not argue.

Simon took off his hat, slapping the felt against his thigh. The tense set of his shoulders relaxed. "I don't wish any harm to befall you, Petra. I don't wish to appear so —"

Obstinate? Controlling?

"—insistent on such things," he finished.

"Of course, my lord." Petra acquiesced. "I apologize if I caused you any undue worry." God, she sounded so...*simpering.*

The tree-climbing portion of her personality rebelled instantly.

"Shall we walk for a bit?" An assured smile crossed his lips.

"I would like that."

Simon dismounted and came around to assist her. Regardless of his rigid nature, Petra had to admit Simon cut an impressive figure. The dark blue of his coat paired with light tan riding breeches tucked into polished black boots set off his athletic build and gave him an air of command. The breeze ruffled his hair and his cheeks were reddened from the slight chill in the early morning air. Who could blame Petra for swooning a bit when he decided to court her? Or for overlooking certain flaws in his character?

A pair of sapphire blue eyes and an unruly mop of black hair invaded her thoughts.

"Stop it," she whispered under her breath.

Simon looked up at her in question, and Petra shook her head. "The horse was twitching."

He helped her down, his hands firm about her waist and lingering not one moment longer than necessary. Intentionally she allowed herself to brush against him hoping for some type of reaction.

Simon stepped back immediately with a murmured apology.

Petra was only mildly surprised. Looking back, she realized Simon had never touched her with anything remotely resembling passion. Not so much as an improper touch of his hand.

"Thank you, my lord." Petra tried to imitate Katherine's seductive drawl. Moving closer, she allowed her skirts to wind around his legs in a deliberate manner.

Simon didn't move away, but neither did he give any indication of interest in her actions. There was no flicker of desire in his eyes, nor did his body coil around hers as Morwick's had. If Simon possessed any passion at all for her, it was buried so deep she couldn't see it.

Because it doesn't exist. I've mistaken his lack of desire for me as respect.

To be fair, she felt nothing either. No tingling of awareness or hint of a racing pulse. The breathless intoxication that was ever present with Morwick was sadly lacking when she interacted with Simon.

Petra turned and looked out across the vastness of the moors, watching the rows of heather wave back and forth in the breeze. The air smelled clean with just a hint of earthy undertone and the faint scent of pine. She inhaled deeply as she took in the glory of White Peak laid out before her and thought of Morwick.

Simon's property, situated as it was in the region of the White Peak, was actually closer to the lower moors and blocks of limestone which made up this part of the district. The moors gave way to gently rolling pastures and farms. She could see a dozen or so sheep from where she stood, looking like tiny swatches of cotton moving about a pasture. A cottage stood nearby with a roll of smoke curling out of the chimney. She wondered at the inhabitants of the cottage. A young man and his wife? Perhaps children?

"It's so beautiful here," Petra said, meaning every word as she glanced at the cottage, her heart full of longing for something she couldn't quite put a name to. The scene before her was so peaceful and...*real*. There was no artifice in the sheep below, nor in the carefully tended garden behind the back of the cottage. "You must find it difficult to return to London after a visit here. The city must feel stifling."

"Not at all." Simon was looking down at the cottage, a mild look of contempt on his face. "This is only a tiny slice of the world. My tenants have been content to farm the same land as their father's for a century and will likely continue to do so for another hundred years. This is my home, of course, but I've never been so enamored of the area as some people I know."

"You're speaking of Lord Morwick," Petra guessed, then added quickly, "Your sister. She told me the three of you grew up together roaming the moors, along with Baron Kelso."

A breeze blew Simon's hair against his temples, momentarily obscuring the frown wrinkling his brow. "We did, though Morwick possessed a wildness I did not aspire to. After a time I found his rebellious nature tiring. Kelso is a bit more of a gentleman, I grant you, but he is no less wild. At least Kelso wasn't running out to dance with the Gypsies who camped in the moors."

So Morwick *had* run with Gypsies. Petra thought of the ridiculous rumor that he'd actually been fathered by a Gypsy, recalling the story Lady Pendleton related to Mother their first night at Brushbriar. She'd no doubt the source of those rumors.

"Morwick and Katherine were always together; as they became older, their relationship bordered on impropriety. Once, I had to retrieve my sister from the Gypsy camp where Morwick had taken her." He turned to Petra, a hard look on his face. "They were dancing before the fire. My sister looked like a common harlot. Because of *Morwick*. Thankfully, Whitfield appeared a few months later and whisked Katherine off to London before my sister could create any more scandal."

No wonder Simon disliked Morwick. Simon, with all of his fear of scandal and upstanding morals, had been worried his sister would be dishonored. Petra inhaled sharply, ignoring the slight pinch in her chest at thinking of the voluptuous Katherine, arms entwined around Morwick's neck as they danced in the firelight of the gypsy camp.

"While at Oxford," Simon continued, not noticing her

silence, "I rarely came home. I preferred to spend my free time either in London or as a guest at some of my friends' estates. Once I was finished with my schooling, the first thing I did was leave Brushbriar and open up our house in town. When my father passed away and I took his seat, I found my calling. The moment I walked into Parliament for the first time I felt..." Simon looked out over the moors.

She'd wanted passion from Simon; unfortunately, the deep longing and desire on his face wasn't for her, but for Parliament. "I hadn't realized you and Lord Morwick attended Oxford at the same time." Petra liked the way the long grass brushed her skirts as she walked.

"Yes, until he was expelled for brawling." Simon's lips ticked up. "Unfortunate."

Smug. Petra wondered if Morwick's expulsion from Oxford had had anything to do with Simon and thought it probably had.

"I hired an excellent manager." Simon snapped his crop against his leg as they walked. "He runs the mines with no trouble. I've spent little time here since, other than to visit my mother who rarely comes to London. I've a highly competent secretary and a solicitor who look after the affairs of Brushbriar and my other estates with precision. I studied law at Oxford for a few years, before my father died and I've found it an excellent basis for my work in Parliament."

It was hard to argue with a man's purpose. "Your political career means everything to you, doesn't it?"

"Yes." He gave her a solemn look. "It's of the utmost importance. I daresay it will be the most important thing I can do with my life. The reforms I'm trying to enact will impact the lives of thousands of people. The bill I'm currently in the process of drafting has to do with the way in which financial institutions deal with the lower classes." He waved his hand. "It's complicated to say the least and the concepts difficult to grasp."

Petra kept her features calm and placid, like the sheep in the pasture below. It would be futile to acknowledge Simon's insult to her intelligence, for he didn't see it as such. Any woman, in Simon's world, wouldn't be considered capable of understanding such difficult concepts. It wasn't personal nor especially directed at her. It stung all the same.

"As my wife, you'll be expected to preside over political gatherings and dinners. I'll expect you to stay informed on current events, though you'll rarely need to speak on them." He gave her a reassuring nod.

"What a relief." The breeze blew through her hair, and more of the pins pulled loose, falling to the ground. She didn't bend to pick them up. Simon's opinions were not unusual; most gentleman considered women less intelligent than themselves.

"Never fear, Petra; I will walk you through exactly what you must say and to whom," Simon reassured her. "I will even write it down if need be and we'll go over the finer points together. You need not fear embarrassment."

"Perish the thought. How considerate of you." Simon thought her incapable of grasping the simplest of concepts yet it was Morwick who she'd been angered at for calling her a pea-wit. How ironic.

"You'll be a splendid politician's wife and an amazing viscountess." Simon went on, unaware of how incredibly offensive he was. "We shall set London on its ear, won't we?"

"Of course." Petra breathed in the desolation of the moors, wishing she need never return to Brushbriar.

"Goodness, the wind has picked up." A scowl darkened his face as he took in the strands of her hair spilling in disarray down the length of her back. "It seems you've lost some pins as well as your hat."

Good God. The small birds hovering about them might be affronted by the loosening of her hair. They might report such a terrible impropriety to Lady Pendleton.

"Shall we go back, my dear? Almost time for tea."

Simon would *never* be late for tea, after which he would walk with his spaniels again and probably speak to the dogs with much more affection than he did Petra. A great deal had been overlooked in her desire to avoid disappointing her parents.

"And I expect you'll want to refresh yourself. You may want to," he waved imperiously toward her head, "do something. I should not wish such a display to be mistaken for something else other than the results of too much wind."

Of course not. Petra gave one last glance at the valley below. The sheep were still grazing, and smoke still puffed up from the cottage chimney, the inhabitants of which were probably blissfully happy and unaware of how Petra envied them.

"Yes, my lord." She twisted her hair into a bun at the base of her neck with the remaining pins. "I should hate to miss tea."

The guests for Lady Pendleton's house party had begun to arrive.

All of Brushbriar hummed with the footsteps of servants as they hurried to their duties. Each room was to have at least one vase of fresh flowers. Every bit of Blue John must be polished to a brilliant gleam. Intoxicating smells came from the kitchen as Cook prepared countless tarts, biscuits and other pastries with which to tempt the guests. The windows to the ballroom had been thrown open to air out the space, little used for many years.

Katherine, more militant than any general, marched about inspecting everything on her mother's behalf. There weren't enough roses in this vase. A smudge was found on one of the ballroom windows. More wine should be brought from the cellar.

Mother had taken breakfast in her chamber that morning, citing exhaustion. She'd been assisting Lady Pendleton in preparing the menus and discussing other diversions, besides dancing, for their guests. Unfortunately, Katherine's fortune teller would not be coming to Brushbriar since she'd been run out of Castleton with accusations of fraud at her heels. Lady Pendleton decided on a room for cards to be played instead.

Petra wandered aimlessly about the house trying to find some way to amuse herself without being underfoot. One day, she could very well be in the thick of such preparations if she were to throw a house party, but becoming the mistress of Brushbriar became less a reality as each day went by.

The ride with Simon the previous day had left Petra with a hollow feeling, as if she were a piece of fruit whom an industrious member of the kitchen staff had scooped the pulp from. The void grew wider and deeper by the hour. The least rebellious part of her, the place where old Petra lived, whispered marriage to a brilliant man of Simon's standing was what every young lady of her station hoped for. Mother and Father would be *so* pleased. The *ton* would flock to pay calls upon her. Invitations to sup at her table would be fought over. The most important and influential people in London would visit her home. Petra would become one of the most powerful women in the *ton* and indeed in all of London. She reminded herself of all those things but felt no reassurance. It didn't help that her thoughts seemed to gravitate toward Morwick and the fact she would see him soon.

Agitated and at loose ends, she decided to see if Simon would walk with her or even play a game of chess.

Asking first the butler, a white-haired man with a superior attitude matched only by that of his employer, where she could find Lord Pendleton, Petra was directed to Simon's study. Finding that room empty except for a maid busy cleaning the windows, she was told Lord Pendleton had gone to have tea with his mother in the family's private sitting room.

As she strode down the hall in the direction the maid had indicated, Petra decided she didn't care at all for the décor of Brushbriar. There was little warmth in Simon's home. The furniture was uncomfortable and formal, every room packed with sculptures, expensive vases, paintings and other objets d'art. Brushbriar resembled a museum more than someone's home. Even the portraits of Simon's ancestors looked as if they'd rather be somewhere else.

I wouldn't have to live here, but in London.

Petra found the thought of London, along with a great many other things, did not appeal to her anymore.

As she neared the room the maid had indicated, voices sounded through the door, which had been carelessly left ajar. She *should* turn around. Go back the way she'd come and seek out Simon another time. Unintentionally eavesdropping had become an unwelcome habit of hers. The results had been mixed to say the least.

"I'm not sure what you are concerned about, Simon. There's *no* map. No survey. Not a scrap of paper duly witnessed. Nothing to dispute the property line as it now stands. I've been assured of it." A cough followed Lady Pendleton's words.

"I certainly hope you're right."

Petra could almost hear Simon frowning in distaste.

"Why would Katherine invite them? Morwick and I haven't spoken in years; not since the debacle in Oxford. Not even when we bumped into each other in Castleton several months ago. And you've never cared for Marissa. Good Lord, I'm not even sure how to refer to her anymore, she's married so many times."

Petra pressed herself against the paneling, thinking how unkind the comment about Lady Cupps-Foster had been. As if it were her fault she'd been widowed and her husbands had died so tragically.

"Don't be unreasonable. In hindsight, Katherine was right to invite them. Morwick *is* our closest neighbor regardless of your rather acrimonious relationship. And he has recently done you a great service in assisting Lady Marsh and Lady Petra. Thank goodness he did so; otherwise, your intended might still be stranded out on the moors. Their coachman should be fired for driving them so far off the main road. I'm surprised he hasn't been. Perhaps I'll suggest such a thing to Lady Marsh."

"Katherine never does anything purely because it's the right thing to do, as well you know. Good Lord, you don't suppose she's carrying on with him again, do you? I thought that was over and done with long ago. She married Whitfield and thankfully moved away. When we were younger, I never understood why Father tolerated Katherine's relationship with Morwick, though now, of course, I see why."

Petra winced at the sudden tightening of her stomach.

Fine porcelain rattled. "Your sister assures me nothing has occurred...*yet*. Perhaps we should allow her to pursue the diversion of Morwick, something to take her mind from Whitfield's loss. She's always had an odd fascination for him. I would have much preferred she pursue the elder brother, but Morwick is rather appealing I suppose, in a savage sort of way. Allow Katherine her little affair. No one outside of Brushbriar need know about it."

Simon cursed. "It's distasteful."

"Don't be such a prig. Would you rather she marry him? I am hopeful she will show an interest in Haddon." The sound of glass meeting china sounded again.

"Mother, really. Drinking brandy this early in the morning? It's a good thing you don't venture to London. I can't have you drunkenly stumbling about. Imagine what my detractors would say. My mother a sot, and my sister—"

"It's for my cough. Dr. Stubbins assured me having a little brandy in my tea was beneficial."

Another cough sounded. "You won't have any detractors, Simon, unless your future wife does something scandalous."

Petra pressed her palms against the wall, careful to make no sound.

"Doubtful. I chose Petra *specifically* for her decorum and obedient nature. She's as docile as can be. Well-mannered. Attractive, but not overly so. And she hasn't a reckless bone in her body. If anything, she's a tad dull. It's unfortunate her family is related to the Duke of Dunbar, but I can turn such a thing into an advantage."

I'd no idea I was so boring and tedious. Petra was clenching her fists so tightly she could feel the press of her nails into her palms. *Nor my family connections so questionable.*

"She strikes *me* as stubborn," Lady Pendleton said. "The way she looked me straight in the eye upon her arrival doesn't speak of a docile nature. Best you take a firm hand with her right from the start."

"What about Morwick?"

Yes. What about Morwick? Petra was sorting through the conversation trying to determine exactly what the point *was*, but all she could think about was Morwick with Katherine and Simon's rather poor assessment of her character.

"There's no proof, so you must cease your worry." Lady Pendleton began coughing again, and Simon stayed silent until she was finished.

When he finally spoke, Petra was surprised to hear fear instead of his usual measured confidence. "If Morwick were to ever *truly* suspect, not even my sister's numerous charms would keep him from the truth. He'd go to his cousin, the duke."

"Yet another reason to keep him and his mother close. And marriage to Petra would assure some relationship with the duke. Sometimes I think it would have been easier if Morwick had..." The words lowered and trailed off.

Petra sidestepped her way back down the hall, careful to make no sound as she did so. Eavesdropping never did anyone any good, *especially* Petra. Simon wanted her because she was dull and possessed not a lick of spirit. Morwick and Katherine's involvement with each other was common knowledge. Lady Pendleton liked brandy in her tea and was potentially a sot. That was the only piece of information she'd gleaned that Petra found amusing. The remainder of what she'd overheard Petra found curious, though she wasn't sure what she should do with the information or exactly what it all meant. Until she did, Petra meant to keep things to herself.

Once she reached a suitable distance, Petra turned and made her way loudly back down the hall again, toward the parlor. "Lord Pendleton? Simon?"

A moment later, Simon's dark head poked through the open doorway. "Are you perchance looking for me?" He spoke in a cheery voice, as if he hadn't just been telling his mother what an obedient dimwit she was. "Shall we take a walk?"

❧ 14 ❧

Brendan crossed and uncrossed his legs within the confines of the coach. Why couldn't manufacturers of coaches and carriages make a conveyance to accommodate a man of his height? He wasn't the tallest man in England, for God's sake. There was a gent in Buxton who was far larger than Brendan, though Big Tom farmed sheep and likely had little need for a coach.

"Really, Brendan. Can you not settle? Even as a child, you were forever flip flopping about like a tiny goldfish struggling to find its way back into a pond." Mother's deep blue eyes twinkled in amusement. "I do miss those days." She straightened. "Whatever are you nervous about?"

"I'm not a child, Mother. I haven't been for some time. Nor am I a goldfish. If you haven't noticed, I have overly long legs and the coach is a small space. Discomfort is what I am feeling."

"Unsettled." She corrected him. "You have been for some time."

"Yes, since we climbed into this coach to head to Brushbriar. The mere thought of eating at Simon's table for the next few days *unsettles* me to no end." Mother didn't know about Oxford; why should she? He'd told no one. Even now, the memory rankled him. He should have allowed Simon to be beaten to a pulp that night.

A very unladylike snort filled the coach. "Fine. Continue to be obtuse. Perhaps you are only wishing to catch a glimpse of Katherine. Awful girl." His mother's nose wrinkled as if she caught a whiff of something unpleasant.

"Mother, I hate to spoil your assumptions, but I've already seen Katherine. I visited Brushbriar a few weeks after her return to offer my condolences on the passing of Lord Whit-field. She's smashing in widow's weeds, by the way."

"I'll not pretend I'm unhappy things didn't work out between you two. You would have been estranged within a year. Tales of her escapades still echo throughout the *ton*. Affairs should be discreet, not be flaunted for all to see."

Mother had worried needlessly. No woman, even Kather-ine, was worth the potential damage to his heart; at least, he'd assumed such.

The slim lines of Petra's delicious stocking-clad legs clasped around his waist, instead of dangling from a tree above him, were all he'd thought of for days. As he'd readied himself for the trip to Brushbriar, Brendan had realized the days in Buxton hadn't really alleviated his desire for Petra. Being in close proximity to the object of his lust, while under Simon's roof, was stupid and foolish, especially since he was certain he wouldn't be able to keep his distance. The mere smell of roses and sugar cookies, and Brendan would lose his resolve. When she was close, terror and desire mixed together in an unwelcome way.

"I've no interest in Katherine," he said, his voice gruff, "so you may put your fears to rest."

"Good, since I assume she'll try to seduce you at some point during the house party." Mother plucked at her skirts.

"There are times, Mother, when I dislike your bluntness."

"How else should I be? I have been married three times and am a Dunbar to boot. Goodness, Brendan, I may be your mother, but I am still a woman. I know what lengths a lady will go to in order to seduce a man."

He shifted in his seat. "This conversation is adding to my discomfort, Mother. May we speak of something else? This tedious house party, for instance. And the fact I am here under duress. You don't even care for Lady Pendleton. You've made no attempt to call on her since you've come to stay at Somerton."

"It would be far truer to say Lydia doesn't care for me. Nor did she like your father. I'm sure we were invited for the sake of appearances, especially after your assistance to Lady Marsh. Imagine if all of the county arrives at Brushbriar and we aren't present. Everyone would gossip. Lydia would never wish to invite such attention. Certainly Simon would not. I suppose Lydia never did forgive Spence for punching Simon in the nose all those years ago, though Simon certainly deserved it. Little tyrant."

"Don't blame Spence; he was only defending me. I was an easy target for Simon." He had been until Brendan had turned fifteen and his stature had nearly doubled overnight. Before then, Brendan had been a small, squat lad with big feet. Easy pickings for the much larger Simon, whom all the boys in Castleton worshipped. "Spence preferred to have the unshared duty of bullying me, and Simon disagreed." Though Brendan and his brother argued about nearly everything, the two were still close. He trusted Spence with his life.

"I miss that little boy." A wistful look crossed his mother's face.

What she enjoyed about the smelly child he had been, Brendan didn't know. Most of the time, he'd been covered with dirt and had bugs in his pockets. He shifted against the squabs again. Mother was often sentimental.

Brow raised, she took in his immense form crowding the small space of the coach. "You're built like your cousin, Nick, and my father. Large, giant men who are fond of ruining perfectly good furniture that does not accommodate their enormous frames. Your brother was fortunate not to inherit the Dunbar build."

True. Spence was an inch or two shorter than Brendan with the natural agility of an athlete. Spence was also quite deadly. His mother surely knew about that aspect of her eldest son's life, though they never discussed it. She continued to tell people Spence was an attaché for the British government in India.

A lie no one in London believed.

"I will be glad to have Spencer home with us at the end of the year. He promises to return to England in time for Christmas. I will expect you in London as well, my love. I wish to have all my ducklings in one place. We have not celebrated as a family in ages."

She had called them that as children. Ducklings. It wasn't enough she raised her two boys alone, but also Brendan's orphaned cousins, Nick and Arabella. She'd had to be mother for all of them while caring for her own ailing mother, Brendan's grandmother. Not to mention defying the elderly Duke of Dunbar when the situation warranted it. She deserved to have them all together if that was what she wished. Brendan would ensure Spence was home. "It's only midsummer, Mother. Plenty of time for you to plan something spectacular. I would not disappoint you for the world."

She smiled indulgently and patted his knee. "I know you will not."

Brendan could see her excitement at the thought of hosting such a gathering, even though it was many months away. Was his mother bored? For years, Mother had acted as chaperone to Arabella, since the death of Lord Cupps-Foster, a man no one missed. He wasn't even sure why Mother had married Cupps-Foster, a hothead with the temperament of a bull. Brendan had detested him. Was she lonely? Now that Arabella was happily settled, Mother must be at loose ends. Perhaps she would take an interest in one of the dozens of charities Arabella seemed always to be involved in. He couldn't imagine she'd marry again. Mother was quite unlucky in marriage and love.

The point of avoiding Petra. Exactly.

"Ah! Here we are. Brushbriar. It's as lovely as I remember." Mother peered out the window as the coach passed through the gates. "You know I *begged* your father to update Somerton, but he refused. His pride, you see, as we most certainly would have needed to use my personal funds, something Reggie didn't wish to do. Somerton wasn't near as prosperous as Brushbriar, especially after Pendleton found Blue John. I'm sure Lydia spent a small fortune to update the estate. She was always more than a little extravagant."

"That's a polite way of saying you find Lydia's tastes to be vulgar."

Mother laughed. "Quite. Money does not buy class, Brendan. Lydia started life as the daughter of a prosperous merchant and was thrilled at her new, elevated station. After the Blue John, she enjoyed throwing her newly found wealth in my face. As if I gave a fig." His mother's voice was light but her face had hardened to stone. "My family could buy Brushbriar and all its contents several times over. I had to remind her *I* was the daughter of a duke." She pressed her nose closer to the window. "In retrospect that may have been what led to her dislike me, as I had to be *very* firm."

Brendan caught the flash of ruthlessness in Mother's eyes. There were many people, much to their detriment, who liked to write his mother off as a tragic widow flitting about the *ton*. It was a mistake few made twice. Mother was her father's daughter, a Dunbar through and through. He expected Lady Pendleton would not misstep again.

"Oh, God, poor Haddon has been dragged into the third circle of Hell with us. That's his coach." Brendan nodded to a splendid set of bays. "I hope he hasn't brought the Haddon Herd with him."

"I'm sure the girls are lovely. Do not refer to them as cows."

"I didn't call them bovines. I only said the *quantity* of daughters Haddon has could be referred to as a herd."

Mother rolled her eyes. "Regardless, I'm sure the poor man does the best he can. It can't be easy trying to raise four young ladies alone with no feminine influence to speak of."

"You've never even met him and Haddon is rarely alone, from what I understand." Brendan gave his mother a pointed look. "And there is a steady stream of governesses through his doors."

"Perhaps I shall offer Lord Haddon my advice in raising young girls." Her fingers drummed against the windowpane in thought. "He may appreciate my experience."

"Pray do not hold up Arabella as an example of your abilities. Besides, the girls are called the Haddon Hellions for a reason. At last count, the Hellions have disposed of *eight* governesses, three dancing instructors and four French teachers."

"*Psh*. It sounds as if Haddon's daughters are merely in need of direction and structure. Arabella has made an excellent match. A *love match*. I adore Rowan and admire his tenacity in handling your cousin." Mother gave him a brilliant smile. "You might learn from their example."

"What is that supposed to mean?"

"Oh, I see the Divets." Mother ignored his question. She

was bouncing in her seat in excitement. "I was so hoping they'd been invited. Mr. and Mrs. Divet have been abroad for nearly two years traveling all over America. The tales they must have! Dinner is bound to be fascinating."

"I somehow doubt that." Brendan pinched the bridge of his nose wishing he was still in the middle of a brawl at the Whistling Pig in Buxton.

15

Petra was late.

Mother was bound to have a fit if she didn't hurry downstairs to the drawing room, especially if Lady Pendleton was forced to delay dinner on Petra's behalf. After several sleepless nights, ones in which she merely tossed about her bed thinking on her current situation, Petra found herself drifting off while reading in the gardens and decided on a late afternoon nap. Morwick, who'd invaded her thoughts nearly every night since she'd left Somerton, was blissfully absent from her dreams today, and she'd fallen into a deep sleep.

Stomach grumbling, she surveyed herself in the mirror. She'd slept through tea and the arrival of most of the guests and was now starving.

Petra looked down at the barely discernable rise of her bosom. "I resemble a small boy dressing up in his sister's clothing." Petra had never given much thought to her figure one way or another. She was slender and small-boned, with the bosom to match. But since meeting Katherine, she found herself constantly comparing herself to Simon's sister. Petra supposed it had more to do with Morwick than anything else. Next to Katherine, Petra was drab and childlike.

"Begging your pardon, my lady, but you do not." Tessie stood just behind her. "You are lovely. And the color of the dress brings out the green in your eyes. Lord Pendleton won't be able to take his eyes off of you."

The pale green dress, the color of spring grass, was one of her favorites, though she couldn't remember the last time the garment had been worn. She hadn't even realized Tessie had packed the dress until Petra saw it hanging in the armoire after her arrival.

"Thank you, Tessie." She hadn't the heart to tell her maid she doubted Simon would notice anything about her, let alone the color of her dress, unless she drew undue attention to herself.

"You'll be late, my lady. I'm surprised your mother hasn't sent for you." Tessie surveyed Petra once more and nodded. "You should go down."

Petra thanked the maid again and hurried out the door only to be halted by a wall of warm muscle smelling of the moors, pine, and vaguely of soap. Her breasts, small things that they were, pushed impudently against the crisply pressed shirt. And it *was* nicely pressed, a change from his usual slightly rumpled appearance. Not a hint of ancient cambric nor a speck of dust decorated the broad chest.

Petra tilted her chin back. There was still a shadow clinging to the line of his jaw. Possibly Woods hadn't shaved him close enough or more likely, Morwick hadn't cared to shave at all. A grimace graced his full lips as he returned her regard. Really, she was starting to consider it more of a smile. A surge of delight filled her at the sight of him.

"Hello, Perfect Petra." The raspy voice tripped over her skin.

"Good evening, Lord Morwick." A sudden unsteadiness

caused her to rock toward him in a most alarming manner, as if she were on board a small boat buffeted by a wave. Her pulse beat wildly, her body thrilled to be in close proximity to his. In desperation to restore her sanity, Petra attempted to move aside, unsurprised to find the lace of her bodice caught in the button of his coat.

Of course the bloody button was caught. She'd been consistently ruining her clothing since leaving London.

"Do not bother to help. The gown is one of my favorites and I would be quite unhappy were it to be damaged. Stay still."

His eyes darkened to indigo, the bits of gold surrounding his pupils glittering in the light of the hallway lamps. Morwick had the most beautiful eyes, like a lake sparkling with sunlight to illuminate the depths below. She found herself wishing to drown in those eyes and not bother to save herself.

Get ahold of yourself, Petra.

"There are some occasions, Petra, when the tearing of a dress is warranted."

The skin of her arms prickled awash with heat.

"I'm not certain there is any instance in which the tearing of a lady's dress is warranted." Only an inch separated she and Morwick. If another guest were to come upon them, the worst would be assumed and Petra would be immediately ruined. At the very least, there would be talk and possibly a scandal.

Morwick *certainly* knew such a thing. Possibly he didn't. He wasn't much of a gentleman.

"When you are annoyed or considering something, your nose scrunches up like a rabbit," he murmured in a soft voice. His breath stirred the small hairs around her temple.

Petra worried the bit of lace stuck on his button, her fingers brushing against his shirt, becoming more clumsy by the second. At last the lace came free. Her hands immediately flew down to clasp before her. "An unwelcome comparison to a creature with prominent teeth and large ears," she stuttered, sounding like the pea-wit she was often accused of being.

Morwick leaned over, words vibrating against the skin of her neck. "I happen to like rabbit."

Petra's body arched as if on command, drawn to the low, erotic suggestion in his voice.

Bollocks. She was beginning to understand the usefulness of cursing. It helped to center a person.

A small, rather smug grin graced his mouth before he straightened. He turned toward the stairs without a backward glance, as if he'd only told her it was raining outside or some other mundane comment.

A wonderful ache spread down Petra's body. She cleared her throat determined to sound unaffected and unmoved by his sudden appearance. "Really, Morwick. You cannot say such a thing to me and then walk away."

He halted and looked over his shoulder. Flames burned in the depths of his eyes, now more black than indigo. "Why not? Are you going to be petulant, Petra?" His gaze flicked down the length of her before returning to her face.

"I dislike you," Petra threw back at him. She felt gloriously alive for the first time in days.

The big shoulders rippled in a careless manner. "Unfortunate, as I happen to like you very much. Petulance aside."

Petra opened her mouth, knowing now was the time to say something incredibly witty in return. She hadn't seen him in over a week. He'd kissed her madly under a tree, insulted her, then fled to Buxton in an effort to avoid her. She was terribly confused by his manner. *And happy.*

Contrary, complicated beast. Heart fluttering madly, Petra lifted her skirts, and made a great show of stomping past him toward the landing.

"Petra, darling." Mother was just at the base of the stairs, annoyance clear as she spotted Petra. "There you are. Finally. I thought I would need to fetch you myself. Come, greet the rest of the guests." A small gasp popped out of her mouth as Morwick stepped out of the shadows of the hall to spy down on her. "Oh, Lord Morwick. You've arrived."

"Indeed, I have, Lady Marsh." Morwick glided past Petra to gracefully make his way down the stairs. He was such a beautiful, elegant animal in his evening clothes, the sight of which banished all memory of his usual dusty, wrinkled appearance.

Upon reaching the bottom step, he bowed low and took Mother's hand, tucking her fingers neatly into his elbow.

Mother's lips parted and then shut, for once not knowing what to say. The top of the ostrich feather in her coiffure trembled even as she nodded to Morwick. Mother was wearing a deep purple gown embroidered with butterflies across the skirt. She looked like a tiny, overstuffed plum.

"Allow me to escort you to the drawing room. It would be my greatest pleasure."

Somehow Petra doubted that. What was Morwick about besides completely unsettling her before dinner?

He turned to look up at Petra, who was midway down the long staircase. His eyes followed the movement of her body with a hungry look. "And you as well, Lady Petra."

Petra reached the bottom of the stairs, fingers trembling as he took her hand. She'd hoped the effect Morwick had on her would have...*dissipated*. She was wrong. The attraction was stronger than ever.

Bollocks.

BRENDAN WAS BEHAVING LIKE THE SAVAGE HE WAS OFTEN accused of being. Polite gentlemen didn't stare at a woman as if she were a delicious bit of roast. And he'd called her *petulant,* which he knew irritated her. The best part had been taking the arm of the annoying Lady Marsh. Petra's eyes had widened in shock as he took her mother's fingers.

I blame the dress. The bloody green dress.

Petra wore the same pale green dress which had first launched his unwanted desire. The same dress she'd worn the day of her brother's wedding. He'd spent endless nights fantasizing about peeling the green silk from her shoulders and pulling the dress from her body. Then she'd gone and pressed those small, delectable breasts against him, smelling of sugar cookies and roses. His mouth had watered with hunger. Brendan wanted to devour her and he was tired of pretending he didn't.

Clarity, when such a thing happened, could change many things. A lifetime of avoidance, for example. Such a thing meant nothing when watching the delicate pink flush come over Petra's cheeks as her fingers fumbled over the lace caught on the button of his shirt. He'd been uncertain, until that very moment, what Petra's feelings were toward him. He'd told himself the entire time in Buxton that she was merely having cold feet over her marriage to Simon.

But when her lips had parted and Brendan had seen the pink of her tongue peek out, the way her head had tilted, begging to be kissed, his heart had beat more firmly. He felt lust, of course—for God's sake, she smelled of cookies and roses—but something else hovered between them. Brendan considered it the most *gentlemanly* act of his life he hadn't dragged her back to his room and ravished her. Because he wished to. He wasn't sure how he would get through the dull dinner before him without falling on her like a madman.

Damn. She had an extensive wardrobe. Why that dress?

Petra's fingers trembled, vibrating against his forearm as he escorted her and her mother to the dining room, catching up with the other guests just now going in. The slow burn of her touch stoked his arousal. Thank God for his coat.

"I fear we're to be the last ones in," Lady Marsh, ever conscious of social propriety, twittered.

"A shame to be sure." Brendan answered politely, pleased he'd missed the requisite sherry before dinner. Watching all of Pendleton's guests bestow false smiles on each other while they discussed nothing of importance was a waste of time.

Gazes lifted as he entered the room with Lady Marsh and Petra. Brendan smiled at his good fortune.

Simon was absolutely furious.

16

Lady Cupps-Foster, Marissa to her friends, watched her son lead in the Marsh ladies much to the dismay of Simon and his harpy of a mother. She and her son were not exactly welcome guests at this gathering, and by escorting Lady Marsh and Petra, Brendan was guaranteed to tweak the nose of his host.

Katherine eyed Petra with unforeseen malice.

This was going splendidly.

Had she not been certain of Brendan's feelings before toward the lovely Petra, Marissa was definitely sure *now*. There was no mistaking the possessive way his larger body hovered over Petra as he led her to her seat, nor the darkening of his eyes as they lingered over the girl. The attraction between the two was difficult to miss, as evidenced by the pout on Lady Marsh's face.

The same attraction had lit the air at Arabella's wedding. Brendan had watched every move the girl had made. Even Nick had commented to Marissa privately on Brendan's interest. When she had confronted her son, suggesting Brendan possibly call on Petra, he had grown angry. Dismissive. He had called Petra a *pea-wit*.

A sure sign of his attraction to her.

Guilt filled her. Her grief over Reggie, witnessed by Brendan and his brother, had distorted their view of love. Maybe to most people, that wouldn't have mattered. Marriages weren't usually based on love, but her own with Reggie had been, brief though it was. She wouldn't trade that time with him, no matter his loss. Unfortunately, she'd not impressed such a thing upon her children.

Brendan must come to terms with his fears or loose Petra —something Marissa didn't think he was prepared to do. She hoped she was wrong about such a thing, as she would hate to interfere without Brendan's knowledge, as she had with Arabella.

But first, she must get through the tedium of Lydia's house party.

With a sigh, Marissa pasted a smile on her face and waved for the footman to fill her wine glass. Perhaps it was time she took another lover. While Marissa was certain she'd never fall in love again, she did adore masculine companionship. She missed having a handsome rogue look at her the way Brendan now eyed Petra. Perhaps once she returned to London.

Contrary to what her sons and nephew surmised, Marissa was not *solely* devoted to her family. While she adored her children, it was difficult to allow herself to be thought of as a woman well past any physical desires or needs simply to spare their feelings. She *did* take lovers, discreetly, careful never to allow her very overprotective children to find out. Her last lover had been a dark, gruff Welshman in Twinnings where she'd joined Arabella in exile last year. There was also the problem of her nephew, His Grace, the Duke of Dunbar. Nick would pretend amusement should he find out she'd taken a lover, but in reality, she feared her nephew would take matters into his own hands and her lover would discreetly disappear. Lord Cupps-Foster, cad that he was, had suffered such a fate. She'd no idea what a misfired pistol could do to someone.

Her eyes ran over Lord Pendleton. Simon. A priggish boy grown into a rigid, unbending man. Simon would destroy Petra and make her miserable within a few months. He would suppress the wild nature Marissa suspected lay beneath Petra's ladylike manner, which would be a terrible pity. Lady Marsh seemed set on the man mainly because she wanted the prestige of having an up-and-coming politician connected to the Marsh family at the expense of her daughter's happiness.

Marissa didn't dislike Lady Marsh, and in fact empathized with the woman who'd never gotten over the death of her eldest child. But she was far too controlling. Lady Marsh and her domineering nature were suffocating Petra. Anyone could see it.

Marissa sipped her wine, pretending to listen to something Lydia droned on about. The woman was dropping names and hints about her vast wealth, boasting about Simon's accomplishments and the stature of the Pendletons. It was laughable, truly. As she looked up, glass hovering at her lips, Marissa caught the eye of the man seated to Petra's left. Lord Haddon.

Haddon toyed leisurely with the stem of his wine glass, as his eyes lowered and fell to her lips. After a moment he looked directly at her again, a lazy smile on his lips. The corners of his eyes crinkled in the most becoming manner.

Heat rushed up Marissa's cheeks. *Goodness.* She hadn't blushed in ages.

❧ 17 ❧

Simon's dark eyes held no hint of welcome for Petra as she entered the dining room and approached the mahogany table laden with silver and fine porcelain. A black, murderous look was thrown in the direction of Morwick. Simon gave a stiff tilt of his aristocratic chin to Petra as she took her seat and adjusted her skirts. Mother received a pursing of Simon's lips which may have passed for welcome.

A soft chuckle sounded from Morwick as he left Petra at her seat, clearly enjoying the disruption he had created.

The moment Morwick's warmth left her side, Petra ached with his loss. She'd not realized how much she missed him until he'd appeared again. She went over their brief conversation in her mind, trying to discern what he had hoped to gain from teasing her in such a way. Her eyes searched out Morwick as he sat down, but he looked away and instead began speaking to Katherine.

Petra looked down at her plate, pretending to admire the spray of blue roses circling about the edges. Given Simon's mood and Morwick's amusement over angering his host,

Petra again considered that perhaps she was only a means for him to annoy Simon. Perhaps this was a game between the two men and she nothing but a pawn.

That's not at all a comforting thought.

The mood in the dining room became tense as Morwick deliberately took his time in finding his seat. Only Katherine looked at Morwick with welcome. *Far* too much welcome.

Petra's hands clutched tightly in her lap. She studied her plate and wished to be somewhere else.

Thank goodness for the Divets.

As dinner was served, the couple carried the bulk of the conversation around the table, regaling those present with their travels across America. Mr. Divet resembled a well-dressed monk, with a fringe of snow-white hair surrounding a bald pate. He laughed uproariously at his own jokes, and drank far too much wine, much to Lady Pendleton's displeasure.

Petra thought him marvelous.

Mrs. Divet was a tall, willowy woman possessed of pale blue eyes, with hair the color of copper. The contrast between their appearances couldn't have been more pronounced. Mr. Divet would have gone unnoticed had he been walking about the docks or sitting in a tavern, while Mrs. Divet was fine-boned and aristocratic in appearance. She clearly adored her shorter, plumper husband, gazing at him in adoration as he spoke. The Divets were completely in sync, finishing each other's sentences or reminding one another of a forgotten tidbit. Their eyes caught and held while they talked and every so often, Mr. Divet would lift his glass in his wife's direction and tilt his head, with a murmured, '*Hear, hear, Mrs. Divet.*' The Divets were an odd pair, mismatched in every way, but clearly in love. When the conversation steered to Simon and Parliament, Petra caught

Mr. Divet winking lustfully at his wife, who batted her eyes in return.

"They are quite a pair, aren't they?" Her dinner companion to the left, Lord Haddon, commented with a grin. "My late wife was great friends with Edith." He pointed a fork discreetly. "Mrs. Divet. I've known them for ages. She's a great help with the girls when called upon for a more feminine hand than I can offer. There was no one happier to see her return from her travels than I."

"How many daughters do you have, Lord Haddon?" Haddon was an attractive man, especially when he smiled.

"Four. Jordana," he pointed to a lovely girl who was seated next to Mrs. Divet, "is the eldest. It's nearly time for her first Season." He took a sip of his wine, and the tiny lines around his eyes deepened. "I shall be buried in laces and fripperies, drowning in gloves and petticoats. The air around me constantly scented with lavender. I had to purchase two male bulldogs so I shouldn't feel so outnumbered."

Petra laughed. Haddon was quite charming. "Your situation appears dire, my lord."

"Indeed. I've not spent much time in London in the last few years as matters here required my attention. And I haven't enjoyed a Season since I courted my wife."

Lord Haddon possessed a dry wit, a handsome face, and was a wealthy widower. He should probably be more concerned about *his* Season rather than his daughter's. She doubted he'd remain unscathed. Haddon would be like a fat goose dropped into the lap of the *ton*.

"Jordana is beside herself to visit London." He shot an indulgent glance to the dark-haired girl across the table. "I do hope she's not disappointed."

"I enjoyed my time in London immensely," Petra assured him. It was only a partial lie.

"I assume that's where you met Pendleton." Haddon lifted

his chin in Simon's direction. "He's highly regarded in Parliament."

"Yes, he is." The Cornish hen turned to dust in her mouth. She'd not thought Simon's neighbors would realize Simon's intent, but of course they would. Why else would she and her mother be at Brushbriar? Petra stared at her plate for the longest time; her interest in the dinner, never strong to begin with, became non-existent.

"Have I said something wrong, Lady Petra?" He shot her a curious glance.

"No, of course not." Petra chewed slowly. "I was only remembering all Jordana has to look forward to. Some of the Season can be a bit daunting."

Lord Haddon nodded as if considering her response. "I may seek your mother's council, Lady Petra."

"She will be happy to help, I am sure."

"You know, as long as I've known Morwick, tonight is the first time I've actually met his mother, Lady Cupps-Foster." Haddon's gaze drifted to the other end of the table where Lady Pendleton sat regarding her guests with a regal tilt to her head. His eyes passed over Katherine but lingered on Lady Cupps-Foster. "Are you acquainted?"

"We are related, of sorts, through marriage." Petra related the rather twisted familial tree which forever entwined the Earl of Marsh with the Duke of Dunbar. "And, of course, Lord Morwick rescued Mother and I when our coach became disabled, and our driver became lost on the way to Brushbriar." She left out the part where she ruined Morwick's boots by becoming ill.

"She has a very tragic past, does she not?" Haddon's eyes never left Lady Cupps-Foster who had lifted her glass.

"I do not think she sees it that way." Petra looked at Haddon directly, noting his interest. Lady Cupps-Foster was still a beautiful woman, her face remaining smooth and unlined and her dark hair showing only a few streaks of gray. Her eyes, a brilliant blue and so much like Morwick's, gazed back at Haddon with returned interest.

Katherine's seductive laughter floated down the table to Petra's seat.

"Morwick, you haven't changed one bit," Katherine cooed.

Petra stabbed viciously at her peas determined not to listen to the conversation at the end of the table.

"Lady Petra, have the peas displeased you somehow?" Simon said next to her, his earlier ire at her gone. "I find coaxing them onto my fork much easier."

Petra laid down her fork, angry at Simon and having no idea why. She was really angry at herself. She formed her lips into the practiced smile she'd used during two Seasons. "I'm so sorry, my lord. I fear my mind wandered from my plate."

"Your mother told me you slept through tea today." He regarded her with an affectionate glance, one which you would bestow upon a treasured pet of some sort. One lacking a brain.

She had the urge to flick her peas into his face. "No, my lord. I simply read late into the night."

"I knew you would love the book of poetry I selected for you."

"Yes, thank you, my lord." He really thought she'd stay up all night to read poetry?

Simon nodded in approval and then turned his attention to Mr. Divet. "Mr. Divet, you were in the United States during an election. Tell me, how did you find their voting process?"

Petra gripped her fork. It had taken him only a moment to forget all about her.

Brendan didn't care for Cornish hen. Nor peas, his least favorite vegetable. And he especially didn't care for Haddon at the moment. Haddon's eyes were lingering on the gleaming tops of Petra's breasts displayed to perfection in the blasted green dress. And Brendan would know, as he'd admired her breasts in the same dress before. Worse, of course, was listening to the droning of Pendleton about how important he had become in Parliament.

Windbag. Talk about something of importance. Like reparations for injured miners. Or the destruction of the Peaks due to lead mining.

Petra laughed at something Haddon said and Brendan's hold on his knife tightened. He was quite good with a knife. From this distance, he could pierce Haddon's jugular very neatly. It would be a shame to kill Haddon, since Brendan actually liked the baron. He just didn't care for Haddon admiring Petra in such a way. You'd think Simon, as her future husband, would do something about it. Or hell, even leer at her himself.

But Simon was busy extolling his own virtues as the self-important ass he was. Lording over the entire room from his place at the head of the table. Petra appeared to hang on Simon's every word. But Brendan noticed the strain around the corner of her lips. She was viciously attacking her peas and stabbing at her Cornish hen.

Simon lifted his gaze while he spoke and Brendan hastily looked away, lest Simon catch him watching Petra.

I'm Hades coveting Persephone, wondering how he could trick her into eating the bloody pomegranate.

He wanted to laugh at the uselessness of trying to avoid Petra, as if such a thing would ease the ache inside of him. The craving for her was like nothing he'd ever known.

Petra turned back to Haddon and as she did so, a honeyed curl fell over her shoulder, dangling impishly just above her left breast. She laughed at something the baron related to her.

Why the fuck was Haddon so amusing? Brendan's eyes traced the delicate line of Petra's shoulder to the curl skimming against the exposed skin of her chest. He longed to trail his lips across her skin, to chase that curl across the tops of her breasts and across the delicate expanse of her shoulder. His cock stiffened and Brendan shifted in his chair.

A stockinged foot slid up the line of his calf.

Good God. He must tolerate the lecherous Haddon, the pompous Simon and now Katherine's foot attempting to insert itself between his legs. He shot her an annoyed look which she returned by batting her lashes at him. She'd been posturing all during dinner, trying to gain his attention and in general behaving as no recently widowed woman should. Katherine licked the rim of her wine glass with her tongue and leaned forward in order to give Brendan a glimpse of her nipples in the shockingly low-cut gown she wore. Possibly he hadn't made his intentions, or rather his lack of intentions, clear enough to her earlier.

Katherine shot him a look full of promise, practically purring as her foot moved further up his leg. Two more bloody inches and she'd be stroking his cock with her toes.

"I've been rather bored since my return from London, my lord." Katherine dangled her wine glass from one hand. "Perhaps you can tell me what types of amusements can be found here or in Castleton?" Invitation swelled in the depths of her dark eyes. "I would even go so far as Buxton."

Katherine had never been known for her subtlety. Their affair had started when she had begged him to meet her on the moors, stating she'd found some interesting fossils he might wish to inspect. He'd gone eagerly, his rucksack thrown over his shoulder, before remembering Katherine couldn't tell a fossil from a plovers print in the mud. She'd been laying across a rock, her bodice loosened and her skirts hiked up to her thighs.

Brendan had been a virgin. Katherine had not.

Their affair continued on and off for years until he had discovered her with the son of a wealthy merchant in a barn in Castleton. He'd toyed with the idea of marrying her up until that point, because he liked Katherine, but didn't love her. Katherine's main appeal. She'd apologized, of course, begged him to forgive her, which he had, but Brendan didn't fancy spending his life being cuckolded. In the end, she'd married Whitfield.

"You are in mourning." Lady Pendleton admonished her daughter with a brittle show of teeth. "You aren't supposed to be amused or seeking diversion."

"Surely a carriage ride with an old friend," she looked directly at Brendan and her toes wiggled against his leg, "wouldn't be amiss, Mother. Why, Morwick and I have known each other for nearly all our lives. Played together."

Christ, could she be more obvious? "I fear I'm rather busy, Katherine, for carriage rides." Brendan shot a glance down the table and saw Petra hastily return her eyes to her plate. Her cheeks were pink as if embarrassed by Katherine's behavior toward him.

Well, he certainly was.

Katherine didn't care for having her request refused, nor did his lack of interest seem to bother her. She was still beautiful, breathtaking if he were being honest, but incredibly self-centered. During his brief stay in London, Brendan had heard the rumors about Katherine. Half the gentlemen in London had been her lovers. He'd no desire to add himself to the list. Besides, he wasn't interested in her. He returned his eyes to the honey gold of Petra's hair.

"Brendan." Katherine pouted. "Are you still traipsing around the moors and picking up rocks? Pebbles and stones and such? You've a perfectly good house in London you never use. A complete waste."

For all that she'd grown up here with him, Katherine had not a shred of curiosity in any of the things Brendan did. She'd never tried to understand why he loved the moors. London and how to get there were all Katherine had ever cared about. And Whitfield had been the heir to a duchy.

"Minerals, Katherine. And I've rented out my house to a man with the unfortunate name of Mr. Crank. He's a well-heeled merchant from Edinburgh."

"Like I said. A dreadful waste."

"The minerals or the house? Or are you speaking of Mr. Crank?"

She rolled her eyes. "You are always so glib. I'm sure you're still climbing about, either up a cliff or down into some dank cave. When we were children, you forced me to venture down below." Katherine shivered to allow her breasts to push against the silk bodice of her gown. "Dripping spears of rock—"

"Stalactites," he muttered.

"Vermin. Spiders. An earl should have more mature pursuits." She gave him a glance from beneath her lashes leaving no doubt as to what she referred. Her toes returned, pressing against his ankle.

"I like caves. I may even discover my father in one of them."

Lady Pendleton dropped her fork, her entire face puckering as if she'd sucked a brace of lemons.

His mother choked on her wine. "Morwick."

Simon gripped his knife as if he'd launch the blade at Brendan.

He could *try*. Simon had never had a very good arm. Wasn't worth a shit for shooting a pistol either.

Katherine pulled back her foot sharply, a pout on her lips. "You have always been a trifle morbid, haven't you, Lord

Morwick? I think you enjoy shocking everyone with your comments."

"I don't find it at all shocking, merely truthful." Brendan leaned back in his chair, wine glass clasped loosely in one hand. Who knew the mention of the long missing Reggie would dampen Katherine's ardor?

The table quieted; only the clinking of silverware sounded as the guests continued their meal, attempting to ignore their mortification at the mention of the long-disappeared former Earl of Morwick.

Mother's hand trembled slightly as she raised her fork, then just as quickly put it down.

"I'm a student of geology as well, my lord." Mr. Divet's cheerful voice broke the silence at the table, deftly averting disaster by turning the direction of the conversation. "There are some incredible fossils to be found in the American territories."

The strained conversation at the table instantly eased and Brendan relaxed. "Tell me more."

18

As seemed their habit, Lady Pendleton and Mother were determined to discuss Petra's future once the men melted away to enjoy their brandy. One would think they'd find something else of interest to discuss.

Haddon's daughter, Jordana, stayed close to Mrs. Divet's side as they retired to Lady Pendleton's garish drawing room to await the arrival of the gentlemen. Jordana's dark eyes flashed with rebellion as she listened to the various rules required to ensure a successful Season and attract the right type of gentleman. The mulish tilt of her head led Petra to believe Haddon would have his work cut out for him in London, for Jordana didn't strike her as particularly obedient.

Petra's attention drifted to the open doorway, wondering if Morwick had joined the others in spite of Simon's dislike. It was then that she noticed Katherine, who'd stayed behind with the excuse that she needed to speak to the head foot-man, hadn't joined the other ladies in the drawing room.

"An excellent nanny will be essential, especially while Parliament is in session." Lady Pendleton intoned. "Simon lives a whirlwind of dinners, meetings and travel outside of

London if he needs to convince someone of a bill he's sponsoring. He's incredibly dedicated. Simon's grandsire, my father, was also politically inclined. Perhaps that's where his interest first began. At any rate, I recall times when I didn't see my parents for weeks at a time or more, such was their schedule."

"Goodness, how exciting," Mother twittered, totally enamored of Petra's future as the wife of Viscount Pendleton, social reformer and brilliant orator of Parliament.

Petra clasped her hands in her lap. She loved children and had no intention of leaving any child of hers for extended periods of time so Simon could pursue his political ambitions. Mother, for all of her faults, had been present in Petra's upbringing and Petra had every intention of doing the same in her own children's life.

"A governess, one fluent in French, will be of the utmost importance." Lady Pendleton's lips were pursed as she laid out her vision of Petra's life.

The urge to stamp her feet and run screaming from the room was nearly overwhelming. Petra could stand the conversation no longer and stood abruptly, ignoring the look of disapproval on her mother's face. "Please excuse me for a moment."

"Are you well, dear?" Lady Pendleton asked solicitously, though there was no concern in her eyes.

"Quite, thank you. I merely need a moment to refresh myself."

Lady Pendleton inclined her head. "Of course, my dear." She waved a gloved hand in dismissal and went back to her conversation.

Petra nodded to her mother, ignoring the tiny hill of disapproval forming on her upper lip. She exited the drawing room, relieved to have a few moments to herself. All her life,

Petra had done what was expected of her, and now the expectation was that she marry Simon.

But I don't think I can.

The last week had shown how incredibly ill-suited she and Simon were, leaving little doubt a marriage would be disastrous, no matter what her mother thought. He'd no interest in her at all outside of the fact that she wasn't reckless and wouldn't cause a scandal. She thought back to the time they'd spent together in London. Mother had always been present and directed the conversation. If Simon and she had happened to have a private moment, they had only talked of whatever social event loomed on the calendar. He was a marvelous dancer, but outside of clever, witty comments about the current gossip swirling about the ton, Simon had rarely asked Petra anything remotely personal.

Dear God. Simon's dancing mixed with clever comments was hardly a decent foundation for a marriage. The suffocating feeling she'd felt on the way to Brushbriar threatened again and Petra actually paused and put a hand to her throat.

Once she was a safe distance from the drawing room, Petra halted. She had no desire to return to the drawing room and decided she wouldn't. Once the gentlemen joined the ladies, Mother would be forced to make excuses to Simon for Petra's absence. Or would she? Simon may be so immersed in showing off his knowledge of American politics to Mr. Divet, he'd barely notice she wasn't admiring him.

I don't care.

As she climbed the stairs to her room, Petra knew Mother would be embarrassed to have to explain her whereabouts, but she wasn't feeling especially charitable toward her mother tonight. Nor Lady Pendleton. Nor Simon. Nor Morwick, for that matter. Returning to her room to retrieve the Lord Thurston novel tucked at the bottom of her trunk seemed a much more pleasing option than spending the remainder of the evening with any of them.

Grabbing a lamp from the table at the top of the stairs, Petra made her way toward her chamber. Dinner had been a trial. Mother was exhausting. This whole bloody house party was ill-advised, in Petra's opinion. The inclination to simply lower her head and obey everyone had abated, leaving nothing but a deep resentment at being nothing more than a chess piece for them all to chortle over. Morwick's manner was the most painful, especially in light of her observation he may only be toying with her to annoy Simon.

As she neared her room, the creaking sound of a door sounded further down the shadowed hall. A soft seductive murmur met her ears along with the swish of silk. Odd. Petra had left the ladies in the drawing room. Except for one lady in particular.

Katherine.

The family's chambers were in the opposite wing of the house. Petra seriously doubted Katherine was directing the servants on last minute details for the guests who would arrive on the morrow. There could be only one reason why Katherine was in the wing where the guests were residing.

With a puff, Petra blew out her lamp before she was noticed.

In the spill of light four doors down, the silhouette of a voluptuous woman, curves displayed and tangled mass of hair falling about her shoulders, showed clearly.

More seductive whispering and the rustle of fabric.

The door opened wider and Petra could clearly see Katherine in the muted light. She appeared to be wearing little but a dressing gown loosely belted at the waist.

Petra pressed herself against the wall as Katherine looked up and peered down the hallway in her direction as if sensing someone was watching.

I really need to stop eavesdropping even if it is unintentional.

A throaty laugh was followed by a hurried conversation in a low tone to whomever lay on the other side of the door. Petra's hand moved to press against her stomach at the sound. The silk swirled around Katherine's ankles as she spoke, catching the light inside the room. She leaned back exposing her throat and probably a great deal of bosom.

A deep, rasp answered Katherine. Unmistakable even from where Petra stood.

Morwick.

After a quiet discussion between the two, Katherine slid through the opened door, closing it behind her with a soft click.

Petra blinked, in part to stop the prickle of water gathering behind her eyes, and also to blot out the sight of Katherine and her ample charms offering herself to Morwick. She felt terribly betrayed even though she had no reason to be. She swiped the back of her hand against the tears falling down her cheek, horrified someone would find her weeping in the hall. Morwick had never claimed to feel anything for her. Not even lust. In fact all he'd done was kiss her, make a few scandalous comments, and warn her away from him. Oh, and he'd said she resembled a rabbit.

Don't let go.

I won't.

Her assumption earlier had probably been correct. She'd seen the faces of both Morwick and Simon at dinner this evening, like two small boys trying to one-up the other. Morwick must have deliberately sought her out in order to annoy Simon. A comeuppance, possibly for something which had happened between them long ago at Oxford. Nothing at all to do with Petra. She was just here, conveniently allowing herself to be practically seduced by Morwick.

A choked sob bubbled up and Petra pushed the palm of

her hand firmly to her lips to keep from weeping out loud. This was far worse than being the dressmaker's dummy her mother trotted out. Or knowing Simon found her acceptably boring. She'd allowed feelings for Morwick to take root inside her heart, a terrible mistake.

Petra clutched the lamp in one hand, though it would do her little good in finding her room. Slowly she made her way by touch to her room and forced herself to stop crying like some jilted bride. Lady Pendleton and Simon had both assumed Katherine would rekindle her previous relationship with Morwick. And truthfully, she thought, fleeing into the relative safety of her chamber where Tessie stood waiting, what man would possibly chose Petra over Katherine?

"My lady?" Her maid came forward, surprised to see Petra so early in the evening.

She wiped at her eyes again. "Dust." Petra answered to Tessie's unspoken question as she set down the lamp. "I sneezed furiously and the lamp went dark." She wiped at her eyes again.

Truly, she hadn't been surprised to see Morwick and Katherine together. She was only shocked at how much it hurt.

☙✦❧

KATHERINE.

Brendan tried to keep the disappointment at her appearance at his door from his face. He'd had some fleeting, ridiculous notion that it was Petra knocking on his door. The object of his desire was probably downstairs in the drawing room. Lady Pendleton would be sitting, surrounded by large amounts of Blue John, like an overdressed gnome guarding treasure in a cave. Petra would perch calmly, her slender hands clasped, as the old crone interrogated her, patiently waiting for Simon to appear and enthrall the room with how bloody important he was.

He absolutely *detested* the possessive jealousy filling him at the thought of Petra adoring Simon in such a way.

"Hello, Brendan." Katherine stood in the hallway, her dark hair loose and flowing down her back, clothed only in a very thin silk robe. He doubted she wore anything else underneath the silk. Katherine had always preferred to sleep naked.

"Aren't you going to ask me in?" There was no mistaking the seductive question. His mind ran over the evening. Had he given Katherine the least bit of encouragement? Any sign he welcomed her advances?

From the corner of his eye, Brendan thought he saw a shadow move down the hall, closer to the stairs. The other guests should still be downstairs, which was why Brendan had slipped away. He'd taken a walk directly after dinner to clear his head of the mounting frustration at seeing Petra, yet unable to touch her. Also, claiming the dinner too rich was an excellent way to escape the traditional brandy and cigar with the other gentlemen. He and Simon, trapped in the close quarters of the latter's study, would not be advisable. And he'd not wanted to pretend polite conversation once the gentlemen rejoined the ladies. He didn't trust himself.

"Brendan," Katherine whispered, this time louder.

He peered into the darkness of the hall but saw nothing. *Thankfully.* The last thing he needed was for Katherine to be discovered nearly naked outside his room. Or in his room. Simon might feel compelled to fight a duel over his sister's non-existent honor.

"You shouldn't be here." He tried to shut the door.

A slender, bare foot shot out, stopping him. "I only wish to speak to you." She pouted. "A moment, only."

He highly doubted she was here to debate the finer points of mining with him. Katherine's forte was not scintillating conversation, at least none that didn't end in seduction. Reluctantly, he pulled her into his room, lest someone see her, and regretted the decision immediately.

Katherine smiled as her robe slid open to reveal the pale side of one large breast. She did have lovely breasts. Unfortunately for Katherine, Brendan's tastes had changed significantly since their last meeting. He fancied a smaller, tidier bosom now, and less generous curves. Preferably a slender, more compact form with spectacular legs.

"Darling," Katherine breathed, brushing her assets against him as she attempted to wind her arms around his neck. "We can *finally* be alone. I gave the excuse that I had to see to some last-minute preparations, which gave me a terrible headache. I'm not sure Mother believes me." A husky giggle popped from her pillowed lips.

Brendan took her hands from his neck and pushed away from her, taking several paces back to put a chair between them.

Surprised confusion crossed her lovely features. She wasn't used to him resisting her and thought he merely played a game with her, as evidenced by the way she pouted and allowed the robe to slide down her shoulder.

"I've never known you to be so reticent, Brendan."

Katherine was stunningly beautiful, now even more so than when she'd been a young girl. Once, the mere sight of her had brought Brendan to his knees with lust. He crossed his arms, not feeling the slightest arousal at the sight of her.

"I know you still love me." She shook her head so a curl fell artfully between the deep valley of her breasts.

He'd *never* loved her. But he had cared for her. He still did. But his affection for Katherine was nothing like this overpowering urge to claim Petra. "Do not mistake childhood affection for love."

She came forward, hips gently swaying. "Father knew we

were meant for each other. He was most distressed we didn't marry." Her brow wrinkled. "Why are you being so difficult?"

Brendan had always found the previous Lord Pendleton's approval odd, since Lady Pendleton didn't care for him in the least. And Simon detested him. But at the time, Brendan hadn't questioned his good fortune. Now, some years later, he found the old man's encouragement to be strange.

"I love you," she murmured, looking up at him with great doe eyes.

A snort of disbelief. "You don't *love* me, Katherine. Nor I, you. Don't mistake fucking for love. It isn't at all the same."

A hiss. Her eyes narrowed. "Are you still mad about Whitfield? He's dead."

Brendan shook his head. "I'm not mad about Whitfield. I never was. And I'm sorry you won't get to be a duchess. You would have been splendid." His tone softened.

"Yes." Katherine toyed with the sash of her robe. "Unfortunate, to say the least. I *would* have made a smashing duchess." She looked him in the eye and shrugged. "I would settle for being a countess."

Another snort of disbelief left him. "No. You wouldn't. You are far more ambitious than that."

She gave him a sideways glance from beneath her lashes before bestowing a brilliant, *genuine* smile. The first one he'd seen from her in ages. Since before Whitfield.

"You've always known me best, haven't you? And liked me in spite of knowing me so well."

"We would never have been happy had we wed," Brendan said. "You know that as well as I. We wanted different things. You'll find another earl or duke."

His playmate, the girl she'd once been before they became lovers, stared back at him and nodded. "I've always wanted to be a duchess. I understand the Duke of Roxbury recently lost his wife, so I have high hopes." She looked down for a moment, her bare toe making circles in the carpet beneath their feet. "I suppose I should leave." Then her chin lifted, and she shot him a saucy look. "Or we could have a tumble for old time's sake?"

"I don't think that's advisable."

"Well, you can't blame me for trying. We were spectacular in the bedroom."

Indeed, they had been. Katherine was a near insatiable lover and very skilled. She should have been a courtesan. "You should go." He moved toward the door.

"Mother wishes me to cozy up to Haddon. He's certainly handsome *and* wealthy enough, though I believe his interests lie in another direction." She walked past him in a cloud of whatever cloying scent she currently favored. "Besides, four daughters? I've no patience for such a thing."

"I agree. You aren't the least maternal. And you'd eat poor Haddon alive."

A small burst of soft laughter from her. "No, I'm not motherly. But as for Haddon, well, you don't know him as well as you should. Remember, *I* was in London. The *ton* still speaks of his escapades. Ask your cousin, the duke." Her eyes gleamed with unspoken knowledge. "I'm sure you'd be surprised."

Haddon's past was of no interest to Brendan. What he knew of the man, he liked and felt no need to delve further. Why would he? "Perhaps."

She came forward, stood on tiptoe and pressed a kiss to his cheek. "You're *very* certain?" The robe slid open further and she tilted her chin in the direction of the large bed.

"I am." He was. Any man would wish to bed Katherine. That he did not wish to renew their relationship proved beyond a doubt that something had shifted inside him. Escorting her to the door, he pressed a kiss to her temple, relieved they could part as friends.

"Good night, Katherine."

"It's her, isn't it?" The dark eyes searched his face.

Brendan's hand on the door stilled. "Who is what? I've no idea what you're speaking of."

She pressed another kiss to his cheek. "I like her, if it matters. She has spunk." Without a backward, glance Katherine slid through the door. "Good luck."

19

P etra slept much later than usual the following morning, the sun well up before she rang for breakfast. While she usually went down for her tea and toast, she wished to avoid seeing the other guests. Hiding in her room was the obvious option, though rather cowardly on her part, but she didn't think conversing with Katherine while they politely sipped tea would help her mood. She needed time to think. Alone.

Mother stopped by Petra's room, but seeing her daughter with a breakfast tray, asked with barely restrained horror, if Petra was ill. Since the stomach ailment brought on by spoiled stew, Mother treated Petra as if she were some frail, delicate young lady prone to bouts of illness.

Petra assured her she was only tired and wished to rest up for the night's dancing, an excuse Mother approved of and didn't question. Today, her mother wore a brushed muslin day dress in a pale shade of mauve. The fabric was sprinkled with what looked to be lilacs. The material was far more suited as wall covering for some elderly matron's parlor than a day dress, and Petra thought she looked a bit ridiculous, but wisely kept her mouth shut.

Assured Petra wasn't ill, Mother hurried off to fawn over Lady Pendleton.

No note came from Simon to inquire about her whereabouts or her health. She was not surprised.

For the remainder of the day, Petra was bothered by no one but her maid. When luncheon was served, she again asked for a tray, citing a need to rest for the evening's festivities. Again, no one questioned her reasons. Apparently, the entire household thought young ladies were so fragile they required constant naps.

Petra spent the remainder of the day in a large, overstuffed chair, a fluffy blanket her maid had procured slung over her knees. She had Tessie position the chair so she could gaze out over the moors while she read. She finished Lord Thurston while she had her breakfast, disappointed she would now only be left with books on geology. Turning to the book on fossils, she leafed through the pages, finding herself intrigued despite having little interest, at least initially, in the subject matter. She tried to imagine Morwick crawling through a dark cave with only a lamp and discovering the outline of a giant seashell. Petra tried to concentrate but as the day drew on, it became more difficult.

The feeling of suffocation that had plagued her since leaving her family's London home weeks earlier had only increased. She'd had a brief reprieve from her dread while at Somerton, but since meeting Lady Pendleton and seeing Simon, the sensation had returned. Petra closed her eyes against the constant chattering of her mind. Torn between her parent's expectations and her own desires, Petra was at a loss. Perhaps defiance came easy for some, and it was coming far easier these days for her than before, but she'd been raised to be obedient. The thought

of disappointing her parents, particularly her mother, was difficult. She was shedding the skin of whom she was expected to
be, and it was a far more painful process than she'd imagined.

She wished desperately to speak to Rowan.

Just after noon, as Petra was about to ring for another pot
of tea, a broad-shouldered man, dressed like a laborer and
carrying a battered heavy pack in one hand, strode across the
back gardens of Brushbriar toward the open parkland
beyond. Dark, unruly curls peeked from beneath his hat.

Petra put down the book and sat up a little straighter. She
wasn't sure why she continued to read about geology, for
certainly it would do her no good in London, but she'd had an
urge to surprise Morwick with her knowledge of the subject.
And somehow reading about rocks and fossils made her feel
closer to him.

Her chest squeezed painfully.

Morwick strolled purposefully through the gardens, never
pausing as he circumvented trees, the small pond and a large
fountain of a Roman deity. He moved with such fluid,
measured grace for a large man. A length of rope hung over
one shoulder. Morwick was going exploring. At dinner last
night, Simon had mentioned a cave a short walk from Brushbriar. She'd no doubt that was where Morwick was headed.

It was easier, in the light of day, to push down the hurt of
seeing him with Katherine last night. Petra wondered at what
point her heart had tethered itself to Morwick, and decided
the timing didn't matter. The reality of her feelings was a
constant, dull ache in the vicinity of her heart, coupled with a
horrible sense of loss.

She continued to watch Morwick until he was nothing
more than a tiny speck on the moors, wanting to hate him,
but missing him all the same. Batting away the moisture
forming at the corner of her eyes, she rang for more tea.

20

P etra stopped before the floor length mirror only long enough to inspect her appearance. The musicians were already tuning their instruments below, and the dancing would begin soon. After spending the day reading and napping, Petra was eager to leave the room. She shifted back and forth on the balls of her feet, watching the material of her ballgown flutter in gentle waves around her hips, silently thanking Arabella for her foresight.

Mother didn't care to have Petra wear anything other than pastels, a color palate that left Petra feeling like an after-dinner mint served at the conclusion of a large meal. Arabella had extended an invitation for a day of dress shopping when the decision to visit Brushbriar had been announced. Her sister-in-law needed a new wardrobe, given that she'd recently found herself with child. The invitation had only been for Petra. Lady Marsh would not be included, since Arabella tolerated her mother-in-law only when necessary and even then, only to please Rowan.

Ironically, after spending a lifetime in dark, unflattering

clothes, Arabella had become something of a fashion plate. She'd shaken her head as the modiste brought bolts of lime and cream for Petra, insisting on something more vibrant. Probably thinking how best to annoy Mother, Arabella had chosen the delicious material and design of the gown Petra now wore.

The gown was the color of a newly bloomed rose, not pink or red but a subtle hue in between. The shade spoke of innocence with just a hint of seduction. Composed of four scalloped tiers edged in silver thread, the skirt fell in graceful flounces over her hips. The fabric draped daringly around Petra's arms, exposing her shoulders, before dipping sharply into a deep vee to gently cup Petra's breasts. A sash encircled her narrow waist, embroidered with silver vines sparkling in the light with every twitch of her hips.

Twirling around, the tiers of fabric all lifted and fluttered about. She felt a bit like a cake she'd once seen at Gunter's, all frosted layers and flowers. Tessie had painstakingly gathered Petra's hair into a smooth chignon at the base of her neck and carefully encircled the bun with fresh roses from the Pendleton gardens.

Petra smiled back at her reflection. *I look smashing.*

A brief knock and the door was flung open as Mother entered, her gown the exact color of a hyacinth. "My good-ness, we shall be late *again*. It is almost as if you wish to antag-onize Lady Pendleton or Simon." She paused, gloved hand on the door. "Hurry now." Her skirts slapped against the door as she halted abruptly. Eyes bugging from her plump face she turned, with a stunned look, back toward her daughter.

"What on *earth* are you wearing?"

"A ballgown, Mother." Petra smoothed the fluttering skirts. Her hands automatically tried to force themselves together in the typical manner of obedience she'd been trained to for her entire life. She resisted and instead, placed her hands, palms flat, against her hips. There would be no more of *that*, ever again. "A very lovely ballgown."

"I can see it's a ballgown. But not a gown I approved. Where did you get such a thing?" Lines appeared in her forehead. "Well," she waved a gloved hand, "it doesn't matter." The tiny hill appeared on her upper lip. "You will not go downstairs in such an unsuitable ensemble. It's completely unacceptable. The dress is much too grand for a demure, unmarried young lady. Flashy, even. Something a more mature woman would wear. Tessie!" She clapped her hands as if summoning a dog to her. "We must hurry so as not to be late. Bring Petra the pale yellow."

"No." Petra picked up the lovely fan, also chosen by Arabella, from where it sat on the vanity. "I refuse to spend the evening looking like a demented buttercup."

Mother expelled a whoosh of air, lips quivering in affront at Petra's unexpected rebuke. "A...*what*? I insist—"

Petra walked toward the door, deliberately swinging her hips to allow the diaphanous fabric to flutter about her waist. "I am wearing a gown of *my* choice, not yours. And I must say, I look magnificent."

"You will not leave this room in that gown. I forbid you to wear such a thing." The declaration was followed by the stamp of her mother's slipper clad foot.

"As you wish, Mother." She wavered as if unsteady on her feet. "Oh my, I'm feeling very ill. My stomach is unsettled." Petra put a hand to her forehead. "I should return to bed. Please make my excuses to Lady Pendleton."

"You wouldn't dare, Petra." Her nostrils flared at Petra's rebellion.

"Try me, Mother." She crossed her arms.

A sputtering noise, like a teapot, came from her mother's

lips. "I do not care for this behavior Petra. I simply *do not*. We shall discuss your...*intractability*, on the morrow."

Petra sailed toward the door. "Indeed we shall. Are you coming?" Not bothering to wait for an answer, she strode down the stairs to the sound of music below.

My God, that felt good.

21

Brushbriar's ballroom was filled with society from Castleton, Buxton and the surrounding area. Liveried servants passed through the swirl of skirts and snapping fans. The smell of pomade and lavender filled the ballroom even as the doors to the rear were thrown open to allow in the evening's cooler air. A flurry of names and faces passed before Petra as introductions were made. She danced first with Simon, then Baron Haddon. Mr. Divet twirled her about the floor, laughing when she stepped accidentally on his toe. A young gentleman, a squire's son from Castleton, next claimed her. Then Dr. Stubbins questioned her health while spinning her about.

Her eyes constantly peered into the corners of the ballroom and through the small crowd, searching for an overly tall man with a mop of unruly ebony curls. She'd promised herself she wouldn't do such a thing but seemed unable to stop looking for Morwick. Surprisingly, Katherine did appear, alone, resplendent in a gown of dove gray silk decorated in lace and black jet. Even as a widow she far outshone every woman in the room.

Petra hastily looked away from her, lest the other woman see the jealously erupting like a wound torn open. At least Morwick wasn't at her side.

Lady Pendleton surveyed the dancing from her place against a far wall. A chair covered in red velvet had been placed upon a raised dais, and there, Queen Lydia perched. A group of older women, including Petra's mother, clustered about Queen Lydia, hanging on her every word.

Lady Pendleton bestowed indulgent smiles to her small court, waving her boney gloved hands and flapping an over-large fan at her bosom. Laughter erupted from the group and Petra heard her mother.

Lady Marsh glared back at her daughter, eyes gleaming with future retribution for Petra's disobedience. She shot a pointed look at the skirts of Petra's gown.

Petra didn't give a fig.

Her mother had ruled Petra with an iron fist for the vast majority of Petra's life. Rules piled upon rules. *Constant* super-vision. Everything decided for her without due consideration for Petra's opinion. She was like a small country who had finally thrown off the yoke of petty dictatorship.

Oh, that's quite good. Unfortunately, I can't share such a thing with Simon to prove my ability to understand simple politics. Morwick, though, would find the comparison amusing. Petra ignored the brief stab at her stomach, thinking of the inti-macy she'd witnessed last night. He was involved with Katherine. She must accept their relationship and acknowl-edge their brief flirtation was at an end.

The day alone, sitting and watching the moors while reading about rocks and minerals, had given Petra plenty of time to think without interruption. While her future was now uncertain, Petra was *very* sure of what she did *not* want. She recalled the conversation she'd had so long ago with the

Dowager Marchioness of Cambourne. She'd made a promise to the elderly woman to follow her heart.

Yes, but follow it where?

Simon claimed Petra for a dance, expertly twirling her about, executing each move with precision. He kept a proper distance between the two of them, careful not to hold her too close, his gloved fingers resting lightly on her waist. He danced with her exactly as he had in London, but now Petra felt none of the thrill she had before. Every so often, Simon would lean in and instruct her to lift her skirt a bit or mind her step.

The guests in the ballroom, observing she and Simon, would incorrectly assume he was whispering endearments in her ear as they danced. Or perhaps Lord Pendleton was taking the opportunity to eye his dancing partner's bosom, so delightfully displayed in the slightly daring neckline of the gown. Nothing could have been further from the truth. Petra felt as if she were whirling about the floor with the dancing instructor from her youth. He'd been so much more charming in London.

Once the dance ended, Simon returned Petra to the group of women surrounding Lady Pendleton, bowed low and brushed his lips against her knuckles. "I think I'll play cards for a bit, my dear. I'll be sure to find you before the buffet is served and claim you for another dance."

Petra dipped. "Of course, my lord." She rather hoped he'd play cards all night.

"Lord Pendleton doesn't care for your dress." Mother hissed below her breath as Simon walked away toward the card tables. "I could see the disapproval in his eyes from where I stand."

Petra gave her Mother an unconcerned look. "Well, then, it's a good thing he's not wearing it."

"May I have the honor of this dance, my lady?"

Marissa nodded in agreement with a polite smile. The conversation amongst the ladies surrounding Lady Pendleton and her throne was becoming tiresome. Brendan had yet to make an appearance this evening, though thankfully Katherine was in the ballroom and dancing with a score of lovestruck gentlemen. Marissa was much relieved, for it meant Brendan was not sequestered with Katherine in a guest room somewhere. She'd been very certain of her son's regard for Petra and didn't wish to be proven wrong.

She extended her hand to Squire Turley. "Delighted." While she had little desire to be hefted about the floor by Squire Turley, Marissa didn't refuse. She liked to dance, even if her partner was a somewhat round, beefy man. Unfortunately, the musicians began the waltz and Marissa resigned herself to feel the press of the squire's sweaty palms against the fine damask of her ballgown. A shame. She liked this gown but it would likely be ruined after dancing with Turley.

Droplets of moisture hovered above Squire Turley's upper lip and beaded on the man's forehead.

Good Lord. Was he unwell?

With a clumsy turn, the squire pulled her into the cluster of other couples circling the dance floor. Hard to believe the waltz was once so scandalous, for she didn't feel anything but terror while dancing with Turley. If he stomped on her foot, he may well break it.

"How are you enjoying your stay, Lady Cupps-Foster?" His eyes assessed her.

Marissa had seen that look before, more times than she cared to. Turley was looking for a wife. "It has been very pleasant." She bestowed a polite smile on his glistening face. Every man assumed a widowed woman couldn't wait to have the shackles of marriage bestowed upon her again. Not Marissa. Three marriages was quite enough, thank you. Besides, her husbands had a propensity for dying quite soon after saying their vows. And Turley was not to her taste.

Turley spun awkwardly and Marissa stumbled, but he caught her swiftly enough, managing to draw her closer to his sweating body at the same time. A practiced move on Turley's part.

Marissa attempted to pull back, but he clutched her firmly. The dress would definitely be ruined. No amount of brushing would remove the sweat stains. "Mr. Turley——"

"May I cut in?" The cultured masculine voice inquired.

Eyes the color of quicksilver cut across Marissa's breasts, lingered for a moment in the exact location of her nipples, then moved down to her still slender waist before returning to her face with singular intensity.

The blush of Haddon's regard rose up to pink her cheeks before Turley could even answer.

"Haddon, the lady and I——"

"Thank you, Turley." Haddon smoothly brushed off

Turley's response. "That's a good sport." Before the puffing squire could say more, Marissa found Haddon smoothly gliding her about the floor without missing a step. Strong fingers wrapped around Marissa's waist and pulled her a bit closer than was strictly polite. He smelled deliciously of sandalwood soap and tobacco.

Turley clenched his fists, indignant, but bowed at being politely vanquished and stumbled off the dance floor.

"That was rather abrupt. Possibly unkind," Marissa said, though she couldn't deny the relief she felt to be out of Turley's grasp.

Haddon had the most curious eyes. Silver gray, but now that she was closer, Marissa could see the hint of green around the edges of his pupils. He used those glorious eyes to make an impression upon women, if any bit of the gossip in London were true. Just now, with her skirts wrapping around the hard, lean lines of his body as they danced, Marissa thought the gossips hadn't done him justice. Haddon was a splendid, handsome beast. It was surprising to Marissa they'd never met before tonight.

"Ah," Haddon spun her about expertly, "you looked as if you were in need of immediate rescue." The silver of his eyes glittered in the light of the chandelier. "Was I wrong? I can always call back Turley. Even now he is eyeing you like a cherry tart. No, wait, my apologies. It's only that the desert table is behind your shoulder."

Marissa raised a brow at his wit. "You're rather incorrigible." Haddon was also charming and at *least* ten years her junior. They'd not spoken directly since being introduced the previous evening before dinner, though she'd noticed his regard for her during the meal.

"I am, aren't I? You, though," his voice lowered to an erotic growl, "are stunning."

Goodness. A heated blush rose up her chest for the second time.

Haddon had been a rake before his marriage, and quite a successful one if the rumors were correct. Marissa was, unfortunately, well-versed in rakes. Her first husband had cut quite a swathe through London before their marriage. And *after* their marriage. Kelso had seduced her and in a burst of honor, married her. Reggie, whom she loved, had also been a bit of a rogue. Cupps-Foster was a mistake. She'd fallen into bed with him and then found herself married. At any rate, Marissa no longer found such men held appeal for her in the long term, though a brief dalliance was certainly an option.

"I appreciate the compliment. Will you next extol the virtues of my eyelashes? My cheekbones? Perhaps the curve of my ear?"

Haddon laughed, a great masculine sound which sent wonderful shivers down her spine. "I thought the tip of your nose, or perhaps your wrist. I am partial to wrists."

Haddon's reputation was well-deserved. His wit paired with the dark, sable hair and silver eyes would make him irresistible to most any woman. Her fingers tightened on his shoulder. No padding in the jacket, either.

The fingers at her waist pulled her closer to the broad expanse of his chest. A delicious ache started just below her breasts, something she hadn't felt in quite some time. Haddon also had the appeal of being far from London and the eyes of her nephew. A very brief dalliance could be had before returning to Somerton.

The silver gaze lingered on her mouth.

When Haddon asked her to take air with him on the terrace, which she knew he would do, Marissa would say yes.

BRENDAN WATCHED THE BALLROOM FROM THE SHADOWS, his eyes lingering on Petra. She looked stunning tonight, for once not wearing a gown of some pale hue he despised. The neckline appealed to him as well, much less modest than usual. He kept imagining trailing his fingers beneath the silk while kissing her.

Petra was making him mad with hunger.

As she swirled about, Brendan imagined the legs beneath the silk and how exactly he would peel off her stockings, careful to press a kiss to each inch of exposed flesh, before pushing her thighs apart. Worse than the lust was the knowledge that he missed her—desperately. Solitary creature that he was, Brendan didn't want or require companionship. At least he hadn't. Besides, Petra was bound to attempt climbing again. He needed to be there, lest she needed rescue.

Christ. He sounded like a lovesick lad.

Grabbing a glass of wine off the tray of a passing servant, Brendan tossed the dark liquid back in one swallow. The wine tasted French and slightly pretentious.

Petra avoided Katherine, though Katherine greeted her politely and with a smile. Even from where he stood, Brendan saw the flash of dislike on Petra's normally polite features, along with the sheen of jealousy.

He was terrible. He liked that Petra was jealous.

Brendan grabbed another glass of the French swill and wondered if the shadow he'd seen in the hallway last night hadn't really been a shadow, but a person, namely Petra. He'd checked, discreetly of course, where Petra's room was located. She was a mere four doors down on the right from his room. Had Simon guessed at Brendan's obsession with Petra, Brendan was certain he would have been sequestered in the stables.

Petra's eyes flashed murder at Katherine, before she was whisked off to another dance by one of Turley's son's. The boy was holding onto her a bit too tightly, practically pawing her. Brendan pushed back from the wall, setting the empty wine glass down. His fists clenched automatically.

Brendan wasn't possessive by nature. He'd never had a reason to be.

Until now.

❧ 23 ❧

The evening passed far too slowly for Petra's taste. Had she once looked forward to such events? Enjoyed them? Odd how without Morwick's presence, the entire evening had gone gray and colorless. She hadn't realized how profoundly she'd wanted him to see her in this particular gown.

Petra danced with nearly every gentleman in the ballroom at least once and dared not dance more for fear of creating a small scandal. Bored, and not wishing to join the women hovering around Lady Pendleton, Petra spoke for a time with Jordana. The poor girl danced awkwardly, almost as if she couldn't hear the music, and blushed profusely every time she missed a step.

"I shall be a country girl with nothing to recommend me, neither dancing nor conversation," Jordana muttered. "I don't even wish a husband."

"You don't?" Petra questioned.

"But I do want to go to London. I've plans, you see." Her gaze was full of determination, clearly intent on something only she could see.

As she suspected, Jordana wasn't near as well-behaved as she pretended. Feeling a kindred soul, Petra wondered what her plans were. She opened her mouth to ask Jordana, but Mrs. Divet, her face wreathed in smiles, requested her attention. A young gentleman from Buxton wished an introduction.

Jordana shot Petra a woeful glance but allowed herself to be led away.

Bored after Jordana's departure and feeling *profoundly* mutinous, Petra decided to leave the ballroom. Mother was fairly howling with laughter at something Lady Pendleton related to her and wouldn't notice her absence. At least, not immediately. Sadly, Petra doubted *anyone* would notice she was gone. Simon had yet to return from the card tables.

If she'd thought far enough ahead, and had something more interesting to do, Petra would have clothed a dressmaker's dummy in the buttercup yellow gown her mother had wished her to wear, and positioned it in a corner next to a plant, and no one, including her mother would have been the wiser.

Strolling around the edge of the ballroom, she wondered again where Morwick was and immediately chastised herself for continuing to seek him out. A moment of respite from the noise and brittle laughter of her mother was what Petra desired. She moved toward the open terrace doors, thinking to walk the gardens. A couple lingered by the doors, whispering to each other, their heads bent together, before escaping into the darkness.

Lady Cupps-Foster and Baron Haddon.

A smile teased Petra's lips. She'd noted Haddon's interest in Lady Cupps-Foster over dinner the previous evening. Unfortunately, Petra could no longer escape to the gardens, though she was happy for Morwick's mother.

Petra moved through a small hallway at the opposite side

of the ballroom from where her mother stood speaking with Lady Pendleton. The first place Mother would look, should she notice her daughter's disappearance, would be the guest room Petra occupied.

Sconces lit the hall and the sound of the musicians became somewhat muted. She'd not been down this way before, though from the positioning of the hall, she thought it might take her to the library. She could sit out the remainder of the evening there in relative peace.

Katherine's laughter, throaty and seductive, floated toward Petra.

Thinking Katherine was in the midst of an assignation with Morwick and not wishing to be seen, Petra opened the first door on her right. Relieved to find it unlocked, she quickly ducked inside. The very thought of witnessing the pair together again made her ill. She shut the door with a quiet click.

The room was dark but appeared deserted. Heavy curtains were open to allow the pale moonlight to stream through the windows. The bit of light illuminated various dark lumps which Petra took to be low chairs and tables. She could just make out a couch by the window next to another dark mass which she took to be a wing-backed chair. The couch was a perfect spot to look out across the moonlit moors.

Making her way to the couch, she carefully spread the skirts of her gown to avoid undue wrinkling and settled herself on the plump cushions of the couch. Her feet ached from dancing and she kicked off her slippers, wiggling her toes blissfully. Her hands automatically crawled from her sides to clasp in her lap, but Petra forcefully pulled her arms apart. How often had she sat quietly, hands perfectly clasped, while Mother instructed her?

Not anymore.

"Are you hiding? A woman who climbs trees to look at Mam Tor can't possibly be a coward."

Petra's hand flew over her mouth to stifle a scream. What she'd taken as a large misshapen chair was actually...*not*. A bubble of excitement pushed up from her heart at the raspy voice. "You scared the bloody daylights out of me. And I am not hiding. I needed a moment of respite."

A dark chuckle echoed in the room, kissing the skin of her arms. "From your future mother-in-law? Or perhaps Lady Marsh? Your mother does have a propensity to be a bit...*challenging*. I've been meaning to ask, why purple? It invites all sorts of unwelcome comparisons."

Her brief happiness at his presence faded as she remembered Katherine, barely clothed, at his door last night. "I'm sure Katherine is looking for you. I just saw her in the hall. Don't let me keep you." She bent to pick up her slippers. "I'd hate to interrupt your little assignation." Petra winced, knowing she sounded like a jealous fishwife.

Silence filled the room before Morwick said quietly, "What makes you think I'm having an assignation with Katherine?"

Petra wished to rail at him. Punch him with her fists for disappointing her and toying with her emotions in such a way. Though in all fairness, she doubted Morwick intentionally sought to hurt her.

"I'm not meeting Katherine."

"Last night was enough for you? You know, you really should be more discreet."

A soft curse filled the air before he said, "Your ladylike decorum is beginning to slip, Perfect Petra. You shouldn't speak on such a subject."

"You object?"

"Perish the thought. On the contrary, I adore the reckless, less than perfect Petra who climbs trees and allows a gentleman to see her ankles. The one who doesn't like the thought of Katherine."

"I misspoke." She ignored the tightness in her chest. "And I didn't *allow* you to see my ankles. Besides, your affairs are your own and certainly none of my business. Just as my life is none of your concern."

"I fear you are incorrect." He stood and without asking, moved her legs over on the couch to make room for himself to sit. Taking her calves he put her legs across his lap.

"There's not enough room." Her voice trembled. It felt far too intimate having her stockinged feet nestled in the warmth of his lap. Far too close to— "Find elsewhere to sit. Where you were sitting was perfectly fine."

Morwick was always so warm. Heat rolled off his body and found its way up her skirts to warm her legs. Ignoring her outrage his hands took hold of her feet. Fingers, big and strong wrapped around her toes as his thumb pressed into the arch of one foot.

Petra bit her lip to keep from moaning out loud which would only encourage him. But, *my lord,* that felt good. She hadn't realized how badly her feet hurt or how much she'd danced until now. Was he rubbing Katherine's feet before Petra's arrival? Was that why she'd been laughing? At the thought, Petra tried to jerk her feet from his lap, but he held on tightly.

"Relax, Petra. I had no assignation with Katherine."

"It's none of my concern with whom you have an affair." When his thumb dug into her arch this time, she bit the pillow next to her head to keep from moaning. She didn't wish to encourage his attentions.

"You are a poor liar," he said in a soft growl as he squeezed her toes, before circling her ankles with his hands, holding her feet firmly in his lap. His thumb rubbed back and forth over her ankle.

"I've been pretending all my life. I should be better, don't you think?" Petra tried to keep her voice light. She wished she could make out his features, but the room was far too dark. "What are *you* hiding from, my lord? Surely, a man who scales the edge of cliffs and explores dangerous caves has little to fear. I saw you today as I looked out across the moors. Leaving to go roaming about."

He was quiet for so long, Petra didn't think he would answer her. Finally he said, "You would be mistaken, Petra. There are a great many things I fear, as it turns out."

The seriousness in his voice, with not so much as a hint of sarcasm, unsettled her. "Perhaps you were concerned someone would find you here with Katherine?" When he didn't answer, Petra tried again to pull her feet away, convinced she was correct and he didn't wish to admit such a thing. "I overheard her laughter, you see. Just down the hall." She twisted, her heart aching painfully.

"Stop, or you will hurt yourself." Morwick trapped both feet with one hand. "Would you like to know the story of Katherine and me? It's not very interesting, I grant you."

"You are lovers," Petra choked out as his free hand trailed up and down her calf, sending flames licking up her thighs. "Let go. Stop toying with me."

"*Were* lovers, Petra. Long ago. I was young and in awe of the beautiful girl who lived across the moors from Somerton. Katherine was my closest childhood friend; eventually she became more. We were young. She was experienced, I was not. At one point I thought of marrying her."

A fist punched into Petra's side. She didn't wish to know anymore and struggled against his hands. "I don't wish to hear about your sordid affair with her."

His grip tightened. "I *never* loved her, but liked her, which

made her a perfect candidate for marriage. Do you understand my meaning? For I can explain it no better than that."

Petra ceased her struggles. She recalled Lady Cupps-
Foster's private sitting room. The portrait of Morwick's
father. His mother's endless grief. What such a thing would
have done to a young boy's perception of love.

"Instead of offering for her, I went to visit my brother,
Spence. I spent some time learning the family business. But,
that's a story for another time."

Petra's breath caught, feeling the tickle of his calloused
fingers at the hollow of her knee. "It's really none of my affair,
Lord Morwick, who you are involved with."

"*Was* involved with. Aren't you paying attention? I want
you to understand I've no interest in Katherine. I've involved
myself with no woman since returning to Somerton from
London. Aren't you curious why not?"

"It's none of my affair," she repeated stupidly.

He shifted, positioning himself beside her. His hand slid
under her buttocks, brushing aside her skirts to pull her
firmly against the hard length of him. "Is it not?" The words
melted against her skin like molten chocolate.

"Not in the least." Petra molded herself against him,
seeking his warmth. She was suddenly ridiculously happy.

"*Brendan.* I have wanted to hear you say it." He growled.
"Please do so."

"Brendan." Petra was entranced by the rough emotion
emanating from him. She sensed fear and restraint, tempered
with longing—for her. The tips of her fingers traced the
dusting of hair on his jaw until she found his lips.

He nipped the edge of her finger. "Dangerous, Perfect
Petra," he said in a low tone. "So dangerous." Nuzzling the
side of her neck, she felt a sharp pain as he nipped the skin
beneath her ear.

"I disagree." She turned until their lips were only a hairs-breath apart. Layers of clothing separated them yet Petra could feel his heat seep through the fabric of her gown. The hard length of him pulsed against her thigh. The deep ache which had begun in her heart the moment he touched her now pumped furiously through the rest of her body.

His mouth covered hers in a sensual kiss.

Petra fell back, sinking into the cushions. Deep and slow, his mouth moved over hers, speaking of longing and want. All will to move, to stop this madness, fled. It was impossible to think of anything else with Brendan's fingers moving in a lazy manner beneath her skirts and his mouth slanted over hers. Petra's hands slid from his face to clutch at the fabric of his coat, bringing him closer.

A deep growl vibrated in his chest.

Brendan surrounded her. Filled her. She could think of nothing but giving herself to him. She longed to be naked before him, a thought which should make her blush with embarrassment. Her body, small and delicate, brushed against the hard planes of his chest, igniting a slow insistent ache between her thighs. Petra arched her back, pushing her hips closer as the scent of the moors permeated her nostrils.

Brendan's tongue traced the outline of her bottom lip, coaxing her mouth to open. She did so without hesitation, twining her own tongue around his. His mouth became rougher, more demanding and she answered in kind, writhing beneath him.

Brendan broke away, his breathing ragged. "*Christ.* What did I tell you about self-preservation?" His palm cupped her knee.

"That I've none. At least, not with you." She was rather shocked to find her legs had fallen apart, open in invitation to him.

"Petra, where is your sense of propriety?" The tip of one blunt finger traced the lace decorating the neckline of her dress. The finger paused briefly, dipping below the lace to find the tight bud of her nipple.

Petra inhaled sharply. *Oh, this felt divine.*

"I adore this gown." His finger brushed back and forth sending jolts of sensation down through her belly. "The color is blessedly not pastel, and the neckline displays your lovely bosom. Though I didn't care to have other gentlemen looking."

"You weren't in the ballroom. And I'm sure no one was admiring my *lack* of bosom."

"I *was* there, watching you. I've spent the last hour imagining the color of your nipples."

Wetness slid between her thighs at the bluntness of his words. Petra's breathing had roughened as he tortured her poor nipple, and she bit her lip to stop from crying out. "My breasts are quite small. Not much to see."

"I would have to disagree with you. They are perfect." His finger circled the hardened peak of her nipple and pinched. "You are perfect."

A low seductive moan left her lips, and her hips rocked forward. She'd not known she could make such a sound nor behave in such a manner. "I don't wish to be perfect. I find it to be vastly overrated."

He cupped the underside of her breast, pushing the flesh upward and the edge of her bodice down. When her breast popped free, Brendan's mouth encircled her nipple, rotating the tiny peak between his teeth and sucking gently.

Petra stretched, one foot dangling off the edge of the couch, begging without words for him to touch her. The skirts of her gown and petticoats were rucked up around her waist. His tongue circled her nipple and more wetness seeped between her legs. His hand stayed on her knee and boldly, Petra covered his fingers with her own, urging him upward.

His mouth broke free of her breast, and he pushed his

forehead to hers, even as his fingers found the slit of her drawers.

"Jesus, Petra, tell me to stop. Aren't you afraid?" His hand toyed with the opening of her drawers, making her nerves pop with anticipation.

"No," she whispered, gasping at the feel of his hand against her mound, the large fingers brushing through the soft down. "I am never afraid of you."

"You bloody well should be." He kissed her again, hard and wanting, before his mouth trailed down her chest. "I've never wanted anything so much in my life." She heard him say against her skin, so low she struggled to make out the words.

A large finger stroked against the damp flesh between her legs.

She whimpered and twisted, trying to force him to do more.

"Here, love?" The finger pushed and circled, teasing her. He caught her mouth with his once more as two large fingers slid inside her.

"Oh." Petra's head fell back as his thumb pressed against the tiny, engorged knot hidden beneath her moist flesh. "Yes," she panted, her body on fire.

"Do you ever touch yourself, Perfect Petra?" The dark growl climbed over her skin, heightening the sensation of his touch.

"More," she breathed, thrusting her hips up toward his fingers. She had too many bloody clothes on. Too many layers.

"Do you?" he said again, sucking her nipple in his mouth and nibbling gently. The combined sensation of his mouth and hand was nearly too much for her. "Tell me."

Heat flooded her cheeks. She had touched herself down there many times, only to become frustrated at her efforts, followed by shame that she'd done such an unladylike thing. "Yes, but I couldn't—"

He moved another finger inside her, thrusting gently while his thumb stroked her flesh.

The most glorious feelings surged down her legs. She had the sensation something was going to burst within her.

"I will catch you," he whispered against her neck. "I won't let go."

Petra gave herself over to the play of his fingers and the mounting sensation within her body. Brendan was all around her, his warmth, his scent. His mouth was hot on her breast, his body cradling hers. When at last the bubble exploded and burst, her cry was swallowed by his mouth, gentle and demanding over hers. He kissed and stroked her until the tremors of her body ceased and she was left sated, floating and safe in the circle of his arms.

Brendan's lips moved against her ear, whispering nonsensical things to her even as his arms tightened. For the longest time he only held her, without speaking, as she listened to the beating of his heart. He was still aroused, hardness pressed against her thigh, but he made no move to ease his own needs.

Finally he pulled her gently to a sitting position, like a rag doll, and adjusted her bodice. The warmth of his lips brushed the top of her breast and he nipped at the flesh.

"Brendan?" She didn't want him to leave her. Something had profoundly changed between them, and she wanted nothing more than to stay here with him, oblivious to the party going on in the rest of the house.

"Close your eyes and breathe, Petra. Count to one hundred before you leave the room."

He gently disengaged her fingers from his coat and stood.

She was trembling, her body still throbbing madly, but she nodded in agreement, even though he couldn't see her. The door opened, and she sensed Brendan had paused, possibly considering coming back to her. Then the quiet click of the door met her ears, leaving her in the quiet darkness of the room.

There was only one thing she could do under the circumstances.

"**D**o you wish for tea, dearest?" Mother sat at a small table in her chambers, a breakfast tray at hand. The tray held an island of toasted bread, fresh butter and some sort of fruit preserves, along with a pot of tea.

Petra's stomach was in knots over the forthcoming discussion. "No, Mother. Thank you."

Mother patted her lips with a napkin and moved to butter another piece of bread. "I *insist* you get rid of that horrid gown from last night. Simon was horrified. Lady Pendleton, though too polite to say so, found the color inflammatory."

"I'm not even sure what such a thing means, Mother. How could the color of my gown possibly inflame anyone?"

Mother's face pinched, not caring for Petra's tone. "You are unmarried. Pale blues, pinks and yellows are better choices. And cream."

"I notice you left out lilac."

The piece of toast was flung down to the plate beneath it. "I've had quite enough of your sass, Petra. I've never known you to behave in such a way. I sense you have fallen under the influence of...Arabella."

"I've no intention of ridding myself of the gown." The gown represented the death of the old Petra and the rebirth of the new. She wasn't sure what her future held. Possibly no more than a return to London. But she was *not* going to marry Simon. After her intimacy with Morwick and the powerful connection she felt to him, the thought of Simon engaging her in a similar activity was repugnant to her. "I'm keeping it."

Mother's eyes flashed. She didn't care to be disobeyed. Once this discussion was over, Petra thought her mother would welcome another argument about the gown.

"I came here to tell you Simon and I do not suit, Mother. He's a lovely gentleman, but we don't get on. I know this to be an *enormous* disappointment to you, and I am sorry, but I cannot marry a man simply to please you." There, she'd finally said it. After having kept such a thing bottled inside her for weeks, Petra was vastly relieved. "We can leave tomorrow if you like. I'll speak to Simon today and explain myself." Outside of being inconvenienced by having to court another young lady, she didn't think Simon would be overly upset.

Mother set down her teacup with a rattle, her face militant. "You are only having *nerves*, dearest. You and Simon are perfect for each other." She dismissed Petra's speech with a wave of her hand. "Now, have some tea and we can discuss your wedding plans."

"Mother, didn't you hear me? We are *not* perfect for each other. How I tire of you using such a word to describe everything you find suitable."

"Perhaps you should lay down and rest." Mother added more milk to her tea and stirred. "You seem to be overly tired from the previous evening's entertainment."

"You aren't listening. I am *not* going to marry Simon. He has not a shred of affection for me, nor do I have anything remotely resembling passion for him."

"What do you know of passion?" her mother said. "It's certainly not required for a successful marriage." She eyed her discarded piece of toast. "Simon is a brilliant match. He is—"

"Yes, Mother. I am well aware. Simon is brilliant. The match is brilliant. He's perfect for me. I'll be a rising political star's wife. I've heard you repeat the litany"—her voice rose in agitation—"until I wish to cover my ears. I spoke to Father before we left London. I was having second thoughts about Simon even then. Father assured me, despite you being enamored of Simon, he would sign no betrothal contract unless I was in agreement. I am to have a choice."

"I was so hoping it wouldn't come to this. Your childish tantrum only serves to reinforce the decision I made before we left for Brushbriar."

Cold fingers of dread caressed the back of Petra's spine. Mother was far too calm at Petra's declaration. "What decision would that be?" But Petra knew.

"The betrothal agreement was signed before we departed." The matter of fact way in which Mother expressed her dominion over Petra's life left no doubt she was telling the truth. "I explained to your father, dear man that he is, you were merely having a case of cold feet. I know you better than anyone; I'm your mother. You are much too immature to decide something as momentous as your future."

"How could you?" Petra closed her eyes, unable to look at the woman before her. She'd known Mother to be overbearing and stubborn when she wished to get her way, but this...she'd lied to Petra. And so had Father. The betrayal bore down on her with a terrible sucking feeling.

"This is all for the best, dearest. Your dowry already sits in

Simon's bank account and the papers have gone to our solicitors. You will be married at the beginning of September. Lady Pendleton and I have agreed."

Petra's hands automatically clasped in her lap. She was going to faint. "Father promised me."

"I'm exhausted with your missish behavior, Petra. You will thank me one day for looking out for your future."

She'd drastically underestimated her mother. "You *lied* to me. I never had a choice."

"You aren't capable of making good, sound choices, Petra."

"You've never allowed me to make *any* choices, Mother." Petra stood abruptly, nearly upending the tea tray. "How would you know whether I'm capable or not?"

Agnes, Mother's lap dog of a lady's maid, popped into the room. She'd probably been hovering just outside the door. "Is anything the matter, Lady Marsh?"

Petra turned away not willing for Agnes to see her in a near state of tears.

"No, Agnes. Nothing at all. Would you mind going downstairs for a fresh pot of tea? This one has gone tepid."

"Yes, my lady." The maid shut the door and scurried away.

"Sit," her mother commanded. "Stop being dramatic. We'll have some hot tea and discuss your wedding gown."

"I'm not sure I can ever forgive you," Petra choked as she made for the door.

"Darling." A frustrated puff. "Please sit." She reached out a hand. "I only want what is best for you. Let us not be at odds during the happiest time of your life."

Petra looked down at her mother's plump, bejeweled hand and curled her lip. "No, you want what is best for you, Mother. I don't care for Simon. And just now, I don't care for you either."

Panic, large and dark, was blossoming inside Petra. She had to get out of here. Away.

Ignoring her mother's gasp of surprise, Petra walked out of the room, not bothering to shut the door behind her.

❦ 25 ❦

Petra wiped furiously at the tears running down her cheeks. Darting down the hall to her own room, she quickly donned her oldest dress and a pair of half boots. She was determined to get as far away from all of them as possible. Simon. Mother. Lady Pendleton.

Her father had promised she was to have a *choice*.

But an earl's daughter didn't get to have choices. She was merely a pawn to her parents' ambitions. They would have her wed, miserably, rather than allow her to make her own decision about her future. Worse, her own father had lied to her about allowing Petra a choice. Her mother's treachery was devastating. How was she ever to look at either of her parents again?

Petra set out across the moors, headed in the direction she and Simon had taken for their ride earlier in the week. Small birds flitted through the heather, scattering before her as she strode angrily, crushing the grass beneath her boot heel. She was so bloody furious, so distraught at the turn of events, she paid no attention to her direction. When the rocks she stepped over became larger and eventually turned into boulders, Petra realized she'd gone in the wrong direction.

Would serve Mother bloody well if I disappeared like Morwick's father out here.

Climbing up one large rock Petra turned in a circle, reassured somewhat to see Brushbriar in the distance, though she had no intention of returning anytime soon.

The boulder was at the edge of an outcropping with a wonderful view of the surrounding woods and hills. Taking a deep breath, Petra inhaled the scent of the moors and told herself to remain calm. Her brief rebellion had come to an abrupt halt. The upper hand had always belonged to her mother. Father may have had good intentions, but he always deferred to Mother.

The betrothal is signed. My dowry sits in Simon's bank. No wonder he'd had no inclination to spend time with her or continue to court her. There was no need to. She already belonged to him, like one of his stupid spaniels. What a fool she was. Priding herself on changing and becoming more assertive. Defying her mother. In the end, she was still the dressmaker's dummy, ready to be hoisted about at Mother's whim, as she had for her entire life. Her fingers flew to her throat, the suffocating feeling so real Petra nearly choked.

Brendan.

For a moment it hurt to breathe.

Petra put her head in her hands and looked out across the moors, wondering just what the bloody hell she should do.

I can't marry Simon.

Unfortunately, unless she did something scandalous or Simon changed his mind, there was little Petra could do to change her impending marriage. She absolutely refused to go to Brendan for help, especially since he'd accused her once before of being a damsel in distress to attract his attention. Besides, despite what happened between them last night,

Brendan had a very skewed opinion of what loving someone did to a person. He'd told her no different last night, only trying to make her understand. Should she go to her brother for help? If nothing else, Arabella would take great pleasure in defying her mother. Besides, Arabella owed Petra a favor. Her anxiety eased somewhat. She just had to get to London first.

Her stomach grumbled. Loudly. How long had she been here? Surely she'd missed the noon meal, and Petra now regretted not taking a scone or piece of toast from her mother's breakfast tray before storming out. She was hungry. Starving, actually, recalling she'd left the ballroom before the buffet had been served.

Standing up, she stretched, hearing the popping of her neck and spine. When she hopped off the boulder a sharp tearing sound met her ears.

"Dear God." She tugged to free her skirt which had managed to wedge itself into a tiny crack in the rock. "I have ruined half my wardrobe on this journey. Nearly every dress I own has a tear in the skirt." Petra took a deep breath as the panic returned. What was she going to do? Deflated, she flopped back on the boulder, her appetite gone.

"You bastard." A male grunt followed the words. "I've got hold of you now."

Petra turned her head in both directions but saw no one. The moors before her were empty. Her distress was making her hear things. She stood again and wiped her hands against her skirts, resolving to go back to Brushbriar.

"Blasted bitch."

Petra jumped at the curse, assuming for a moment it was directed at her. She stepped off the boulder. The echo of pebbles and rock being dislodged met her ears along with the sound of heavy breathing.

Could an animal be trapped somewhere nearby?

Yes, of course. The area is known for cursing goats.

Another grunt. "Damn you." More rock pinging about.

Petra followed the sounds, stepping cautiously until she found herself at the edge of a narrow crevice which split through the field of gritstone.

"Bloody, fuc—"

"Morwick?" She interrupted his disparagement of the crevice and peered over the edge. "Are you down there?"

A large hand appeared just below her feet, and Petra stepped back. The hand was followed by another, then a mass of unruly ebony hair and broad shoulders.

Bare, completely shirtless shoulders.

Petra's heart fluttered madly and it was not from absolute *certainty* Morwick wasn't padding his coats.

Powerful muscles, glistening with sweat, twisted and bunched, struggling to lift Brendan's weight. His forearms strained with effort, fingers digging into the earth.

Good Lord. Petra paced back and forth. Should she help him? Make a rope out of...she looked down at her torn dress... skirts? "Should I—"

Another loud grunt interrupted her question, followed by a muttered curse that made her ears pink before Morwick pulled himself up and over the side of the crevice. He was wearing only a worn pair of overly tight leather breeches and a scuffed pair of boots. His battered rucksack hanging from one shoulder. As he crawled over the top, he released the pack and tossed it in Petra's direction before flopping over on his back, eyes closed.

Petra had never really seen a *man* without a shirt. Her brother once, but that had been when she was little more than a child. Besides, brothers didn't count. Her gaze ran over the hard planes of his torso, glistening with moisture, the flat stomach and the crease of his hipbones. A dusting of dark hair covered his chest, trickling down to his navel. Muscles rippled up and down with each breath he took.

A slow burn pulsed beneath Petra's skin, similar to her feelings of the night before. He was beautiful, a large, rather savage animal sprawled at her feet. She had the urge to kneel and press a kiss to the hollow of his throat. Touch the hair trailing down to his navel. Petra couldn't look away.

I'm looking at him as if he were a large, tasty tea cake.

"Hello, Perfect Petra." Brendan flashed a grin at her, clearly unconcerned by his appearance.

The old Petra would have turned, excusing herself at the sight of a half-naked male. But she was no longer that girl and she certainly didn't miss her. Instead Petra allowed herself the simple pleasure of gazing at the man she loved.

And she *was* in love with Brendan. Perhaps from the moment he'd first kissed her at Rowan's wedding. Or maybe it had happened when he'd climbed the large oak tree to rescue her. He was complicated and often sarcastic. Terrified of caring too deeply for anyone. None of that mattered to her heart. She hoped someday he would love her back.

The sapphire eyes popped open. "Out walking? Without proper escort? Simon's not about, is he?" Brendan made a great show of looking around, pretending to be scandalized.

Petra couldn't take her eyes away from the play of muscles across his torso. Amazing how he managed to climb with nothing but his hands. She could see the very end of a rope peeking out of the rucksack, unused.

"I'm quite alone. And I've no idea where Simon is. Probably drafting yet another bill to govern something incredibly important."

"My sarcasm has rubbed off on you." A dimple showed in his cheek.

"However do you do that? Climb in such a way with no rope?" She'd wondered about the callouses on his palms and fingers, thinking them from working outdoors, but the callouses were from climbing. Those capable hands had caressed the inside of her thigh, touched the very core of her. She could still feel the press of his thumb against her flesh. A burn slid down her body just thinking about doing such a thing with him again.

"Very carefully." A deep laugh filled the air. "It's taken me years of practice. I always bring a rope and hook just in case I get myself into a pickle." His eyes crinkled. "Climbing is good for the soul."

"A good walk wouldn't do?" Petra teased, so happy to see him, she was giddy. His current state of undress was a lovely unexpected surprise. "Nor a stroll through the gardens? Instead you must climb the face of a cliff?"

"Technically, that is a crack in the gritstone. A crevice, not a cliff. And you shouldn't be out here alone." His gaze flicked down to the tear in her skirts. "I see you've had another clothing mishap." He looked back to her face. "It's unfortunate the entire skirt didn't come free."

"You're very bad." Petra's heart thudded.

"Exceptionally." A frown appeared on his lips. "But you really shouldn't be out here alone. There are holes one can fall through."

"I knew he would eventually appear, the Morwick I know so well. Frowning. Usually at me. The pea-wit." Petra rolled her eyes.

"Don't do that." His look became serious. "I wish to never hear such a thing from you again, Petra."

Petra couldn't resist any longer. The urge to touch him was simply too strong. "Do what?" She came forward and kneeled next to him. The glistening skin of his neck and torso begged for her touch. Possibly her lips.

"Make yourself to be less than you are." His voice grew soft and raspy. "It pains me to hear you refer to yourself as such. That I did in a moment of anger was...unforgivable."

"I was only teasing you. I know I am not a pea-wit." Then

she reached out and trailed her fingers down the length of his chest.

DAMN.

In spite of the warmth of the day and the exhausting climb, Brendan felt himself stir. After he had left her last night, after she'd come apart in his arms, moaning his name, Brendan hadn't returned to his room. Instead he'd found a quiet bench in the garden and contemplated just what the hell he was going to do. He was torn between wanting Petra and being terrified of having her, *then* losing her. But if he did nothing, he would lose her to Simon, which he found completely unacceptable.

"Petra," he sat up and grabbed her by the wrist. "Don't."

"Why not? You're beautiful, Brendan. Like a statue carved from marble."

Brendan was well aware of his rough-hewn looks. He'd never lacked for female companionship. But hearing Petra speak her desire out loud to him was different. Despite the exhausting climb, his cock throbbed painfully.

"Petra, I beg you, these breeches are very unforgiving."

"I can see that." She looked down before meeting his eye.

His cock twitched. Brendan was sure he'd sell his soul for a glimpse of the gorgeous legs beneath her dress. "You've become very brazen in an exceptionally short amount of time. I blame myself."

"Have I? I think I've slowly been shrugging off my lady-like decorum in small bits over the last few months. Like a snake shedding its skin, although that's an unwelcome comparison." She looked down at the tenting of his breeches and giggled. "I could clasp my hands, turn my back to you and implore you to cover yourself. Or perhaps you'd rather I faint at the sight of your near nakedness?" A hand flew to her brow and her lip trembled. "Oh dear, I think I'll need the smelling salts."

"Your imitation of Lady Marsh is quite good."

At the mention of her mother, an odd look entered Petra's eyes. "Years of practice."

A strand of hair pulled out of the careful bun at the base of her neck, landing just above her left breast. He could still feel the curve of that breast in his hands. The taste of her nipple in his mouth. His hunger for her came bubbling to the surface. "I want you." He stated in a gruff tone. "I mean to have you."

A wisp of a smile tilted one side of her mouth. "You should put on a shirt lest I am overcome with lust. You do have one, I assume?" Her eyes were soft on him. Warm.

He stood, groaning at the soreness in his arms and shoulders. Grabbing his pack, he pulled out the shirt he'd discarded earlier. "There are some things we should discuss." Namely how in God's name he could allow her to marry Simon.

Petra wandered over to a small pile of rocks. She stooped and picked up a stone, holding it up, ignoring his request. "Is this anything?"

A rush of longing for her filled him. She'd no idea how desirable he found her. "No. Just a rock. I thought you'd done some reading on geology. My library is filled with books on the subject." He shook his head as if disappointed.

"I only got as far as the mining of lead before we left Somerton. I did take one from Simon's library, and I've been studying fossils. What about this?" A brilliant smile crossed her lips.

"Gritstone." *Christ,* he wanted her. "Nothing special."

He turned his back on her as he donned his shirt. "Stop picking up pebbles and such. If the guests at Somerton see you out here traipsing about the rocks with me, your reputation will be in jeopardy." Her reputation was already destined to be ruined. He was even now contemplating how best to persuade her to refuse Simon. Brendan didn't think he could spend more than a month at a time in London without losing his mind, but he would do so for her. He'd even cease renting the town house he owned and have it redone to please her. *Christ.* He'd have to attend a ball or two.

"Petra, are you listening? We should go back."

A scattering of pebbles greeted his words along with an odd, muffled sound. He turned and saw nothing but the rocks and open moors.

"Petra?"

❦ 26 ❦

The fall happened so fast Petra had little time to think, let alone yell for help. At one moment, she was picking up a rock she thought might be somewhat interesting, and the next she was coughing up copious amounts of dust.

Petra lay quietly for a moment on the hard ground, wiggling her fingers and toes. Nothing appeared to be broken. Just bruised. The air around her was filled with dust from her fall, making it difficult to see. A meager beam of sunshine struggled through the small hole in the limestone she'd fallen through.

I'm in a cave.

It wasn't much of a cave, at least not the type Petra had imagined or read about in one of Brendan's books. Carefully, she came to her feet, blinking and coughing. The sunlight coming through the narrow hole she'd stepped into wasn't much, but she could make out that the cave was no bigger than her room at Brushbriar. Looking up, Petra could see she hadn't actually fallen very far at all, maybe fifteen feet. Her fall had been broken by a small bush, struggling in the depths of the cave and growing toward the stream of light.

She'd have a few bruises and her knee hurt where she'd banged it against the side of the cave coming down, but miraculously, she'd survived. The same could not be said for the bit of shrub that broke her fall. It looked far worse for the wear.

"Petra!" A panicked Brendan was yelling for her, his voice sounding muffled and far away.

"I'm," she choked out, waving away another cloud of dust. "I'm here!" She cleared her throat and tried again. "Morwick! Brendan! I'm down here."

Pebbles rained down on her from his footsteps. He was stomping about above her like an enraged bull. "Petra!"

He can't see the hole or hear me.

Petra moved to stand directly in the circle of sunlight. "Sorry," she said to the broken bit of shrub. "Brendan! There's a hole. I've fallen down a hole." She wasn't sure he could hear her. Picking up a rock she tried to toss it up through the hole but was only successful in having more dust rain down on her. She tried again. Maybe he wouldn't see the rocks, but possibly the dust cloud coming out of the hole.

After tossing up nine or ten rocks, something large blocked the light. "Petra? How the hell did you...are you hurt?" The strain and worry in his voice was evident.

"I'm all right. I've found a cave," she stated triumphantly.

"Bloody Hell. Are you certain you aren't hurt? Hang on, sweetheart."

"I'm fine." Was it wrong under the circumstances to feel so pleased he'd called her sweetheart? "I landed on a small bush of some sort. Can you believe there was one tiny little shrub struggling to grow down here and I fell on it?"

He didn't answer. Brendan was still stomping about, his

footsteps sending the dust swirling and bits of dirt dropping on her shoulders.

"I'm coming down." His face appeared above her.

More pebbles bounced off her head. She brushed off her shoulders and found a tear in the shoulder. "That's a total of two day dresses and one traveling dress ruined beyond repair," she said out loud.

"I can't hear you. I'm coming down." A rope trickled down through the hole to dangle just above her.

"I was just saying I've ruined another dress." She thought of Brendan's broad shoulders and looked askance at the hole. "Perhaps you should just pull me up. I don't think you can fit through the opening. You're much too large."

"I'm coming," he insisted.

As she waited for Brendan to come down, Petra walked over to the other side of the cave, measuring the length with her footsteps. She'd read to do that in one of the books she'd skimmed on caves. Something glittered against the far wall and Petra looked up to see another hole in the limestone, with a bit of sunlight coming through.

"Brendan, there's another hole. Possibly a bit larger. Something is shining on the far wall. Does Blue John shine?" Although, if she found Blue John it would be on Simon's property. "We don't have to tell Simon."

Cursing echoed in the small chamber. Brendan was having difficulty fitting through the hole. She *had* warned him.

"Petra." Brendan grumbled somewhere above her. Another string of curses followed.

Whatever was on the far wall glittered where the light hit it. She walked forward, careful to move slowly so as not to trip over anything on the floor of the cave. A circle of light appeared in the right-hand corner. "I was right, there is another hole." She looked up.

"What? Petra, wait for me." She could hear him scrambling down the rope but instead of waiting she moved toward the bit of sunlight. Birds sounded above her and the floor inclined up. This portion of the cave couldn't be very deep at all. Petra moved closer, but stopped abruptly, clapping her hand over her mouth to keep from screaming. Not that it would have mattered if she had screamed. Her companion in the cave was well past hearing.

⚜

THE THING HE'D FEARED THE MOST HAD HAPPENED.

The most sickening feeling had clawed up inside him when he'd turned and found her gone with nothing but the trickle of pebbles to announce she'd been swallowed up by the limestone. He immediately knew what had occurred. The area was laced with holes and small caves.

He wasn't very good at praying, feeling it an occupation best left to elderly matrons and vicars, but Brendan found himself pleading. Begging. He wouldn't touch her again, he promised, just let her be all right. Brendan ran for his rucksack and the length of rope. His eyes searched between the tall grass and sprinkling of small bushes looking for where she could have fallen.

I'll even let her marry Simon.

Possibly not the last part. He didn't think he could allow that.

When he heard the muffled sound of her voice coming from somewhere beneath his feet and saw the cloud of dust she was kicking up, Brendan almost wept with relief.

The hole wasn't very wide, barely big enough for him to lower himself down. After securing the rope from his rucksack, he rolled up his sleeves, twisted the length of rope around his arm, and slowly made his way down.

His shoulders stuck, scraping against the edges of the limestone. One of the scrapes started to bleed. As he moved, the wind began to kick up, dirt rising to the air to stick to his still sweat dampened face and throat. Brendan glanced up at the sky.

A storm was rolling in. He needed to hurry.

Brendan could see the outline of Petra in the cave. She said something about another hole than moved from his sight.

What the bloody hell...he was rescuing her. The least she could do was to stay put until he could do so.

She reappeared a few minutes later, below him again, her face tilted up as he snaked down the rope.

Brendan dropped the rope and fell to the floor of the cave. He immediately grabbed her, wrapping his arms around her slender form. Pressing a kiss to her temple, he held her tightly against him, telling his racing heart to cease its panicked beating. Petra was safe. Unharmed. And struggling.

"Brendan." Lips moved against his chest. "I can't breathe."

He loosened his hold but didn't release her. Instead he cupped the side of her face with one hand.

"I'm fine, Brendan. I promise." She assured him. "Nothing broken. A tiny tear in my dress. Much smaller than the one you made." Her lips turned and she pressed a kiss to the palm of his hand.

His head thudded. Hard. "You were stuck in a coach. What else was I to do?" Brendan looked back up at the hole he'd recently come through.

"You needn't have come down. You should have just pulled me up or told me how to get out." Petra said. "Though now that you're here, I've something to show you."

"It's only a cave, and not a very exciting one, I'm sure. Besides, I've no lamp with me. And there's a storm brewing across the moors. We don't want to be caught in it."

She shook her head. "This will only take a moment. Then

you may haul me to the top like a sack of grain. I could probably climb, but not in skirts." She looked down at his leather breeches. "I'd need a pair of those. Jemma has several. She tells me His Grace seems to like them."

Brendan thought of Petra's beautiful legs encased in leather breeches. His cousin probably had a point.

She took his hand in hers and led him forward. "Do you see the other patch of light? Another hole? This one is slightly larger but there is quite a lot of vegetation around the opening. I heard the birds and looked up.

Brendan did indeed see the sunlight dappling the far end of the cave. Something was glimmering in the shadows. "Have you found treasure?" He knew some of the caves had been used for smugglers in the past. A man in Castleton had found a cave several years ago filled with relics he thought were from the time the Vikings roamed the area.

"I suppose you could say so."

The floor of the cave began to slope upward and the space became much tighter.

Petra stopped below the tiny bit of sunlight. "The opening isn't much larger than the one I fell through and with the tree above, well, I don't think anyone would ever see the hole unless you knew it was there." She squeezed his fingers. "The ring on his finger was sparkling in the light. It's what drew me to him. I thought maybe I'd found Blue John, but instead I found him."

Brendan came closer, releasing her hand and falling to his knees before the skeletal remains of a man, bits of hair still clinging to his skull. The tatters of a hunting jacket hung on the bones of his shoulders and rotted bits of leather surrounded his feet. The boney fingers of one hand were stretched over his heart, as if he'd died in pain. A signet ring still encircled his pinky.

"It's him, isn't it? Your father?" Petra said quietly. "He's wearing the same ring in the portrait at Somerton."

The soft press of her fingers moved over his shoulder. "Yes." He was finally looking into the face of his father. Reginald Lorne, former Earl of Morwick, had departed this world in the depths of a limestone cave within walking distance of Brushbriar. But how had he come to be here? Scores of men had scoured the countryside looking for Reggie, but in the opposite direction, closer to Somerton, not near Brushbriar. No one would have thought he'd be so far from Somerton on foot. He would have had to ride here and leave a horse. But if he'd done that, wouldn't someone at Brushbriar have known?

"The fall must have killed him," Brendan mused. "It's not far, but maybe he hit his head?" He stood and Petra's hand fell away. The skull was intact. He looked down at the way the left hand cradled the skeleton's chest.

Carefully, he lifted up what was left of his father's hand, allowing the ring to slide off into his palm. As he did so the wrist bones gave way and the entire hand fell to the floor.

Petra gasped from behind him. "Is that—"

Brendan looked at the shattered bones of the ribcage, knowing exactly what such a thing meant. "A hole in his chest? Yes." Someone had *shot* his father. The evidence was staring him in the face. What was left of Reggie's jacket was torn and ragged around the hole. "He was shot and then left here to die." His father, mortally wounded, had been flung into this hole, far from where anyone was looking for him. It could only mean one thing.

"Someone shot him intentionally," Petra whispered.

He didn't want to state such a thing, but it was obvious. Brendan could have assumed a hunting accident if Reggie had been found above ground. But tossed below, wounded in a tiny cave? His father had deliberately been placed here. Worse, the Earl of Morwick had still been alive, entombed in this cave and alone, probably in great pain. Whoever had done this had done so with malice and foresight.

Pendleton, Brendan's mind whispered.

Petra crouched next to him. In spite of the dust and dirt, she still smelled of sugar cookies and roses, a scent Brendan thought the most intoxicating in the world. Her nose brushed against his arm as if she were nuzzling him.

"Stop distracting me." Brendan parted what was left of the hunting jacket and ran his fingertips over the ancient fabric. He wasn't sure what he was looking for, but there must be some clue as to why his father was dead of a gunshot wound and hidden in a cave.

"Ah." A distinctive crackle sounded at the lower corner of the coat. A secret pocket. With great delicacy he extracted a small oilskin pouch.

"How did you know to look there?" He could feel Petra's breath against his shoulder. A strand of honey-colored hair trailed along his forearm.

"My father was always picking up stones and other bits as he walked the moors. Every coat he had was layered with hidden pockets. He had his coats specially made for his excursions by a tailor in Buxton. Once, his valet lifted Reggie's coat to shake off the dust and bits of ore, and a plover's nest and a curious piece of limestone fell to the floor. Mother was still finding things Reggie squirreled away long after he died. He made a game of it, hiding trinkets he'd found for her. A lovely rock he'd say matched Mother's eyes, a love note he'd written, or a fossil. He would beg to be searched and often she'd be forced to undress him in the process." Brendan glanced at her. "A little shocking to think of my mother in such a way."

Petra had seen Lady Cupps-Foster wander off with Baron Haddon the evening before but thought better of mentioning such a thing. "Your father was an original. He loved her very much, didn't he?"

"He did. When I was a child, she would set Spence and I on some task to keep us occupied. Then she would sneak out into the garden and read something he'd written her. My brother and I found her behind a spray of tulips once, sobbing into the ground, a letter clutched in her hand. When you fell I—"

He looked away not wishing her to see the truth in his eyes.

Petra's fingers snaked down his arm to take his hand. "Nothing happened to me, Brendan. Only a torn dress and a small scrape."

Brendan stood and released her hand, hearing the small sound of frustration she made at his withdrawal. When he glanced at her, she merely raised a brow. Not put off in the least.

I don't want her put off. He would rather live with Petra and no small amount of fear than with the emptiness of his life without her. *Christ*, he was even open to staying in London on a temporary basis. That had to mean something.

He opened the pouch and withdrew a square of parchment, faded with age. A moment went by before he could breathe, feeling as if he'd been hit square in the chest. The parchment was thin, the writing faded, but it was still incredibly legible.

"Did you find a love letter?" Petra asked.

"No, it's a survey map."

୧୫୬

"A SURVEY MAP?" SHE WAS STANDING OUTSIDE OF THE drawing room again, about to find Simon and try to persuade him to be passionate about her. What a waste of time. Lady Pendleton was coughing and drinking brandy in her tea.

'There's no map. No survey.'

'If Morwick suspects he'll go to his cousin, the duke.'

"Brendan—"

"Son of a bitch." Brendan looked back at her. "The property line is all wrong." Then he hastily folded the paper again, placed it back in the oilskin. "We need to go."

"He moved the property line, didn't he? Simon's father?"

Brendan gave her a hard look. "How would you know that?"

She hated the suspicion in his tone, as if she'd been in cahoots with the Pendletons, but Petra chose to ignore Brendan's sudden mood shift. He had just found his long-dead father's remains in a cave, likely murdered, and he was now holding the reason for that murder in his hand. And she was betrothed to the man whose father had likely committed the crime.

"I was eavesdropping. Accidentally. At the time, I didn't have a clue what they were talking about, but now...well, now it makes sense." She related the conversation she'd overheard, leaving out the part where Simon found her to be docile and boring.

His lips tightened into a hard, unyielding line. "Were you ever going to mention such a thing to me? I suppose you couldn't, Simon being your betrothed and all." Brendan fairly seethed with anger. "I admire your protection of him."

"That's rather unfair, don't you think, Morwick? Especially after..." She blushed thinking of the night before. "Things." She waved about her hands. "I told you I didn't know what to make of the conversation. How would I know what such a thing meant? When was I supposed to impart such information to you? And for the record, I was not attempting to protect Simon."

239

The look on his face told her he didn't believe her. My God. Could he actually believe she *wanted* to marry Simon? "You are not to mention you saw me today or what we found. Do you understand? It's for your own good."

"You really think I withheld this information from you?" She walked past him to the rope dangling down from above. "No, don't answer. I can see that you do. Fine. I'm ready." Now she was angry as well.

He came up behind her, looming over her smaller form. "I'm going to go up. Then I'll send the rope back down with a loop in it. You'll sit in the loop like you're merely on a swing. I'll pull you up very slowly. You stick out your feet and pretend you're walking up the rock like this." He moved his fingers to mimic what he wished her to do.

"Got it. I understand," she said pointedly, wishing she didn't want to burst into tears. Brendan was behaving like an idiot. He'd told her he meant to have her and now...well, now he'd found a reason *not* to have her.

Petra watched him crawl back up through the hole. Hurt, distraught, and filled with purpose.

When he pulled her up from the rock, Brendan waited while she put herself to rights, using the water from a bottle he carried with him to wipe her face clean. His manner was polite and nothing more.

Thunder grumbled again in the air around them. The wind had picked up since she'd fallen into the ground, and she could smell rain coming. The sky had gone dark, shadowing the moors. If she didn't return soon, she'd be soaked to the skin.

She'd seen no one this morning but her mother, so it was likely no one had noticed her fleeing Brushbriar for the moors earlier. Her mother would be too embarrassed to admit to an argument with her daughter and had likely told everyone Petra was resting.

"Go in through the servants' entrance," Brendan instructed her. "Go directly to your room."

"Of course, my lord," she said, satisfied by the way his eyes narrowed. He clearly didn't care for her attitude, which now matched his own.

Without a backward glance, Petra set off for Brushbriar.

❦ 27 ❦

Brendan watched the streams of water running down the window and knew as much as he wished it, he and his mother could not return to Somerton tonight as he'd planned. He'd have to spend one more night under the roof of the family who had murdered his father.

As soon as he had seen the survey map and his father's remains, Brendan had wished to destroy Brushbriar and everyone in it. He'd lashed out at Petra, unfairly, and intentionally driven her away. At the time all he could think of was his mother's grief and Pendleton's treachery. He'd accused Petra of protecting Simon.

Christ, I'm such an ass.

The urge to confront Simon and Lady Pendleton made his skin itch, but he did not. There was no real proof save the map he held in his hands. His grandfather, Henry, would have cautioned patience, ruthless old bastard that he was. Henry, were he still alive, would have quietly destroyed Pendleton and Brushbriar brick by brick for the insult done to his daughter. He would have advised Brendan to do the same and get started on doing so immediately.

He'd declined to go down to dinner, citing exhaustion and over exertion from his climbing. His host would be relieved at his absence. Besides, Brendan didn't think he could look at Pendleton or his mother over roasted pheasant and not scream his accusation out loud. As he visited his mother in her room, thinking to tell her of the day's discovery and its implications, he found he could not. She'd been humming and chattering about nothing in particular and seemed oddly eager to go down to dinner.

He would tell her once they were home at Somerton.

Brendan unfolded the survey map again, showing the original property lines between the Earl of Morwick's holdings and those of Baron Pendleton, later, Viscount Pendleton. The map he held was dated over two hundred years before the birth of Reggie and had doubtless been lost to time. In an ironic twist, Baron Pendleton had been the nephew of the Earl of Morwick. Brendan and Simon were *very* distantly related.

At some point over the last two centuries, the property lines between the two estates had become blurred. The map he held had been filed away, and new surveys drawn. No one seemed to notice that Pendleton's property now extended several acres further into Morwick's. The land was desolate and good for very little. The rich deposits of lead, copper and other minerals were much farther to the western portions of both estates. No one would have cared if the property line blurred between the two as the land wasn't valuable.

Until it was.

Reggie, jealous of his neighbor's good fortune and puzzled by the presence of a vein of Blue John so close to his own property, must have done some digging, literally. He would have taken samples. Walked the property line. Surveyed. The third largest deposit of Blue John in England was a very big deal. At some point, Reggie probably started searching the library for any record of the mineral on his estate. He would have pored through dusty boxes of old receipts, letters and building plans. It's what Brendan would have done. Reggie had probably found the original survey by accident.

His mistake had been in confronting his neighbor and friend with the information.

Brendan wondered how Pendleton had lured Reggie out to that specific outcropping. He thought about his father, dying below the earth in a tiny cave, knowing his wife would never find him and he'd never meet his son.

At least now Brendan knew why Simon's father had encouraged him to court Katherine. Insurance in case Reggie was ever found.

Brendan held tightly to the neck of the bottle of scotch he'd pilfered from Simon's study. He hadn't even debated about doing so. The scotch had likely been purchased with proceeds from the Blue John which rightfully belonged to the Earl of Morwick. Simon and Lady Pendleton had known Reggie was murdered and why based on what Petra had overheard. Brendan could even imagine Simon's mother hatching the scheme herself.

Brendan took another mouthful of scotch. Before he left Brushbriar on the morrow, Brendan intended to have a very lengthy discussion with Simon, one that involved murder and Blue John.

❦

"HOW DID YOU SPEND YOUR DAY, DEAREST?" MOTHER, seated on her left at dinner, said to her in a low tone. "After our discussion at breakfast I grew concerned when I couldn't find you for tea." Her plump form shifted in the deep lavender silk as her lips tilted in welcome to her daughter.

Mother's eyes were a touch too bright, as if she were struggling to maintain her decorum.

"Your concern overwhelms me, Mother." Petra briefly looked her mother in the eye. "I do hope I didn't cause you any worry." She spoke politely, but without feeling.

"Petra." Mother's hand reached out followed by a small sob as Petra flinched from her touch.

After leaving Brendan on the outcropping of gritstone, Petra had started for Brushbriar. She found herself running partway when the rain began to come down in torrents. Gasping for breath and soaked to the skin, she had made her way to the servants' entrance, startling one of the kitchen maids in the process. Petra calmly explained she'd gone for a walk, gotten lost and fell, all the while assuring the girl she was fine. Tessie, bless her, knew better than to ask many questions. She took one look at Petra and ordered a hot bath.

"I am concerned, Petra. You've barely eaten." Mother tried again.

"Do I eat the potatoes," Petra flicked at a portion of potato in a cream sauce, "or do I not? I'm afraid I can't choose. You know best, Mother. Do I like potatoes?"

It was immensely gratifying to see her mother's cheeks redden in an unbecoming way.

"Petra." Her mother tried to take Petra's hand beneath the table. "Please cease this behavior. I don't wish us to be at odds."

Petra wrenched her hand away and proceeded to ignore any further attempts on the part of her mother to engage her in conversation. Mother had quite a lot to answer for. Rowan had resorted to issuing his mother an ultimatum. Petra didn't think she'd have to do that. If things went as Petra hoped they would, Mother would decline to speak to Petra again.

At the moment, such a thing sounded blissful.

Brendan had not come down for dinner, nor had she seen

him since their discovery earlier in the day. Somehow, she'd expected that. Petra was still angry with him.

Lady Cupps-Foster sat directly across from her, laughing quietly at something Lord Haddon said to her. Haddon was flirting shamelessly with the older widow, and Lady Cupps-Foster was blushing in pleasure. It was obvious from her gaiety Brendan had not yet told his mother of the discovery of the former Earl of Morwick's remains. She thought him right to wait until Lady Cupps-Foster was back at Somerton. The news would certainly devastate her.

Lady Pendleton sat with her toothy smile in place at one end of the table, hanging on Simon's every word as he related a dinner party he'd attended while in London. The prime minister, Viscount Melbourne, had been a guest. Katherine was engrossed in a conversation with Mr. Ulster, a wealthy merchant who'd come for the dancing and stayed, ensnared in Katherine's seductive web.

Petra ate little and spoke not at all. It was a relief when dinner ended.

After dinner, the gentlemen went to have their cigars and brandy while the ladies retired to the garish drawing room. It was difficult for Petra to sit calmly amongst so much Blue John, knowing now how the Pendletons had come to have it. But settling the score with the Pendletons belonged to Brendan and his mother. For her part, Petra wanted to ensure she would not marry Simon, nor anyone not of her *own* choosing.

She'd given much thought to her situation and how best she could avoid becoming part of this deceitful family. There was only one way to ensure Simon would jilt her and break the betrothal. A solution which would also guarantee Mother would absent herself from Petra's life. It was rather simple, and Petra couldn't believe such a thing hadn't occurred to her before now. Perhaps the girl she'd been wouldn't have considered such a thing, but old Petra had been foolish and docile.

After an hour, Petra excused herself, pleading a headache. Mother shot her a look of disapproval, the tiny hill forming above her top lip, but wisely didn't press Petra into staying.

Mother would be so much more displeased tomorrow.

Luckily, Tessie had taken a liking to one of the Brushbriar grooms. It was an easy thing to encourage the maid to go to the object of her affection after Petra had readied for bed, especially since Petra swore no one, especially Lady Marsh, would ever find out.

Hands shaking, she discarded the plain, cotton nightgown for the small tissue-wrapped package at the bottom of her trunk. Another parting gift from Arabella who'd noted Simon's lack of passion. Of course, Arabella had no idea Simon would never see this particular nightgown.

Petra threw the wispy piece of cotton, silk and lace over her shoulders, careful to tie the pink ribbons at the shoulder. She knew the risk she took. Brendan had said today he wanted her and meant to have her. But she was of a mind to take things into her own hands lest she find herself married to Simon.

Petra meant to make her own decisions from this moment forward.

Brendan took another sip of the scotch, wishing he was drunk and disappointed he was not. Simon probably watered down the alcohol in the sideboard. Or Lady Pendleton did. You'd think with the money they were stealing from his family, Simon would have a better quality of liquor available in his study. The poor scotch only added to Brendan's opinion of Simon.

Fucking prig.

Quiet footsteps sounded in the hall outside his room. A soft click of the door and Brendan instantly regretted not throwing the lock. He'd impressed upon Woods not to bother him this evening. The valet had been hovering about him like an elderly grandmother since discovering the small gash on Brendan's arm.

"Woods, I told you I do not need your services tonight. My arm is fine. It's only a scratch. Begone. Find something to amuse yourself."

The room stayed silent except for the crackling of the wood in the fire. Whoever entered hadn't left. He knew it wasn't his mother, for she'd be talking to him. Besides, he had a sneaking suspicion something was going on between Mother and Haddon, which he would have to deal with at a later time.

"It's not Woods. It's me."

Brendan nearly dropped his glass of scotch, and he cursed softly. The length of his cock hardened immediately at the sound of Petra's voice. Turning, he watched in surprise as she came toward him, her bare toes curling into the carpet. She was clothed in a ridiculous bit of lace and pink ribbon. If he squinted just a bit, Brendan could make out the dusky circles of her nipples and a delicious shadow between her legs.

Jesus.

"I need to speak to you," she murmured, toying with the ribbon at her shoulder holding what he was sure was supposed to be an innocent young lady's nightgown. Shouldn't such a thing be made of thick cotton? It offered no more protection than an oversized napkin.

"You are wearing what amounts to a doily, Petra. I don't think you are here to talk."

Her eyes were heavy lidded, watching him with an innocent hunger that sent another pulse to his cock. "No," she whispered, coming closer until he was engulfed in the scent of roses and sugar cookies. "I am here for something else." She tugged at the ribbon on her left shoulder.

"You don't know what you're saying. Or doing." This was not exactly how he had intended to spend the evening, though he was far from disappointed. Thoughts of revenge fled his mind. His mouth fairly watered as the tiny bow pulled free and the lace slid down the skin of her shoulders, catching on the hardened peaks of her nipples.

"I'm exhausted with everyone telling me what it is I should want, Brendan. I'll hear no more of it, not even from you." Her chin tilted mulishly. "I know exactly what it is I want." An impish smile graced her lips. "And as for this," she waved over the silky lace, "Madame Moliere's. I wanted some-thing pretty."

The silk was barely clinging to her breasts. He didn't care that she'd probably had it made with Simon in mind. One shrug and the night rail fell down around her waist. She was trembling, either from the chill in the room or her bold behavior. Petra was lovely. Her small breasts were high and full, the nipples hardened and begging for his attention. He'd been right about the color. Pale pink.

"Do you want to know why I was wandering about the gritstone with no escort when you found me today?"

"You actually found me, if we are being truthful."

"My God, must you always be so contrary?"

"Yes." Actually he *had* been wondering why she'd been out there alone and so far from Brushbriar. But with the discovery of his father, his anger at her, misdirected as it was, had caused him to forget. Of course, at the moment, he could barely think straight. "What happened?"

A wiggle of her hips and the nightgown slid down her legs to pool around her ankles. With her hair spilling down to her waist and the fluff of a nightgown amassed on the floor at her feet, Petra resembled a painting he'd seen once of Aphrodite rising from the foam of the sea. He couldn't for the life of him remember the artist. Not that such a thing was impor-tant at the moment. And he didn't give a shit about art.

"It's not important. You said you wanted me and meant to have me."

"Yes."

"Then take me."

PETRA STOOD BETWEEN BRENDAN'S LEGS, NAKED AND trembling, afraid he'd find her wanting in some way. Would he reject her? She knew he desired her physically. He'd told her so. Why was he just staring at her?

I love him. She did. No matter what happened after this evening, she wished her first time to be with the person she loved. Her choice. *Her decision.*

His eyes roamed over her body as he took one last sip of the scotch, setting the glass none too gently on the table. Hunger crossed his face, so intense she nearly moved away from him, but she held her ground. A big hand came out to splay possessively against her stomach and she shivered, desire for him coursing through her veins. His fingers ran down through the soft hair covering her mound, before one digit slid between her legs, stroking her.

"Are you certain?" He leaned forward and pressed a kiss to her stomach, gently nipping at the soft skin.

"Yes." She shivered at the warmth of his mouth. "I wish to be thoroughly ruined. Simon would never marry me under such circumstances, especially knowing it was you." Her words choked out as his mouth lingered over the curve of her hip and the small hollow at the juncture of her thigh. "If I am no longer a virgin, I'm no longer suitable. Mother won't be able to find me a brilliant match and I'll be free."

"So what you are saying is, you'll have me ruin you. Then you plan to tell your mother and Simon."

Petra looked down. "I will not ask you for anything else, if that is your concern." She tossed her head. "This isn't a ploy to have you do the honorable thing, Brendan. Nor force you... I would never force you into such a decision."

He saw the truth of her statement in her eyes. Petra, who had never been allowed to make her own decisions about anything, would never take away someone else's choice. He realized she hadn't believed him when he had said he meant to have her, or at least not in the permanent sense. What he should have told her was, he meant to keep her. "You'll be ruined, Petra. A virtual pariah in London. Don't you care about your reputation?"

A sheen of wetness in her eyes. She blinked and raised her chin. "No. This is my choice. My decision."

Brendan blew against the soft hair and she shivered. His finger slid down back and forth over her flesh sending ripples of pleasure through her. Pressing another kiss to her stomach, he sank a finger inside her.

Petra sucked in her breath, grasping his shoulders as another finger joined the first.

"You've thought quite a bit about this, haven't you?" Thrusting gently inside her, his thumb moved up, coaxing the most sensitive part of her. His free arm wrapped around her waist.

"Yes." A deep sigh came from her as his thumb rotated over the sensitive nub, stroking and teasing. He tugged her toward him until she lay splayed across his lap, her legs spread to his questing fingers. "I told you I hadn't accepted Simon, and I didn't. But Mother...the betrothal papers have been signed without my consent or knowledge." A gasp of pleasure followed her words.

He placed his hand over hers, guiding her fingers down to the sensitive flesh. "I see. Touch yourself. Show me how I should please you."

Tentatively, Petra reached down a forefinger and stroked herself. Her arousal was intensified knowing he watched her, his eyes dark and hot. His mouth fell to hers, and his hand settled on top of hers, moving in unison.

All that came from her lips was a low, sensual moan. He leaned over, and his tongue found the tip of one nipple, sucking the peak into his mouth.

Petra cried out as waves of ecstasy washed over her. Her hips jerked forward as pleasure burst deep inside her. His hand was warm on hers, helping her to ride out each tremor, milking each bit of bliss from her climax. His lips whispered against her ear even as she bucked against him, telling her all the dark, wicked things he meant to do to her.

"Yes." She moaned. "Anything. Everything."

⚭

HIS HANDS SLID UNDER HER KNEES AS HE STOOD, SCOOPING her up and carrying her to the bed. He placed her down gently on the coverlet and padded towards the door.

She propped herself up on one elbow, the waves of her hair covering her breasts as she watched him first throw the lock then discard his clothing.

Her eyes never left his as Brendan slid his trousers down over his hips. His arousal jutted out, hard and almost painful. While she watched, his fingers wrapped around the length. "What is it that you want?"

"You," she said without looking away. Petra moved back across the bed and, as he came forward, allowed her legs to fall apart. His eyes flew to the center of her. Pink and beautiful, begging for his touch. He told himself to show restraint. He didn't want to frighten her. Or, God forbid, change her mind.

"That's rather...*large*," she whispered, looking at his cock. There was no fear, only curiosity glowing in her eyes.

"No more than average."

"Somehow, I doubt that, Morwick." Her back arched gracefully as he came to her on all fours. "I think you are anything but average."

⚭

PETRA COULDN'T SEEM TO CONTROL THE SLIGHT TREMBLE of her body as Brendan came toward her. His body was so

253

different from hers and his...what should she call it? She knew what was supposed to happen. Mother's version was that she fulfill her wifely duties and be still. Her cousin, Jemma, however, had been much more detailed and positive about what would happen. But seeing things from the current perspective was far different.

He must have noticed her slight nervousness. "We can stop, Petra. I'm going to —"

"No." She held out her arms to him, tracing the dark line of his beard across his jaw. "I'm very sure I wish to be ravished. By you." She looked down at his arousal. "And that."

A slight twist of his lips, the half-frown she so adored, appeared. His dark head lowered to her stomach, ebony curls skimming her belly as his tongue traced a line around her navel. Tiny nibbles traveled across the soft skin of her thighs. His head moved lower until she felt his breath against the soft hair of her mound.

"Are you—" How wicked. Jemma had told her of such a thing, but Petra hadn't quite understood.

"Going to taste you? Yes. I dream of kissing you there."

"You do? Well, I never thought—" Her words dissolved into a soft mewl, the kind a cat makes as it is stroked. The feel of his tongue there was so delicious Petra thought she may well die from such a thing. Whatever censure she endured after this night would be worth it.

Brendan's tongue rasped against her wetness. Teasing. Searching.

Petra's legs opened wider. Her hands ran over his broad shoulders, threading through the unruly locks of ebony hair. "Brendan," she whispered as the rush of sensation intensified. Her legs wrapped around him as he found the tiny source of her pleasure with the tip of his tongue. Stroking her he gently took her into his mouth. Sucking. Licking. Until Petra bit her lip to stop from crying out. Her release came swift and hard. The spasms rocked her body, pushing her thrusting hips toward his eager mouth. She moaned his name into the pillow, her thighs tightening around his neck and shoulders.

Before she could regain her breath and marvel at the bloodless feel of her limbs, thick hardness pressed between her thighs as he settled himself between her hips. His mouth ran up the side of her neck before his lips met hers. She could taste her own pleasure on his tongue, and Petra kissed him back with all the love and desire she felt for him. Twisting her hips, she pushed upward, toward him, eager for this. For him.

"Petra, love, this may hurt. You're sure? We can stop."

"I don't wish to stop." Jemma had told her the first time felt like a pinch.

"I want you, Petra. I will always want you."

Petra's hands ran down his back to clasp the lines of his buttocks, marveling at the play of muscles beneath her fingertips. Brendan was all hard muscle and lines. Rough sinew and bone. So beautiful and different from herself.

His mouth fell over hers as he thrust inside her, one hand beneath her buttocks, holding Petra in place, the other clasping her hand.

She bit his shoulder at the slight burning sensation, knowing he'd breached her maidenhead. Brendan's heat filled her, stretching and forcing her body to accommodate his.

A growl. "Christ, don't do that. I'm trying to be gentle."

Petra took a deep breath. The sensation was odd. She was full. Pulled taut. Not entirely unpleasant now that the pain was fading, but certainly this wasn't like the feel of his mouth on her.

Brendan's breathing was heavy and slightly ragged, as if he were trying to restrain himself.

Well, restraint wasn't warranted. She bit him again.

"Dear God, Petra." He moved back and thrust again,

nipping her shoulder. "Stop doing that." Another stroke, this one deeper. "Move your hips, love."

Petra complied, loving the way her body held his. She moved her hips up at an angle and Brendan sank further inside her waiting flesh. She wanted him deeper. Her fingers clutched at his back, her nails rasping against his skin.

"Harder," she whispered, her lips pressing to the side of his neck, tasting the saltiness of his skin. "Ravish me."

"I don't want to hurt you," he said against her ear as he groaned, thrusting harder. His fingers moved between their bodies, finding and teasing the small bit of flesh until Petra became mindless with need. She begged, pleaded with him.

Brendan swore. Hooking one of her legs over his arms he filled her so completely, Petra cried out. His thrusts were deep and slow, each one bringing Petra closer to the edge until her body tensed and began to shatter. She climaxed so violently spots appeared before her eyes. Her teeth may have found their way into his shoulder again. Her body tightened, clasping and pulling at his until he moaned out his own pleasure into her hair.

After, she and Brendan lay together, limbs entwined, as their breathing slowly returned to normal. He ran one finger along the crease of her hip. The finger dipped between her legs, exploring her sensitive flesh until her blood became heated once more.

When he took her again, her world breaking apart in a million pieces as he held her in his arms, Petra pressed a kiss over his heart and whispered out her love for him.

Brendan may never love her enough to put aside his fears. She accepted she would be returning to London a scandal-ridden, ruined young lady.

By her own choice.

So much for best laid plans.

Petra was sound asleep next to him, curled up like a kitten. Even now he wanted her, and he'd already taken her three times until Brendan felt like the savage he was often accused of being. He traced the outline of her nose with a fingertip, careful not to wake her. She was brave and clever. Uninhibited in bed. Resourceful. She may even make a decent climber one day.

Lady Lydia Pendleton would ensure Petra was raked over the coals by the *ton*. Petra would never be received again. She would be gossiped about. No one would call on her. Lord and Lady Marsh would need to distance themselves or lose their own place in society. Lady Pendleton would be especially vindictive in light of Simon's political career. Nothing must tarnish her brilliant boy.

Except murder would certainly take the shine from Simon, wouldn't it? And Simon would have to find a girl with an enormous dowry after the profits of the Blue John were gone.

Petra stirred, disturbing his thoughts of revenge. She murmured something in her sleep. His name. Her fingers were curled over his. Trusting him.

Don't let go.

Never.

Heart aching, Brendan crept silently from the bed and dressed. First, he needed to wake his mother and advise her to pack as quickly as possible for the return trip to Somerton. He wanted her waiting in the coach before he spoke to Simon and dared not tell her why they were leaving until they were home. Woods needed to be located immediately.

Brendan looked down at Petra, smiling at the tiny, ladylike snores she made. Pressing a kiss to her temple and pulling up the blanket around her shoulders, he quietly left the room. If all went well, he'd be gone before she awoke.

✣ 29 ✣

Petra awoke to the sound of her mother's raised voice.

That in itself wasn't terribly unusual. Her mother was prone to hysterics. On any given day one could hear Lady Marsh expressing her displeasure to a maid who hadn't used enough beeswax on the floors downstairs. Or voicing her displeasure if her tea became tepid. Petra snuggled back under the covers.

Mother's voice was coming closer. Becoming louder.

Petra's eyes popped open. She wasn't in her bedroom at the Marsh home in London. She sat up and the bedsheet fell away.

She was naked and also alone in the big bed. She turned and saw the indentation of Morwick's head on the pillow next to her. The room outside the bed curtains was disturbingly quiet.

Bollocks.

"Brendan?" She took the sheet and pulled it up all the way to her chin. As she shifted on the bed, Petra winced. The soreness between her legs told her she was ruined. Ravished.

She smiled to herself. Brendan had seen to that several times over.

She'd fallen asleep, despite her best intentions to slip back to her room before dawn. Why hadn't he awoken her?

Bloody Hell.

Mother's voice was growing louder. Footsteps sounded outside the door followed by the twisting of the doorknob.

Good Lord. Mother knows I'm in here.

The door flung open.

"Petra!" Her mother's plump form appeared, clothed in lilac silk, her face mottled with horror and disapproval. The girlish ringlets at her temples quivered and a plump hand clutched at her throat. "What have you done?" Mother let out a long wail like the sound of a cat being choked. "Peee-traaa." Then Mother fainted, collapsing into a clump of purple. She fell to the floor with a loud thump.

Petra stared at the unconscious form of her mother, wondering what she should do. It wasn't unusual for Mother to dramatically faint, but typically one of the Marsh house-maids arrived immediately, armed with smelling salts when Mother was overcome. Petra wasn't sure how to rouse a person without smelling salts. On the bright side, at least she need not delicately explain how she had come to be ruined and was now unable to marry Simon.

Unfortunately, now the entire household would know the culprit was Brendan.

She'd not meant to have her lack of virginity announced to all of Brushbriar and the guests of the house party in such a way, but possibly this was better, though she doubted Lady Pendleton would think so. Petra lifted her chin.

At least I'm not a party to murder.

Petra looked up as Woods, Morwick's valet, appeared in the doorway. He took one look at her mother, stepped over her prone form and immediately shut the door.

"My lady." He bowed. "May I offer you some assistance with your..." his brow furrowed as he looked down at Mother, "situation?"

Petra clutched the sheet tighter, horrified the valet had found her in Morwick's room, though Woods seemed rather nonplussed at her appearance. "I would be in your debt, Mr. Woods."

"We must get you back to your room before your mother awakens. If nothing else, it should keep her from screaming. Do you have something to wear?" His eyes scooted about the room and spying her discarded nightgown, rushed it to her. "Hurry, put this on. The other guests will soon be going down to breakfast." He turned his back. "I beg you to hurry, my lady."

Petra slid out of bed, her toes sinking into the plush carpet. She pulled the cream silk and lace over her shoulders, securely tying the ribbons into place. "How did my mother know I was here?" she said, more to herself than to Woods.

"I'm not certain, my lady." Woods hesitated. "Though I did see Mrs. Leonard, Lord Pendleton's housekeeper, speaking to your mother's lady's maid earlier." His mouth curled. "That horrid, unpleasant woman. Annie. Annabel..."

"Agnes," Petra informed him. *Damn.* "What will you do with her? Should I...help in some way?" Maybe, she thought looking at the mound of purple on the floor, she could convince Mother she'd hallucinated.

"I will give Lady Marsh some smelling salts and inform her I found her collapsed on the floor while I was packing Lord Morwick's valise."

"You're packing his things?" A heavy weight pushed into Petra's stomach at the news. She pressed against the spot, willing the disappointment to go away. She'd known, when she had made her way to Morwick's room last night, that this could be a possible outcome.

The tips of the valet's ears went pink and his mouth pulled in disapproval. "He has left Brushbriar, Lady Petra. As has Lady Cupps-Foster. Before breakfast was even served."

"I see." Petra blinked, unwilling to have Woods see how upset she was. Perhaps Morwick had wished her to be discovered, though she hadn't considered he'd be so thoughtless.

Woods opened the door, his head turning as he looked both ways. "Go directly to your room, my lady, and I will handle Lady Marsh." He waved her forward.

"Thank you, Woods." Petra stepped over her mother, praying no one else would see her, and ran down the hall.

"**M**y lord, may I come in?"

Petra stood, hands clasped lightly in front of her, awaiting permission to enter Simon's private domain. The study was filled with heavy, masculine furniture with thick drapes the color of claret hanging from the windows. A massive oak desk sat facing the door from which the master of Brushbriar, surrounded by stacks of paper, was working. Her stomach lurched in a sickening manner at the confrontation before her.

"Of course." Simon didn't look up. "Shut the door."

His two spaniels sat at attention, watching Petra with suspicion as she approached the desk. Several moments passed as Simon scratched away at something, ignoring her.

"My lord," she said. While she attempted to sound calm, her anxiety threatened to overwhelm her.

"Almost forgot you were there. You were so quiet and *unassuming.*" Simon sat back clasping his hands over his chest. The dark eyes held nothing but contempt.

He knew. Petra swayed a little at the realization. She'd hoped to explain...well, what could she say? If Mrs. Leonard told Agnes, it was likely the housekeeper had told the entire staff before Petra even opened her eyes this morning.

She lifted her chin, determined to brazen it out. "We do not suit, my lord—"

"A gross understatement. Had I known what low morals you possessed, I wouldn't have ever spoken to you, let alone offered you marriage. Cuckolding me in my own home during a house party given in *your* honor." A sneer crossed his lips.

"I was hoping I could speak to you before...I wanted to be the one to tell you. It was not done to shame you, my lord, nor to hurt you in any way."

A puff came out of his mouth, the ugly sound lingering in the quiet of his study. "Is that supposed to make me feel better, Petra? Am I to nod, pretending I understand, and absolve you of your behavior? Perish the thought."

Simon was right. Had she assumed he'd be thrilled to have her ruined? "I am sorry my behavior hurt you—"

"Hurt me?" An ugly laugh sounded as his features filled with contempt. "Can you imagine the lengths I've gone to this morning to ensure the rest of our guests don't know of your transgression?"

Petra looked away and pressed her eyes closed for a moment, trying to compose herself. His distaste for her was justified, she knew. "Simon—"

"Lord Pendleton. You are never to address me by my Christian name again."

Her head snapped back to face him. Fine. Let him hate her. He need only release her from the betrothal. "Given the circumstances, I ask most humbly that you release my father and myself from our betrothal agreement. I hope that we can...keep this incident to ourselves, my lord."

"I release you." The words left his mouth in a hiss. "I have this morning penned a letter to your father's solicitor and mine. A messenger is already on his way to London. Your dowry will be returned to you. Our unfortunate association is at an end. I would no more marry you than a common harlot."

A whoosh of relief left her, even though she strongly disagreed with being compared to a lightskirt. "Thank you, Simon. I am sorry—"

"No, you aren't." He pushed back from the desk and walked toward her. "If you had any scruples at all, you wouldn't have done such a thing. I bid you good day."

She swallowed, knowing he might very well ask her to be removed from his study should she continue. "I know I've no right to ask, but I would appreciate your discretion. I know under the circumstances you may not feel charitable. But for the sake of my family in London—"

A flush stole up Simon's cheeks as a black, murderous rage filled his dark eyes.

Petra stepped back from him, afraid for a moment he meant to do her harm.

"You've nothing to fear, Petra. Not a whiff of this...unfortunate incident will follow you to London. Neither my mother nor sister will breathe a word of the reason for the...*dissolution* of our betrothal. Nor the staff. The guests will be told you were called back to London unexpectedly."

"How kind of you." Given his dislike of her, why would he do such a thing? "I am deeply appreciative of your concern for my reputation."

"I didn't do it for *you*, Petra. Perish the thought." A vein bulged in his temple. "I've no wish to have my name linked with a woman of your ilk. I have a brilliant career ahead of me and my own reputation to protect."

"Of course. Whatever your reason, I am grateful." She'd been preparing herself since leaving Morwick's room for her potential disgrace and future as a pariah. It was almost surreal he didn't mean to punish her in such a way.

"Pack your things. I want you out of Brushbriar immediately."

Petra shook her head and walked toward the door, pausing for only a moment. She felt terrible having done such a thing to him, but he and Mother had left her with little choice. Turning back she said, "Did you ever have any affection toward me, my lord? As one would a wife?"

"No," he said without hesitation. "My offer for you was based solely on the size of your dowry and your obedient, docile manner. You were attractive enough to preside over my table but not too beautiful to draw unwanted attention. In truth, I found you rather unintelligent and boring."

She'd known that, of course, but had hoped for at least some indication he'd borne her some affection, no matter how small. "I bid you goodbye, Lord Pendleton. Thank you for your hospitality."

As she closed the door with a shaking hand, Petra told herself to breathe, the worst was over. How could Brendan have left her to face such a thing after last night? She knew he cared for her, possibly not enough to discard a lifetime's worth of fear of love, but if nothing else, she'd thought he would help her navigate through the situation at Brushbriar. He'd left without a word to her.

Pull yourself together, Petra.

She straightened her shoulders and pushed back from the door, meaning to go upstairs and tell Mother they'd been asked...no, *commanded*, to leave.

"If I had my way, you would never be received again, anywhere."

Petra turned to face a hostile Lady Pendleton a few feet away. They stared at each other for several moments before Petra said, "I would expect nothing else from a woman of your *murderous* intent."

A snarl echoed in the hallway. "You whore." Lady Pendleton's fingers curled at her sides as if she would fly at Petra. She stepped toward her. "I don't care what he—"

"Mother." Katherine appeared from the shadows of the hallway to take Lady Pendleton's arm. "I think you are in need of some tea and perhaps a bit of toast. Remember, we have guests."

Lady Pendleton shook her daughter off and with a huff, strode in the direction of the breakfast room.

Petra took a deep breath and started up the stairs. If Katherine meant to spar with her as well, she'd not give her the chance.

"I was wrong."

The words stopped Petra but she didn't turn.

"You will appreciate fossils much more than I, I'm certain of it."

Petra gripped the bannister, the Blue John ice cold beneath her fingertips. "I'm not sure what you mean, Lady Whitfield," she replied, but only silence met her. When she looked down, she saw Katherine was gone.

Petra approached her room, considering Katherine's odd comment. The door was ajar and the sound of Mother arguing with someone filtered into the hallway.

"I insist you give that to me or I will have you dismissed."

Petra entered her rooms and shut the door, relived to see Tessie had her trunks packed. She was *not* relieved to see Mother charging at the poor maid, arm outstretched toward Tessie who was stubbornly shaking her head.

"No, my lady. I'm so sorry, but I cannot." Tessie lifted her chin, lower lip quivering in fear. "Whether you sack me or not, I gave my word. I am to hand this over to Lady Petra and *only* Lady Petra." Tessie turned in her direction, nearly weeping with relief at Petra's appearance. The maid had a small square of paper clutched in her hand.

"I have every right to review my daughter's correspondence. I am her mother." A scowl hovered on Mother's lips. "Your maid is disobedient."

"As is your daughter," Petra returned. "I won't have you bullying Tessie."

Mother's chin wobbled and her eyes held the sheen of tears. "I shall *never* live this down. We will be shunned by everyone in society for your reckless behavior. I'm sure even begging Simon for forgiveness did you no good. Lady Pendleton will write to every acquaintance she has in London. You will never be received again. First your brother, and now you." Mother flounced down on the bed dramatically.

"I didn't beg Simon for anything, Mother. I asked to be released from the betrothal contract he's signed with Father, and for my dowry to be returned. Simon has agreed."

Her mother's face blanched. "What else was he to do? Marry a strumpet?" She placed a hand to her head as if preparing to faint. "I had hopes he would be willing to over-look your transgression, but I suppose that was foolish on my part."

Petra winced. "I'm not a strumpet, Mother."

"Lady Pendleton has cut me to the quick. She sent a note to my room informing me we must leave immediately, without saying goodbye. As if we haven't been her guests." Mother's voice raised an octave. "And Lady Cupps-Foster has already left in utter shame over the dishonor of her son and your loose morals. He even had his horrid valet try to convince me I was imagining your presence in his room. Morwick has ruined you beyond repair and left you to face the wolves alone."

Petra had been considering the exact same thing, how Brendan could abandon her to such a mess. But, she'd known the risks. "Simon has assured me that not a bit of my trans-gression," she looked her mother in the eye, "will reach

London. Not from his mother or Lady Whitfield." While Simon had promised not a hint of scandal, Petra wasn't sure about her own mother.

"I would demand Lord Morwick do the honorable thing except I will *not* have another Dunbar relation in my family. Thank goodness Lord Dunning is still available. I'm certain he'll be willing to overlook this incident. I'll write to him the moment we arrive home. He's not Simon, but he'll make you an adequate husband."

Petra wanted to scream. "I'm not going to marry Dunning, Mother. Or anyone, unless I wish to."

Mother's face puffed up like an overstuffed squirrel. "Your father and I will cut you off. I won't receive you."

A bitter laugh came from her. "I thought you wished to punish me? I'll live with Rowan and Arabella. Or perhaps Jemma."

"My lady," Tessie said in a quiet voice.

Petra had almost forgotten the maid was in the room. Mother and her anguish took all of Petra's attention.

"I beg your pardon." Tessie dipped into a curtsy as she nimbly side-stepped Mother to make her way to Petra. "I don't wish to interrupt your discussion with Lady Marsh." She held up the square of paper.

"Tessie!" Mother popped off the bed with a squeak. "I insist you give that to me immediately." Her hand shot out in a futile grab for the note Tessie held.

Petra blinked back the wetness gathering behind her eyes, trying to keep from collapsing into a fit of tears. The last twenty-four hours had seen her ravished and abandoned by the man she loved. She'd been called a harlot and a strumpet more than once. Threatened with a blackening of her reputation and now treated to a display of dramatics by her manipulative Mother. Petra wanted nothing more than to once more be beneath the oak tree within the circle of Brendan's arms.

'You will appreciate fossils much more than I'

Petra took the note from Tessie's hand, struggling to keep her hand from shaking. Hope bloomed inside her heart.

"Lord Morwick said I was to hand this to you and only you, my lady." She shot Lady Marsh a look of remorse. "I'm sorry, my lady. But he made me give my word."

Mother tried once again to snatch the note away.

"Thank you, Tessie," she said, taking the note. Perhaps it was only an apology. A goodbye note. How would she endure the journey back to London with Mother? "Tessie, will you finish the packing and find a footman to have my trunks taken down?"

The maid bobbed and left.

Petra's name was scrawled across the top in a bold, masculine hand. Unfolding the paper, she read the words, then read them again, before refolding the note and putting it in the pocket of her dress.

"Well," Mother looked satisfied. Smug, even. "Let us get on the way to London. We can discuss Dunning on the way home."

Petra bit her lip to keep from shouting with joy. "We aren't going to London, Mother," she explained with great satisfaction. "At least, not immediately. We have a stop to make."

A tic appeared in Mother's cheek. She must have understood Petra's meaning. "Absolutely not. I forbid it."

"Mother, I don't wish you to have a fit of apoplexy. I would be most distressed." Petra's fingers ran over the note in her pocket as happiness made her lightheaded.

'Your choices are your own, Petra. I would have you decide your life, not I or Simon and especially not Lady Marsh. Should you choose not to return to London, I will wait for you. I won't let go. Ever.'

❧ 31 ❧

Petra tapped her foot with impatience.

"Mother, do hurry along."

The footmen had already loaded her trunks on the smaller of the two coaches, the one Agnes and Tessie had traveled to Brushbriar in. Mother would return to London in Father's more comfortable coach. She'd opted not to stop at Somerton with her daughter.

"Jenkins," Mother commanded, shooting Petra a self-assured smile. "Please place my daughter in the Marsh coach." Mother tugged at her gloves not looking at Petra. "Restrain her if necessary."

"You've got to be joking." Was there no end to her mother's need to control her life? "Jenkins, don't you dare."

Jenkins, bless him, bowed deeply to Mother. "I beg your pardon, Lady Marsh, but I will not put my hands on the daughter of an earl. Lord Marsh would have my head."

"Jenkins. I insist." Her mother stamped her foot, becoming agitated. "You must do it. You must."

Petra stepped forward. "Mother, stop. I'm not going back to London with you." She hugged her mother's plump form.

"I love you, Mother. I do. But you will not dictate my life any longer."

"Petra." Mother tried to take her hand. "My baby," she sobbed, "please don't do this. You must come back to London with me. Don't go to him." Her head shook. "He's wrong for you."

Petra gently pushed her mother into the Marsh coach. "I love him, Mother."

"How can you after what he did?" Her mother wept, refusing to shut the coach door.

How could she not, after what she suspected Brendan had done for her? And she knew now the depth of his feeling for her.

"Goodbye, Mother." Petra pushed the coach door closed.

Mother's tear-stained face watched Petra from the window of the coach as Jenkins drove the Marsh coach away, back toward London where Petra's father would have to endure Mother's anguish and disappointment over their daughter.

As the groom assisted her into the smaller coach with Tessie, who'd opted to stay with her, Petra felt a huge weight lift from her shoulders. Freedom was a heady feeling.

The light was fading as they drew closer to Somerton, and Petra found herself tapping a foot impatiently. Finally, the coach pulled up the long drive. She looked out at the pile of stone covered with unruly vines and knew she was where she belonged. Home.

The coach had barely slowed before Petra jumped out. "Tessie," she instructed her maid, "inform Lady Cupps-Foster we've arrived. I feel certain she has been expecting us."

"Yes, my lady." Tessie reached out and took Petra's hand. "Good luck, my lady."

Petra smiled, hitched up her skirts and began to run, stretching her legs as she followed the path leading through the Somerton gardens up into the tree line. There was really only one place he would be waiting for her.

A hitch started in her side just as she approached the large oak dominating the small clearing. Mam Tor loomed in the distance. The pins holding her hair had loosened, and the honey-colored mass now hung down her back. As she approached the tree she saw a shadow moving up in the canopy above.

Petra put her hands on her hips and leaned back to look upward. "Are you coming down?"

"Where have you been?" He sounded annoyed and was probably frowning at her. "I've been waiting for hours."

"My goodness. I've run all the way from Somerton. I'm out of breath and it took some time to pack and evade my mother."

"Good God, Lady Marsh isn't here, is she?" A rustle of branches sounded and a shadow moved across the limbs. "I may change my mind about coming down if that's the case."

"No. I've sent her on to London, where she belongs. You're quite safe." She hesitated a moment. "Brendan, were you afraid I wouldn't come?"

Dead silence, then he came into view, scuttling down the tree, his large form sure-footed and agile. He dropped to his feet in front of her, large and magnificent, the sapphire of his eyes shining in the rapidly dimming light.

"Yes." His voice was raspy and broken. "Terrified, actually. If you hadn't come, I would have had to go to London to retrieve you. I would have resorted to kidnapping, probably. I'm not certain. I suppose I could have courted you properly and begged your father for your hand." He laced his fingers with hers.

"You would have retrieved me? You detest London." Her heart thumped wildly in her chest.

"It's true. But I would have gone to that horrible city and found you."

"Even after you went to such great lengths to ensure I would have a choice?" She took his hand, pressing a kiss to the middle of his palm. "Oh, Brendan."

Brendan refused to meet her eyes. "I would not have you hurt, nor made a pariah for loving me," he said in a low raspy tone.

Petra's entire chest expanded with the most exquisite happiness. "You threatened Simon."

The broad shoulders shrugged as he turned to look down at her. "Threatened is a strong word. Let us say I came to an *understanding* with Lord Pendleton and his mother that you be released from your betrothal immediately. And in addition to his continued discretion, he will have to lease the mine from me. Lady Pendleton was a bit put out, and she hates *you* by the way, but I reminded Lydia I was asking for very little in comparison to what the rumors of murder would do to her and her darling son. I'm afraid she had me escorted out of Brushbriar by pistol. I only had time to leave you a note." He looked contrite. "Simon is very lucky he possessed something I wanted. Something more precious to me than Blue John or revenge."

A tear ran down Petra's cheek. "Me."

"Yes, you. I hope to make a decent climber of you and teach you to organize my samples properly. Things a wife should know how to do."

"Is that all?" God, she loved him. Every complicated, frustrating bit. "Are you sure, Brendan?" She knew how difficult this was for him.

"I'm in love with you, in case you haven't noticed. Of course I'm sure," he said, frowning down at her.

"I noticed. I love you too."

The sapphire eyes flashed indigo. "It's bloody frightening."

"I'll help you through it." She squeezed his fingers.

He brushed his lips against hers. "But I promised I would never let you go. And I meant it."

"I won't let you go either." Petra wrapped her arms around him. "Ever."

EPILOGUE

The breeches he'd had made for Petra were his best idea in years, but incredibly distracting. She looked absolutely smashing in them. He could see the outline of her gorgeous legs as well as her other attributes. Brendan found it difficult to take his eyes from her backside.

"How about this?" She held up a small white stone. "Anything?"

She sounded so hopeful he decided to humor her. Petra rarely picked up anything of value. Her job as geologist's assistant was more to keep her close to him than anything. "Maybe."

Her eyes narrowed. "You're lying." She tossed the rock to the side. "I'm not very good at this."

"You're bloody terrible," Brendan agreed. "Your talents lie in another direction."

His wife bent over to pick up a different stone, giving Brendan yet another delicious view of her backside. He took off his hat and fanned himself. The day was unseasonably warm with just a hint of the impending autumn. Soon, he and

Petra would have to leave the relative safety of Somerton and venture to London for the upcoming holidays.

"This *must* be something." Petra held up another rock, smooth and brown with a thin line of green.

"It is something," Brendan assured her, remembering the pebble he'd found so long ago that reminded him of her eyes.

She brushed a lock of hair out of her eyes, leaving a streak of dirt across her cheek in the process before she smiled back at him. "Finally."

Brendan's fears had quieted in the last month, though the terror was still there, buried away. His love for Petra had only deepened since they had wed in the village church in Castleton. He'd offered to be married in London, but Petra had refused. He had sensed she wasn't ready to see her parents. But if they were in London for the holidays, Petra would have to confront Lord and Lady Marsh then. He did not want to be the cause of her estrangement from her parents.

"Brendan. You're not even looking at it." She held up the rock again, wiggling it before his eyes. "What if it's something precious?"

With one step he reached his beloved wife, wondering how he'd survived so long without her. Wrapping his arms around her, he held her tightly to his heart.

"Very precious indeed."

❦

THANK YOU FOR READING TALL DARK & WICKED, I hope you enjoyed the story of Petra and Brendan. If so, please leave a review. Reviews keep me writing and help other readers discover my books.

Click below for the NEXT IN THE SERIES and keep reading.

STILL WICKED.

AUTHOR'S NOTES

I've taken some liberties with the Peak District (as my readers in the U.K. will probably notice). Blue John, the source of the Pendleton wealth, is a semi-precious mineral and a form of fluorite discovered by the Romans. In Britain, it can be found in one of only two places; Blue John Cavern and Treak Cliff Cavern, both outside of Castleton in Derbyshire. Pendleton's Blue John is purely fictional.

Blue John was in high demand during the 19th century. It was used for everything from vases to windows and can be found in some of the finest homes in Britain, including Buckingham Palace.

ABOUT THE AUTHOR

Kathleen Ayers has been a hopeful romantic since the tender age of fourteen when she first purchased a copy of Sweet Savage Love at a garage sale while her mother was looking at antique animal planters. Since then she's read hundreds of historical romances and fallen in love dozens of times. Kathleen lives in Houston with her husband, a college-aged son who pops in to have his laundry done and two very spoiled dogs.

Sign up for Kathleen's newsletter:
www.kathleenayers.com

Like Kathleen on Facebook
www.facebook.com/kayersauthor

Join Kathleen's Facebook Group
Historically Hot with Kathleen Ayers

Follow Kathleen on Bookbub
bookbub.com/authors/kathleen-ayers

ALSO BY KATHLEEN AYERS

Manufactured by Amazon.ca
Bolton, ON

28564209R00166